Praise for *The Christie Curse*

"Deftly plotted, with amusing one-liners, murder and a dash of mayhem. There's a cast of characters who'd be welcome on any Christie set."

—*The Hamilton Spectator*

"With a full inventory of suspects, a courageous heroine and a tribute to a famous writer of whodunits, *The Christie Curse* will tempt her legion of devotees. Even mystery lovers who have never read Christie— if any exist—will find a pleasing puzzle in Abbott's opener." —*Richmond Times-Dispatch*

"The mystery was first class, the plotting flawless."

—*Cozy Mystery Book Reviews*

THE
SAYERS
SWINDLE

VICTORIA ABBOTT

BERKLEY PRIME CRIME, NEW YORK

THE BERKLEY PUBLISHING GROUP
Published by the Penguin Group
Penguin Group (USA) LLC
375 Hudson Street, New York, New York 10014

USA • Canada • UK • Ireland • Australia • New Zealand • India • South Africa • China

penguin.com

A Penguin Random House Company

THE SAYERS SWINDLE

A Berkley Prime Crime Book / published by arrangement with the author

For information, address: The Berkley Publishing Group,
a division of Penguin Group (USA) LLC,
375 Hudson Street, New York, New York 10014.

ISBN: 978-0-425-25529-2

PUBLISHING HISTORY
Berkley Prime Crime mass-market / December 2013

PRINTED IN THE UNITED STATES OF AMERICA

10 9 8 7 6 5 4 3 2

Cover illustration by Tony Mauro.
Cover design by Jason Gill.

ACKNOWLEDGMENTS

First we would like to thank the late Dorothy L. Sayers, who peered over our shoulders, whispered in our ears and whose own words inspired this mystery. Lord Peter Wimsey and Harriet Vane are characters that enchant us still. Hats off to all the legion of readers who, like us, still treasure the books from the "Golden Age of Detection."

We are grateful to the many people who let us know that they enjoyed the first in the Book Collector Mysteries and were waiting for the second. It is delightful to learn that you connect with our characters and that they bring you as much fun as they bring us.

Where would we be without the on-going support of our agent, Kim Lionetti; the cheerful good counsel of Tom Colgan, our editor at Berkley Prime Crime; and the help we receive from Amanda Ng, and, of course, our mysterious but long-suffering copyeditor? Any errors are our own.

We've appreciated the willingness of booksellers, librarians, bloggers, readers and reviewers to help us get the word out. The Ottawa Public Library was a terrific and efficient source of material for the research that went into this book.

Thanks to our family and friends for putting up with us when the going gets tough and the deadlines loom, especially Giulio Maffini, and that man of words, John Merchant, and our friend Linda Wiken, who has been in our lives for many years, and may have developed some sort of Stockholm Syndrome, because she has long since stopped trying to escape. Even with her own flourishing career as Berkley Prime Crime author Erika Chase, Linda always takes the time to read our work and cheer us on.

The writing life is more fun for being part of Mystery Lovers Kitchen (mysteryloverskitchen.com) and Killer Characters (killercharacters.com) and of course, those dangerous dames, the Ladies Killing Circle.

Then there's the real "Real Candy," aka Candice St. Aubin, Victoria Maffini's thirty-three-year pillar of strength, transept of trust and flying buttress of mischief. She keeps Victoria in stitches, trouble and dogs.

Last but not least, we owe a debt to Irma Maffini and Lina Arno for exposing us to the tasty secrets of their great Italian kitchens, or as much of them as they were willing to divulge. These women know their way around a kitchen and have created a legacy of heavenly food.

Eat! Yes! You!

CHAPTER ONE

—◆—

I WAS FALLING for an older man. He was blond, sophis-
ticated and wealthy, an English aristocrat. In fact, he was
far too aristocratic for someone like me, but still, I wasn't
ready to give him up. Or the idea of him, anyway. I hadn't
bothered to share this with anyone, as it was just a matter
of time until some friend or relative remarked that I was
twenty-six years old and the first person in the history of
my family to go straight. Of course, someone else would
point out that while Lord Peter Wimsey was indeed the son
of a duke and a great detective, he was also pushing one
hundred and twenty one. I'd have to snap back that he was
aging well. On the other hand, he *was* a fictional character,
which is really the kiss of death for a relationship.

I wished he were real. I could have used his skills and
insights with the serious challenge I was facing in my job.
One that could mean the end of it.

It was a fall day with a nip in the air and the kind of wind
that rattled the windows and sent you hunting for an extra

sweater. It was always too hot or too cold on the main floor of the historic Van Alst House where I lived with my employer, the noted book collector and grouch, Vera Van Alst. One of the windows in the conservatory had been removed to be repaired, which meant we were having lunch in the formal dining room. I didn't stir the pot by asking how they had finally found someone to repair that window. After all, my employer was the most hated woman in Harrison Falls and the surrounding towns. Van Alst House could crumble to the ground and most people wouldn't lift a finger to help Vera Van Alst, regardless of how much they were paid. Property maintenance was a big issue. I fully expected to find myself wielding a hammer one of these days.

At the other end of the long Sheraton table, the sound of Vera growling penetrated my consciousness. I blinked and came back to reality. Mind you, my reality was pretty unreal. I could imagine Lord Peter feeling quite at home in this splendid room with its priceless antiques.

Vera was in the seat of power, her wheelchair parked by the side. As usual, she was a vision in a dusty beige sweater, with frayed wristbands and a matching moth hole on each elbow, the kind of thing that doesn't make the cut at church bazaars. Vera's high standards for her spectacular collection of mysteries did not extend to her all-beige wardrobe. I'd had one minor triumph in getting her spruced up, but one blue silk blouse does not make a new way of life, and she backslid immediately. Still, I was happy to spot one of her Art Deco pins nestled in the blandness. I'd learned to pick my battles about the clothes, but I was truly envious of Vera's jewelry collection, and I was content when any of her pieces saw the light of day.

In her inimitable gravelly voice, she said, "Miss Bingham, will you consider joining us?"

Us? What us? There was only Vera Van Alst, currently growling, and me, Jordan Bingham, lost in another fantasy of Lord Peter Wimsey and emerald-cut sapphires set in sterling silver. I hate sarcasm, unless I initiate it.

I'd learned not to say "sorry" to Miss Van Alst, as it conveyed weakness and was sure to breed contempt on her part. Life was complicated enough without that. I worked for a wealthy woman who couldn't care less that she was despised by most people. She despised them too. Rare books and first editions—that's what mattered to Vera.

I kept my "sorry" to myself.

"Just thinking about your missing Dorothy L. Sayers first editions," I said. That was the truth but nowhere near the whole truth.

"Oh yes, you mean the biggest disaster that has ever befallen my collection. The disaster that coincides with your arrival in my employ, Miss Bingham. I would hope you'd be concentrating on that during your every waking hour. That's what I pay you for. And I pay you well to get what I want. I want those books back." She kept tugging and straightening the cuffs of her tattered cardigan. Clearly, the loss of a chunk of her collection weighed heavily on her.

This might be a good time to mention that what Vera wants, Vera gets. And when Vera wants something, she wants it the way she wants it and she wants it yesterday.

Unfortunately for me, things weren't working out quite that way. Vera was deliberately ignoring my role in solving a murder and stopping the total plunder of her collection. She seemed to blame me for the theft of her Dorothy L. Sayers very fine firsts. This was unfair, even for Vera, and under normal circumstances, I would have set her straight. Maybe I was mellowed by thoughts of Lord Peter. Or lunch. Or generally how much I liked my life.

I found Vera's collection of rare books irresistibly appealing. I adored the endless corridors of historic Van Alst House and the cozy attic accommodations that came with my position. The food was to die for. It *was* looking good for me to be the first person in my family to go straight. That was my plan and I was sticking to it.

Really, Vera was the only fly in the ointment. Too bad the fly controlled the checkbook and owned the ointment.

"A bit of thought before action usually pays off," I said. I didn't mention where fantasizing fit into the equation.

"Where are you with the so-called thought and action in that case?"

"I know you are anxious to get the Sayers books back."

"Miss Bingham, I do not get anxious."

No, but you're a carrier, I thought.

She pointed a bony finger at me. "Perhaps you mean to say 'eager,' as that is correct usage. If your education is as you insist, I shouldn't have to remind you of that."

I did know the correct use of "anxious" and "eager." Vera can make people, even me, experience anxiety, although with my relatives you'd think I'd be immune.

She rattled on, "That is a valuable and irreplaceable collection. I must have the books that were stolen from me. That is your job. And at your salary and benefits, you should be *more* than eager."

I smoothed my silky vintage Pucci print scarf against my collarbone, took in a deep cleansing breath and let that go. "The books will be located. Count on it." I didn't mention that the missing first editions were hardly a matter of life or death. I'd found out the hard way that there were dangers in dealing with Vera's rare book collection. Vera hadn't been the only danger by a long shot.

"You have them in your sights?" There was that obsessive

gleam in her eye. She paid no attention to the blue point Siamese that leapt onto the table and was making its haughty way toward her. There was an identical one under the table at my end too. I was taking no chances and as usual wore a pair of boots to prevent new scars. Vera reached out absentmindedly and stroked the cat.

"I repeat, do you have them in your sights, Miss Bingham?"

"Not yet, but I have a strong lead."

Even from the other end of the long table, I could see that wasn't quite doing the trick.

"Strong leads will not fill gaps in shelves," she snapped.

"I think you'll be pleasantly surprised," I said with totally unmerited confidence. "The person who sold them—in good faith, might I add—is trying to track down the buyers."

"In my lifetime, Miss Bingham."

At this moment the swinging door from the kitchen banged open and Vera's cook, Signora Fiammetta Panetone, advanced bearing a fragrant mountain of seafood linguine on a giant platter. The signora is somewhat startling the first time you see her: small, round, dressed in black with a wide white apron, pushing eighty, with her unlikely ebony-colored hair pulled back so tightly it seemed to be painted on her head. The signora is unclear about what constitutes a lunch for two.

"Eat," she said firmly to Vera, as she does during every meal. Didn't someone once say that the definition of insanity is doing the same thing over and over and expecting the outcome to be different? If so, the signora was out of her gourd, but she'd made some delicious soup out of it first.

Vera accepted what looked like three strands of pasta and a breath of Parmesan cheese and waved the platter away.

I, on the other hand, smiled the smile of the successful locator of lost and stolen books. I was about to have a tasty treat that would make up for having Vera Van Alst as an employer.

"Who is this lead?" Vera said. Any superhero would have been jealous of her penetrating glance. X-ray vision couldn't compare.

I hated to offer my friend up as a sacrifice, but I said, "Karen Smith seems to have sold them. In good faith, as I said. When she acquired them at the Cozy Corpse, she had no idea they'd been stolen from your collection."

This was not the entire story, but Karen was truly sorry for her lack of attention to the provenance of the Sayers volumes.

Vera snarled, "So get the name from her. What's the holdup?"

The signora lurched toward my place and said, "You eat, now."

No problem with that. As usual I said, "Sure thing," to the signora. I added, for Vera's benefit, "Karen's memory is still iffy since she was attacked. It's not even five months, as you know, and brain injuries take time."

Of course, Vera was well aware of all that, but most days Vera is all about Vera.

I added, "Karen and I are working at reconstructing the sale. I know it will come back to her. It's really just a matter of time." I managed not to remind Vera yet again that Karen Smith had come close to death because of that same attack and that we should all keep our sense of perspective. I hadn't completely lost my marbles.

Lest I forget my place in the pecking order, Vera said, "Don't take forever, Miss Bingham. I have other projects I need you to work on."

Yes, there was an ever-growing list of titles I was tasked with finding, and I couldn't wait to roam freely in the musty back rooms of flea markets and bazaars. It was also fun to poke about online.

Vera added, "You don't get paid to lie around. Remember, you're not the only person who can do this job."

Idle threat?

More likely just mean for the sport of it, but with Vera, who knew?

It wasn't the first time I regretted loving this job so much, not to mention needing it desperately if I was ever to save enough to get back to grad school.

I resisted the urge to defend myself and let the linguine work its magic. The dreamy look on my face was not only because of Lord Peter.

A girl's got to eat.

SIGNORA PANETONE PACKED me off to Karen Smith's home with a coffin-sized container of seafood linguine, a bowl of washed crisp green leaf lettuce, a jar of homemade *maionesa* and enough almond cookies to fill a suitcase. I hesitated because Karen had a tiny, cluttered kitchen in the flat over the Cozy Corpse mystery bookstore. Would there be room? She didn't have a microwave either. But as usual, resistance was futile.

"For Signora Smith! Sick! Head hurt! Must eat!"

No problem.

"And this." *This* turned out to be a baggy of wine-sautéed chicken livers for Karen's dog, Walter the Pug, currently residing in style with my uncle Mick and my uncle Lucky until Karen could manage to care for him again.

I piled it all into the powder-blue '61 Saab that had been my mother's and drove off into the brilliantly colored swirling leaves on that windy October day. I love the fall and love

Halloween. Unfortunately, I couldn't imagine any children in Harrison Falls trick-or-treating at Van Alst House. I'd have to spend the evening with my uncles.

With that thought, I changed direction in order to drop in on those uncles. For one thing, I figured I could pick up a microwave for Karen, resolving the coffin-load of linguine problem. For another, I was happy to ditch the chicken livers quickly. I figured Karen would already have eaten some lunch and would need a bit of time to build up an appetite for the signora's food.

Uncle Mick and Uncle Lucky were in the kitchen in back of Michael Kelly's Fine Antiques, the family business. As you know, I am a Bingham, but the Kellys are my mother's people and they are mine too. This kitchen had been the heart of my home, and nothing much had changed since my childhood. As much as I loved my digs at Van Alst House and enjoyed being out from under my uncles' watchful eyes—I *am* an adult now—I always got a warm feeling sitting around the vintage chrome and Formica dinette table in the safe haven my uncles had created for me. Before they unexpectedly became my guardians, they would have been footloose and fancy free, to use Mick's words. Enjoying travel, cars, clubs, whiskey, cigars and, to hear him tell it, clouds of glamorous women. My uncles claim they never regretted taking me in as a small child and didn't miss their old lives for a second. Even so, I sometimes caught a faraway look in Uncle Mick's eyes.

I beamed at my uncles, who pretty much filled the room even before I got there. Not sure if I've ever mentioned it, but both my uncles are what you could call men of substance, although Uncle Lucky is a man of more substance.

Uncle Mick was resplendent, as usual, his shirt open to show his copious ginger hair and the gold chain that went so well with it. Naturally, he had on his "Kiss the Cook" apron with the downward arrow. He was busy serving up fried baloney and formerly frozen crinkle fries. Lunch as we know it at the Kelly homestead. Walter was thumping his curly tail. I interpreted that as pure happiness. Walter's eyes bulged, and his back wriggled and writhed in excitement. I dropped the baggie of sautéed liver on the counter. It was labeled *Cane*, which I'd come to learn meant "dog" in Italian. Lucky opened up the bag and sniffed, his nose crinkled. I knew he did not deem this treat good enough for his new companion. Only the very best for Walter.

"I don't suppose you know of any microwaves that have become available at good prices lately," I said. "Karen could use one as the signora keeps sending her food."

That translated as "I need a free microwave. Today."

Mick glowered. "Not sure if all that foreign food is good for you, my girl."

I suppressed a grin.

"You hungry?" he added, slapping a piece of sizzling and slightly singed baloney onto a plate next to a glob of green coleslaw with an unearthly glow. Next on were the previously frozen crinkle fries.

"Sorry, love to, but I'm in a real rush," I lied. "If only I'd known you were serving lunch. So, a microwave? The smaller the better. Karen has such a tiny kitchen."

"Check in the storage room. There's a couple still in the box. From an estate sale. If you find one you like, take it. Anything for that lovely lady," Uncle Mick said, with a glance at Uncle Lucky. "Tell her Walter's doing well."

Uncle Lucky has no hair except for his giant ginger eyebrows, and he never says much, but his expression told me that there might be what the Kellys call "issues" if Walter had to be returned. But I couldn't worry about that. I knew that

Lucky had developed a soft spot for Karen as well as Walter. That would work out well. I left them as Lucky was cutting up a round of baloney for Walter. He wasn't sure about the chicken livers. It was a dog's life for sure at chez Kelly.

Uncle Mick cleared his throat. "We have something to tell you."

I smiled. "Tell away."

"Your uncle Kevin's going to be here for a while."

I kept a straight face. "Really?"

"Really. A small disagreement about a large amount of money."

"Oh."

"Some fellas down in Albany with not much patience."

"That would do it then."

Lucky nodded grimly. Mick sighed. "He'll need your bedroom and bathroom."

"I'm glad we can accommodate him."

"If you say so. Come on. Let's take a peek at those microwaves."

I WAS STILL chuckling to myself as I deposited a small, sleek stainless microwave onto the passenger seat of the Saab. The uncles were unique and I adored them. I remembered describing my home to my college roommate and BFF, Tiffany Tibeault. She found it hard to believe, especially the secret hiding places and unseen exits. Not everyone's way to live, but it worked for us.

I suppose in a way I was responsible for the construction and décor of the converted apartments behind and above the delightfully jumbled shop where Uncle Mick supposedly made his living. Besides the uncles, the best part of this secret world in back of the antique shop was the collection of hiding places. My uncles have a unique form of claustro-phobia, meaning they always need to know how to get away in case of visits from unfriendly agents of the law. I felt a little wave of nostalgia for the good old days when I would race through the place, taking shortcuts through the hidden staircases or pressing the lever to make the bookcase full of Danielle Steel and Sidney Sheldon novels open in the garage. Even as a preschooler, I'd been trained to use my own secret exits and to call my other uncles in case of anything that didn't "end well." The special phone is still in operation, and I know that number as well as I know my name.

Of course, I could never tell my school friends about this private world, and until I met Tiff in college, I'd never once mentioned the hidden spaces, exits and special numbers. I'd always enjoyed the secrets though.

It didn't make up for not having a mother, but it was all fun, like living in a Nancy Drew book.

Now Uncle Kev was moving in. Uncle Mick and Uncle Lucky would be pushed to the limit and I would miss all the fun.

For a fleeting moment I felt homesick.

IT SHOULD HAVE been a cakewalk getting the informa-tion about Vera's pilfered Dorothy L. Sayers pristine first editions. My friend, Karen Smith, the pleasant proprietor of the Cozy Corpse, had acquired and sold those copies in good faith, as I kept assuring Vera. Let's just say the pur-veyor was paying the price for that and other crimes, includ-ing the near fatal blow to Karen. But Karen's traumatic head injury had brought her business to a standstill. Not to be unkind, but her record keeping left a lot to be desired and there was no information on the person to whom she'd sold the Sayers firsts. Everything had been in Karen's head, and Karen's brain was still a bit scrambled.

She had a long way to go before she would be better. Still I figured that working with her and going over the thousands of scraps of information in her totally chaotic shop office and mildly chaotic apartment would pay off in a lead.

Karen was not in the shop when I drove over to the neighboring town of Grandville. The "CLOSED" sign hung in the door of the lovely old brick two-story building. Even the jaunty skeleton in the window looked forlorn. Five months after her attack, although she could struggle up and down the stairs, because of her brain injury Karen was still unable to run her business or even put in a shift. I made my way to the back of the building, swishing my vintage plaid Pendleton coat—a legacy of my mother's closet—and rang the doorbell for Karen's flat over the store.

I was psyched to get started. It was just a matter of time until we found a name and that name sparked a response. When that happened, I planned to continue to visit Karen. We'd bonded over our love of books and sugary baked goods in the months since we'd met under less-than-ideal circumstances.

"Come on up," Karen called out. "It's open."

It would take a couple of trips to get everything upstairs to her apartment over the shop. As I lumbered along the driveway carrying the microwave, the pale and lumpy man who lived in the house on the right-hand side of the driveway turned and glared at me. What was that about? I ignored his glare and staggered up the stairs into Karen's living room, which was jammed with stacks of books and knickknacks on every surface. Karen was lounging in an overstuffed armchair covered in faded brown corduroy. Her madly curling red hair had grown back a bit after her surgery. It was barely held under control by clips and bobby pins. Her smile was brighter than the reading lamp by her side. She was also a vulnerable woman alone in an apartment.

"Shouldn't your door be locked?" I blurted out in a bossy moment.

Her eyebrows lifted in surprise. "Why?"

This was from a woman who'd recently been attacked and left for dead.

I said, "Well, because, as you know . . . things happen."

She shrugged and then with another luminous smile said, "But as long as the door stays locked in the slammer, there's no reason to believe bad things will keep happening. This is Grandville, Jordan. A safe little town."

I loved Karen's naïve and unspoiled outlook on life; even after having been beaten and left for dead, Karen was open and eternally optimistic. But the Kelly in me knew there was a dark side to every town.

Karen must have grown used to gifts from the signora and from my uncles. She didn't even comment about the new microwave.

I kept going into the dollhouse-sized galley kitchen and tried to negotiate a place for the microwave on the counter. There was only one cupboard, so the cooking pots and pans hung on hooks and the olive oil, vinegar, salt and pepper were lined up by the sink next to a crooked pile of cookbooks. The tea towels and Karen's apron hung from the bar on the stove. Not an easy room to cook in at the best of times. I had no choice but to dislodge the vintage *Moosewood Cookbook* and a couple of others and stack them in the living room, on the floor. Lots of other book stacks were there to keep them company. Karen was using one stack as a side table. It was a decorating look that I quite liked.

As I headed downstairs again for the food, I said, "Grandville is a safe little town, I suppose. But you will remember that we had a murder and considerable mayhem in our midst only a few months ago."

Perhaps if my uncles had more conventional employment, I'd worry less about doors and locks. And maybe if that neighbor hadn't seemed so hostile.

In the middle of my trip, the lumpy man was joined by a scrawny, scowling woman. They seemed to be trying to give me the evil eye. What was this about?

"You tell her to keep that disgusting dog out of here," the woman hollered.

Did they mean Walter? How could anyone not love Walter? And how could anyone not love Karen for that matter? You have to be very mean-spirited to deny a recovering woman a few visits from her much-loved dog.

I didn't dignify their comment with an answer.

As I chugged up the stairs, Karen called out, "People can get past locks if they really want to."

I couldn't argue with that. I could get past locks myself. Hadn't I received a set of lock-picking tools for my sixteenth birthday? One of my most prized possessions. I chose not to mention that to Karen, especially as I only used them for good. And not often, may I add in my defense.

"Did you know that the great Lord Peter Wimsey was skilled at picking locks?" I said.

She twinkled at me. "I had forgotten that and about a million other facts. I'm not surprised. The man had a lot going for him."

"Tell me about it." I sighed. "On paper he's perfect."

"But unavailable."

I laughed. "Don't make a girl weep."

"Speaking of weeping, I finally remembered who acquired most of the stolen Sayers books."

"That's wonderful. Why would I weep? This is the best news I've had in months."

"It might have been, but I didn't write it down and now I can't quite remember anymore."

I tried to keep the disappointment out of my voice and struggled to find something positive to say.

"Easy come, easy go. And maybe easy come back again. If you remembered it once, then it's stored in your brain somewhere and it's bound to resurface."

"I hope you're right. I feel like a complete fool. You've been waiting on me and bringing me food and cleaning up my place for such a long time and I can't even come up with one simple name."

"Happy to do it, but I would feel much better if you'd keep the door locked. I have a key. I can get in if I need to. I don't like the look of that couple next door. They're very hostile."

"Oh yes. I miss the Sweeneys. They were so sweet. But these new people! Walter got through the hedge the day they moved in. Lucky couldn't squeeze through after him. I guess Walter left a little housewarming present."

I hooted. Couldn't stop myself.

She added, "I believe sandals were involved when the present was found."

I was still smirking when I made the last trip to the car to pick up a small vintage chalkware bank in the shape of a pug, my gift for Karen to fill in for Walter. I know it was wrong of me to let those neighbors see my smirk. Even if they did start it. Surely they could see that Karen was in fragile shape, using a walker.

Once I finished lugging, I heated up Karen's late "lunch" and puttered around the apartment while she ate. I made small talk about her book business as I tried to put things in order. I hadn't known much about the rare book trade until I'd taken the job with Vera in the spring. I may have indicated otherwise in my interview, but let's not dwell on that.

The signora would have been pleased with Karen's appetite that day. As I whisked the dishes off to the kitchen, she said, "If that doesn't fix my brain, I don't know what could."

I grinned. "On that optimistic note, would you like me to make you a cup of hot tea? It might cheer you up and make me forget how unavailable his lordship is."

"Lovely. Use the Satin Shelley set. That rich orange color is a lovely pairing to this fall day." Karen let out a sigh. "I wish I could be useful."

I loved that about Karen too. She'd been through hell, but that didn't mean she couldn't take comfort in her beautiful collectables. It must have been so frustrating for her to struggle with her memory like this, but she kept cheerful and wanted to be useful. I tried for a light note. "Hey, I have an idea. Close your eyes and try to picture the person who bought those hot books." I added, "Even though you didn't know they were stolen property at the time."

I came up with this approach after thumbing through my old Intro to Psychology textbook the day before. Although I'd discovered in college that I didn't want to know what's going on in other people's minds—chances are it's messy and ugly and none of my freaking business—Karen was a special exception. The chapter on hypnosis and repressed memory made me think we should try the DIY version. What could it hurt?

Karen leaned back and closed her eyes as instructed. "I know I didn't find anything in my client files." She gestured toward a chaotic pile of file folders and loose papers. I would have been surprised if she had found anything in that. "I'll keep trying."

"I don't want my tombstone to read 'killed by a woman in beige,' meaning Vera," I joked, turning back to the kitchen.

"Oh boy, I don't want to be responsible for Vera's crimes against you *and* fashion! Such a worry." She chuckled and relaxed a bit. I got her breathing deeply and stayed quiet in the hope that the right memory would pop into her dented noggin.

"Feel no pressure."

"If only it hadn't been the Sayers collection," Karen said. "Such elegant and witty books. So intricate."

I stuck my head back into the living room. "I agree. They're quite complex. You can't just sit and read one in a couple of hours. They are layered and there's a lot to be learned about the twenties and thirties in English society."

"Not all of it good," Karen said, a smile twitching her lips.

"Agreed. It's pretty shocking how matter-of-factly she reflects the prejudices of the day."

"I do like Wimsey and Harriet Vane though," she said.

"Me too. I especially love how the police just let him handle corpses and investigate crime scenes and order constables about. He can walk into and out of people's homes at will."

"Pays to be an aristocrat."

"No kidding. I wish I had a bit of that," I said with a grin, before getting back to my tea making.

"You have more than a bit of it, Jordan."

"Ah, but no, just a simple Irish family." I left out "of crooks," although I had a feeling it didn't bother her much.

"You carry yourself with confidence. I am sure you could walk into and out of people's homes at will. Who would question it?"

A few minutes later, I emerged from the tiny kitchen with

a bone china pot full of Darjeeling tea, with milk and sugar in matching pieces and a plate of amaretti.

"Signora Panetone sent you a fresh batch of her special almond cookies," I said. "She's taken a shine to you. Make sure you eat them all or that could change and you'll regret it for the rest of your life."

Karen had cleared off the small octagonal table by the armchair and stacked those books on the floor. "I don't deserve those cookies. I'm still drawing a blank."

"Everyone always deserves cookies." I settled things and poured the milk into delicate china cups in shades of orange and gold. Karen liked the milk in first. I'd learned to prefer it that way too.

I decided to help Karen's memory as I added sugar and poured.

"Tall or short?" I said.

She blinked. "I don't remember. They were sitting down."

I passed her the teacup. "Man or woman?"

"They are almost always men, in my experience. I mean my customers who collect fine first editions."

I did know that. "I guess Vera's the exception."

"She is unique. In many ways."

"No arguments here."

I said, "Hair or no hair?"

"Hair!" Her face lit up. "Lots of silver wavy hair."

"Excellent. Man? Woman?"

Karen's forehead crinkled. "Man. I suppose that's a bit of a help. A man with a great head of hair." She paused. "But also long hair, I think. I have a tiny memory of hair. Long hair."

"A man with long hair? It's not a good look for most people."

"Not a man. A woman. The woman had beautiful long

straight brown hair. A man and a woman." Her brow furrowed as she struggled to clear her mind. "The man was with a woman. She was helping him, I think. I can see them."

"Wonderful. Name?"

The smile slipped. "No names yet. But I can see their faces. She is younger than he is. A daughter perhaps. Or a trophy wife."

"Enjoy your tea. It will come back to you. We've just made progress."

"I feel terrible about this, Jordan. I had no idea that those books had been stolen from the Van Alst collection or I never would have touched them. I know you are under a lot of pressure to find them. There were some lovely volumes in that batch of books. I remember how excited I was when I was offered that collection. In perfect condition. I think I made quite a bit of money on them."

We sat chatting and nibbling on the almond cookies for a while.

I said, "I know you've checked it, but how about we go through your receipt book? Together. I can read out the names and . . ."

She shook her head. "Sorry. I think they were cash transactions. I don't usually put the person's name."

That would have been one hell of a cash transaction. But I didn't digress into the economics of cash transactions. None of my business. My business was getting the books back.

"Right. How about your mailing list? You do keep that?"

"Of course."

"If I run through the names, I could see if anyone sounds familiar."

"We could certainly do that. It will take a while."

I grinned. "Listen to the patter on the windows. It's

started to rain. So now it's a rainy Friday afternoon in October in beautiful downtown Grandville. I don't have a million things to do and I'm happy to hang out with you."

More than that, I needed to find those books for Vera or she was likely to make me miserable, or even fire me. I wouldn't have put it past her.

Karen said, "I'm glad of your company. I'm really pretty much stuck here until I recover from this . . ." She pointed to her head.

I tried not to remember what Karen had looked like when I'd found her wounded. I didn't want to revisit that image or those emotions and made a mental note to make sure Uncle Lucky was bringing Walter to visit Karen today. "How about a fire? Or is that gorgeous fireplace just for effect?"

"It works. I keep some faux logs in the basement. They're easy to light."

"I'll get them."

"There's a mason jar with matches. Bring some of those too, if you don't mind."

I stood up. "I'll get a couple of logs while you fish out the mailing list."

The basement was exactly the type you'd expect to find under a shop called the Cozy Corpse and also exactly what you'd expect from Karen. For starters, she had a triple dead bolt and it had a key on a Cozy Corpse key chain stuck in it. Why inconvenience your home invaders?

It was crammed with stacks of paper, battered books and broken tools. I was briefly distracted when I bumped into a large craft table parked in the middle of the only corridor. After one quick glance I concluded that at one time or another, Karen must have tried and abandoned every known pastime, from macramé to decoupage. There were cans of spray paint, small tools, a saw, turpentine, a huge jar of faux pearls and another one with buttons. You name it. Maybe the shop could be called the Crazy Corpse. I thought I could give her a hand with a garage sale. She could use a few dollars and the basement would be safer if it were cleaned out. I kept going and continued to bump into things, stacks of empty paint cans, musty books, dented cookware. It was very dark because ancient and dusty curtains hung on what must have been the windows. From the harvest gold, avocado and orange print, I dated them somewhere in the late sixties. Besides being dark and musty, the basement was full of unidentified lumps, shadows and creatures with eight legs and bad attitudes. Every piece of junk and the surface it sat on was covered with dust. Luckily, it didn't take long to find the stack of faux logs and the mason jar of matches next to a huge old stockpot on a shelf in the creepy basement. I figured Karen must have come down to pick up logs fairly often, because the area around them was relatively free of dust. I wasn't sure what else she might keep on those shelves, but I stopped wondering when a spider descended in front of me. I grabbed the last three logs and a half-dozen matches from the jar. I dashed back upstairs as fast as I could, brushing possibly real and possibly imaginary spiders from my hair. I hate spiders, real or imagined, and that's all I'll say on that topic. We spent the afternoon combing through the mailing list, correspondence and even emails. I kept a lid on my impatience, but I could tell that Karen was stressed by her inability to remember. She kept rubbing her forehead.

I fiddled restlessly with my smoky topaz cocktail ring until a thought finally popped up. "How did you send the books? Did you use a courier? That would be traceable."

"I don't think so. I don't have any record of it if I did. I've already checked."

"Mail?"

She shook her head.

"Or did he, or possibly he and she, pick them up? Because if so—"

Her eyes widened. "I delivered them!"

"Wonderful! Where?"

She frowned in concentration. "I'm not sure. It couldn't have been that far. I remember driving and pulling up in front of the house. But I don't remember where the house was. I feel so stupid."

"Please don't feel stupid. You're doing great and you're starting to remember."

"You know what? I do remember the house. It was a gorgeous Craftsman style."

I inhaled. I adored Craftsman-style houses.

She said, "Not that it will do us any good. A house without an address is pretty useless. It could be in any town. I wonder if we'll ever find those books for you, Jordan. You've been very kind to me and so has Vera."

I didn't want to tell Karen that kindness wasn't in Vera's makeup. No point in giving her anything else to worry about.

She said, "I really want to remember. It's useless, isn't it?"

"Not useless," I said. "But tell me, Karen, did you usually deliver books yourself?"

She shook her head. "No. So this must have been a very important customer. But then you'd think I'd remember him and/or her."

"Maybe it was someone you wanted to become an important customer. Someone new. Someone you didn't know all that well."

She smiled a slow smile. "That could be it. Something has to explain it."

"I have an idea. If you delivered books to these people,

then maybe other dealers would have done that for them too."

"Of course!"

"I think it's worth it for me to talk to a few other dealers."

Karen nodded. "I wish I could help you with some names but . . ."

"Don't worry about it. The Antiquarian Book and Paper Fair is back in Grandville this weekend." I heard a sharp intake of breath and glanced at Karen to see if the mention of the book fair had upset her. She was always pale. Was she a bit paler now?

Best thing was to act naturally and help her to feel that all the places in her world could soon be normal again.

I said, "It's quite possible that the same buyer has seen some of the other vendors and possibly asked for purchases to be delivered. I think I'll pop by tomorrow and sound people out."

Karen's face fell. I knew she was sad about missing out on the book fair and yet probably apprehensive about going. There was so little I could do for her. But I could do this.

"So tomorrow, got any plans you can't break?"

CHAPTER TWO

➖➤●➤➖

A T ELEVEN ON Saturday morning, I felt my back stiffen as we turned the Cozy Corpse van into the parking lot of Saint Sebastian's Hall and the Antiquarian Book and Paper Fair. The van did not handle nearly as well as my Saab, but we needed it for Karen's walker. In the passenger seat, she was breathing quickly. Never mind. It was time for both of us to get back on that horse. With Karen's disability parking permit attached to the rearview mirror of the van, we eased into the space next to the door. I could feel my heart rate rise. I could only imagine what Karen was feeling, returning to this spot. Still, Saint Sebastian's was where the fall book fair was happening and it was where we needed to be. I extricated Karen's walker from the side door of the van and set it up. She was trembling slightly as she got out of the passenger seat and gripped the handles. Together we walked toward the table to pay our five-dollar entry fee. The woman behind the table dropped her coffee cup when she spotted Karen. She paid no attention to the brown liquid spreading on the patterned carpet. "No charge for you!" she squealed. "Welcome back, Karen."

Karen's grin was shaky. But that was a good start.

There was no charge for me either, which was excellent, as most of my money went automatically into my college savings account. I was in my usual state of flat-busted broke, to use my uncle Danny's expression.

We wobbled through the big double doors into the exhibit hall. Karen's knuckles were white on the handles of her walker. We'd nicknamed the walker Winged Victory one day while joking about a drag race between Vera and Karen. I noticed the carpet had been upgraded to a smart, modern filigree pattern in a neutral color. It still had the triple underpadding. Nice. I guess the bloodstains never did come out. That under-padding certainly made it nicer for the folks that were on their feet all day working these events.

I inhaled the familiar and tantalizing smell of aged paper and leather bindings. I stared back at the clump of pale, gawking faces. I heard nothing. Not a peep. The room was silent. Then the tall, stooped, gray-bearded man at the map booth began to clap. Soon the room erupted in applause. "Welcome back, Karen," the woman from the booth with the vintage children's books shouted.

Karen was well on her way to putting the ghost of her attack behind her. I'd had my own trauma about this place, but this visit helped me to see it the way it should be and not as it appeared in my nightmares. In those nightmares the building was darker and my feet were heavier and I didn't get there in time to save Karen.

But I still had my task to take care of: finding some clue to the person who had bought the Sayers collection from her. As people pressed toward her, I helped her to a chair where she'd be able to hold court with everyone who wanted to say hello or squeeze her hand wordlessly. I leaned in and whispered, "If something shakes a memory loose, let me know right away." I didn't want to diminish the moment by adding, "before you forget."

In the meantime, I made the rounds, admiring the books, maps, old photos and sketches. I loved this stuff. I could only imagine how much Karen had missed this part of her world these past few months.

Finally, I reached Nevermore Mysteries, where I spotted George Beckwith with his elegant silvery hair. As usual he peered at me over the reading glasses at the end of his nose. His whole life was "just so." You could tell this guy was no fun to live with. From his sock drawer to his alphabetized refrigerator, Master Beckwith had to be in control.

There was no sign of his wife, Jeannette. Too bad, because I liked her more than I liked him.

"Jordan Bingham," he said, in his plummy British accent. Not for the first time, I wondered if that accent was real. "How nice to see you."

I wasn't so sure he meant it, but I would take what I got. He wasn't curling his lip, so that was promising.

"Looking for anything in particular?"

I wasn't likely to let George know that Vera was after something. By now he was well aware that I represented her, and that was enough to drive up the price of any desirable object. George being George, I wasn't sure he'd give me the information I wanted, just because I wanted it. Better not to let him think it was anything other than a friendly visit.

I picked up a pristine copy of *"B" is for Burglar* and said, "Just taking Karen around for a spin. She can't get out by herself yet."

I gasped as someone grabbed me. I spun, but before I could use the old Kelly standard uppercut, I realized it was

Jeannette Beckwith, George's much-better half. She had me in a bear hug. She might have needed a hip replacement, but she hadn't lost the strength you get from years of schlepping boxes. I was laughing when she let go. "Thank you for bringing Karen," she said, with tears in her eyes. "That was so kind."

"My pleasure."

Jeannette sank into a chair and winced. I sure hoped she'd get that operation soon.

I sank into the chair next to her. The Beckwiths had a double booth and always plenty of room for a customer to sit and be talked into a purchase.

Jeannette said, "It must be hard for her, being out of the mainstream."

"She's getting better."

"How's her memory? That's what I'd worry about after an injury like that." Jeannette's round, kind face was full of concern.

"She's making the best of it, trying to remember people. The other day we had a bet that she could remember a certain client's name. She was lusting over their Craftsman home where she delivered an order, and when I mentioned I would be auditing an American architecture class online, it just popped into her head. It wasn't even an important client, just suddenly this house and person were in her mind, then poof, blank. She couldn't remember who or where." I was making it up as I went, not wanting the Beckwiths to pick up on the real reason for our interest.

George decided to poke his longish nose into our conversation and I began to worry. Even his immaculately pressed shirt was annoying. I stifled an urge to somehow smear newsprint on it. I was sure that if George knew Karen needed to know someone's name, he was quite likely to see if there was anything in it for him. Rumor had it he'd been a ruthless trader in the days before he retired.

I wouldn't have put a bit of "client-napping" beyond him. Just as I went to change the subject, one of the regulars, an impossibly tall man in a trench coat, sidled up. I was glad of the distraction, but I wondered where he bought his pants.

Jeannette seemed unaware of my feelings about her husband and didn't appear to notice the unusual height of her customer. She chattered away. "We all forget things."

"Absolutely," I said. "I was thinking that going back to the house would jog something for Karen. She seemed to have it in her mind so clearly. If she were there again, maybe she'd remember more. Besides, I want to see this place. I love everything to do with the whole Arts and Crafts movement. I guess I'll just have to wait until this person reorders and then insist on delivering the order with her." I tried to sound offhand.

Jeannette said, "Oh, I know who that is!"

I was just about to ask who when George glanced over curiously. I leaned in toward Jeannette and said, "Who?"

"Oh, let me think! Gosh. Karen has an excuse. What's mine? I can't remember my own name lately. George insists it's my pain medication, but I'm not giving that up."

I tried not to bite my lip in frustration. Just as George turned back to fawn over a well-dressed male customer, Jeannette said, "Isn't that funny. I remember the house and the town, but not the name. We delivered a stack of lovely books over to Burton not that long ago. A very keen collector and a gorgeous example of Arts and Crafts near the downtown, not far from the statue of Hamilton Burton. It was almost enough to make me think of leaving Nevermore."

There wasn't much chance the Beckwiths would ever give up their charming yellow clapboard farm on its mani-cured acres, and little more that Jeannette would remember the name of the collector. But I almost did a dance of joy. With luck, I had enough to go on.

It was not easy to extricate Karen from the fair. I've had less trouble dragging Uncle Lucky away from a winning hand at the poker table. Every dealer had to have a word and the more demonstrative needed a hug or a hand squeeze. At least Karen would have something to hold on to: the thought of getting back to business and getting her life on track. For the moment, she was almost too exhausted to hobble back to the van. She leaned on her walker, swaying slightly.

"Tomorrow," I said when she was settled and comfortable, "we go to Burton."

All I heard back was a charming little snore.

It didn't matter. The town of Burton wasn't that far away, and how hard could it be for the two of us to find a single distinctive house?

BREAKFAST IS SERVED at eight sharp at the Van Alst residence, and you are on time if you know what's good for you.

Vera was already installed in the conservatory when I arrived slightly breathless, my hair still damp from the shower and pulled back into a twist.

Although the windowpane was now repaired, Vera's wheelchair was parked at an angle from the table so that she didn't face the gorgeous grounds, and she was sporting a moth-eaten blanket on her lap. Black Watch tartan, unless I was mistaken. Like every other morning, she was working at the *New York Times* crossword. That was fine. With the exception of regular stern reprimands and dismissive comments, I never expected small talk from her in the morning, or anytime really.

Even though Vera never kept the heat at a reasonable level, I loved the conservatory almost as much as I loved the signora's mountains of food. Again today the autumn leaves glowed magically outside the massive windows. Three sides of the Van Alst property were ringed with trees, a mix of deciduous and evergreen. We got all the benefits of every season.

Vera glowered at me.

I believe it was Tina Fey who coined the phrase "Blerg." *Blerg*, I thought, channeling Liz Lemon in *30 Rock*. This was not a great start to the day, but I was used to it. Plus my uncles have always taught me to act the way I wish things were.

"Spectacular foliage," I chirped as the signora bore down upon us with a platter of scrambled eggs and Canadian bacon. Perhaps a few lumberjacks were about to pop in and join us. "Eat! Good for you! Eat! You eat, Vera."

Vera ignored her and continued to scowl.

"Nothing but a nuisance."

I gasped. Vera could be harsh and insensitive, but it wasn't like her to actually insult Signora Panetone.

She added, "I hate leaves. Nothing but a big mess."

Ah. Just a little nature hating with our meal.

Of course. We were without a gardener or a handyman at the moment. No big surprise, as Vera wasn't the ideal employer and word travels. If you are the most hated woman in your community, it can be very inconvenient keeping your acreage pristine. The way they spoke about Vera in Harrison Falls, you'd think trees wouldn't even grow here. Most likely no one in any of the surrounding communities was willing to work for the daughter of the man who closed the Van Alst shoe factory and brought the area to its economic knees. It was a long time ago, but feelings still ran high.

Vera, being Vera, did nothing to improve that situation.

And as Uncle Mick would say, "Sometimes people need someone to hate."

It crossed my mind that life might be more congenial if I could help her find a replacement gardener. Of course, I had no idea who that might be, but I was definitely going to give it some thought. I didn't rejoice in the idea of spending weekends riding on the tractor mower, an activity that Vera was perfectly capable of requesting under "other duties as required" in my constantly changing job description.

The signora launched another stealth attack, depositing thick rustic toast, with lovely melted butter, on Vera's plate. I thought Vera's face would break at the sight of it.

"Is there zucchini in that bread, Fiammetta? You know I detest that vegetable and it is one more thing to loathe about the fall."

"Zucchini good! Vitamins! You eat, Vera."

Good luck with that, signora, I thought, gratefully accepting a couple of pieces for myself.

"Bah. No zucchini. Take it away. I can't stand the sight or the taste of it."

Since the signora's small, bizarre garden seemed to have produced enough zucchini to feed the county, I figured Vera would have a job avoiding it. I hadn't thought about it in the bread, which was delicious.

"And you, Miss Bingham, what is the progress on my Sayers collection?"

Well, I had found the town it was probably being held in, but I couldn't see that placating her for long. Nor would she be impressed with our optimistic plan of combing through the streets of Burton with Karen peering out the window over the tops of her gold-rimmed glasses in the hopes of recognizing her client's home as we rolled by.

"We have an excellent lead," I said with a big false smile, a Kelly family specialty.

"Make sure it pays off," she said before going back to her crossword. End of conversation. Was it my imagination or was Vera's glance even more antagonistic than usual? I knew that the Van Alst resources were strained. Was Vera thinking that she could do without me and save my salary and food costs?

What would I do? I was socking away most of my money to get back to grad school, and I couldn't even go back home. Anyway, Uncle Kevin was now installed in my former digs until things cooled down in Albany. Or someone died.

Outside the window, crimson, gold and orange leaves continued to drop to the ground, while Vera grumbled to herself over the *New York Times* crossword and I stuffed my face. I was worried though. I loved this job and I had a feeling that I'd better get my game on if I wanted to keep it.

A HALF HOUR later I was banging on Karen's door. No answer. The lumpy man next door stuck his head out the door and said, "Keep it down or I'll call the police. People are trying to sleep."

I tried opening the door. Unlocked as usual. I was in a panic when I burst into her second-floor apartment. No Karen in the book-strewn living room.

"Karen?"

I thought I heard a moan from the bedroom. I tripped over a pile of elderly cookbooks on my way and stopped, sagging with relief on the door frame.

Karen stared at me blearily from the bed, her unevenly cut red hair wilder than usual.

She smiled weakly. "I'm sorry. I know we're supposed to

go to Burton this morning to look for that client in the Crafts-man house, but I don't think I can even get up. All that excitement at the book fair knocked me off my feet. I can hardly stand up."

Big mistake on my part. I should have realized how tir-ing it would be. Karen wasn't supposed to get exhausted. She was supposed to rest and heal. She had many months to go before she would be anything like normal. I was new to this arrangement. I had to adapt.

"I'm so sorry. I shouldn't have put you through all that."

"Don't be crazy! I loved every minute of it. That's the nicest my colleagues have ever been to me. All those hugs. If I'd realized the benefits, I would have gotten hit on the head years ago. Anyway, it did me a lot of good and now I know I can go back to that world when the time is right. But today, I can't even get out of bed."

I said, "Don't worry. I'll drive over and have a look. But I don't suppose you remember anything more about the cli-ent? Besides the hair?"

She shook her head.

"Was it short and silver like George Beckwith's?"

Her eyes widened. "No, not George's. There was a lot of it, past his collar. Kind of a Beethoven look. Very dramatic. And he was courtly. I remember that. No one could call George courtly. Just uptight."

"Nothing else?"

"I wish."

Me too.

I left Karen with hot tea, this time served in a lovely oversized blue-and-white Royal Copenhagen cup. I'm partial to that soft blue-and-white combo. Books weren't Karen's only love. She had quite the china collection. I loved it too. I wanted to Pin almost everything in the cabinet to my Pretty

Things board on Pinterest. I quickly made some toast, added marmalade and collected a nice selection of old magazines for her. There were no new magazines in the apartment or in Karen's life. She liked it that way. She protested that she was perfectly happy. I put on her favorite bit of Mozart, but it still seemed wrong to leave her alone in the apartment.

"Get out of here," she said with a weak grin. "You're eating into my reading time."

"Fine, but I'm locking the door for your own safety."

That settled it. I would have to volunteer Uncle Lucky to start coming by twice a day. Karen needed more help than I could provide without risking her business. And if her business failed, she'd lose the building and her apartment too. It was getting a tad too chilly to sleep in the Cozy Corpse van. Karen was proud, but she'd just have to deal with having someone help out. Uncle Lucky could use Walter as a cover for doing just that. It might help disguise the fact he was besotted with Karen.

I had more than the missing Sayers collection on my mind when I finally left. I felt the weight of Karen's entire survival on my shoulders.

I HAD THREE reasons to head for my uncles' house. Only one had to do with Karen.

I prepared myself to dodge invitations to join them for breakfast, but it was not to be. Uncle Mick's ginger hair was uncombed and his face was the color of the signora's late-season tomato crop. I could already hear him fussing as I approached the kitchen in the back of Michael Kelly's Fine Antiques.

Uncle Lucky sat silent, but obviously vexed, his inch-thick ginger eyebrows furrowed. In front of him, the bowl of Frosted

Flakes that sat untouched and rapidly getting soggy said it all. Uncle Mick was a Count Chocula man and his bowl was in the same condition.

Only Walter seemed happily able to eat, as his doggie bowl was shiny clean. I couldn't help but notice that he was being served in a Wedgwood soup plate, a step up from cheap imports with doggie designs. His eyes bulged over the rim in delight.

"Everything all right?" I said.

Lucky sniffed.

Mick glowered at him. "What your uncle means to say is that life isn't always easy."

"You're kidding," I said. "I never heard that before."

"Don't start now, my girl. I know you haven't had it easy with your father disappearing like that when you were just a newborn babe and your poor darling mother . . ."

Uncle Lucky cleared his throat warningly at Uncle Mick. What was the matter with the two of them?

I had actually been thinking the source of the tension in the room was more likely the fact that Uncle Kevin had moved into my former digs. Kevin takes a little getting used to. As long as I remembered, he'd been a problem for his brothers. Why would they be surprised? Why wouldn't they have a plan B? Now he was a problem for me because I had no plan B place to go if Vera had a nuclear meltdown over the missing books. No point adding to the fallout by bringing that up.

I held up my hand. "It's okay. I don't own all the bad luck in the world. What's happening to upset the—?"

A crash from upstairs distracted all of us. A thundering on the stairs followed.

"Saints help us," whispered Mick. "That Kevin is going to be the death of poor Lucky."

"Ah," I said. "Of course. He's been here nearly twenty-four hours now, hasn't he?"

"Sixteen hours. He'll be flyin' under the radar for a bit," Uncle Mick said. "Feels like forever already."

Lucky nodded.

At that second Kevin burst through the door. "Going stir-crazy here. There's nothing to do in this place. I don't know how you two stand it at all. Are you a hundred years old?"

I was pretty sure Lucky rolled his eyes.

Mick said, "Why don't you detail the cars again, Kevin? Just keep the garage doors closed this time."

Uncle Kevin seemed to like this idea. His handsome, craggy face lit up. The mesmerizing blue eyes took on their signature twinkle. If there'd been a woman in the room, she might have been smitten on the spot, the poor thing.

I said, "How about if you do the Navigator first? I'm hoping to borrow it."

He was through the door in a flash.

"He seems, um, restless," I said.

Uncle Mick slammed the fridge door. "He's a giant pain in the—"

"What about if he helps in the shop?"

I heard a gasp from Lucky.

Even Walter looked at me as if I'd lost my mind. His flat, black, wrinkled mug frowned in concern.

"What? Would that really be so very bad?"

Uncle Lucky shook his shiny bald head, sadly.

Uncle Mick spoke as if I were just a touch slow. "You do remember that there was a small dispute about a *large* amount of money? And that is why Kevin is keeping a low profile."

"Ah."

"You really think the people involved would never think to look in our shop for Kevin?"

"Point taken."

"They are not the kind of people who listen to explanations. Kevin has seriously annoyed them. The rest of the family could be in an awkward situation." He glanced to Lucky and Walter and laid a hand on my shoulder.

"Awkward situation" is kind of a code in our family. Uncle Mick was more than a bit upset that Kevin had plunged the family into some unknown dangers.

"I get it. So Kevin has to keep out of sight, but being Kevin, he is restless and you're being driven around the bend."

"You hit the nail on the head, Jordan. He's like the poster boy for ADHD. Lucky and I enjoy our quiet life. Now we're at the end of our—"

"Maybe he can come along with me today. Karen is really not doing well and I have to hunt for a certain house over in Burton. I sure could use a driver so I can concentrate."

Uncle Mick brightened. Uncle Lucky managed a small smile. Even Walter wagged his twisty stump of a tail. But then he does that no matter what you say. Still, his eyes bulged in a way that could only mean "Get this guy out of here."

Of course, there's always a downside.

Uncle Mick said, "But everyone knows you're our niece, and most people know the Navigator too."

I said, "I don't plan to look anything like myself when I'm scoping out Burton. And please don't try to tell me in all that parking space that you don't have a single vehicle that isn't officially registered to a Kelly. I wasn't born yesterday."

Uncle Lucky made meaningful eye contact with Uncle Mick. I kept a straight face.

At last, Mick said, "Well, there's always the Kia. We've been saving it for an emergency."

I said, "Would you classify Uncle Kevin as an emergency?"

Walter barked.

Mick said, "I'll get the keys. Registration and insurance are in the glove compartment."

"Good. I'll be back soon."

Mick said, "Take your time."

THE GOOD NEWS was that the Harrison Falls Public Library opened at noon on Sundays and my friend was on duty. Equally pleasing was the fact I'd been able to send Uncle Kev off on an errand. He'd have fun at the vintage costume rental shop and I'd have a Kev-free conversation. The bad news was that a visit to the library always made me a tad flustered. Lance, the reference librarian, was a handsome flirt, but he'd been my true friend since we were in our teens and he was an information gold mine. Too bad he has such an effect on me. I hoped the bright pink on my cheeks subsided before I got to the reference desk.

Dapper as usual in Banana Republic chinos and a crisp blue gingham button-down, Lance's eyes sparkled, picking up the cornflower blue of his tie. "Is it cold out there, mademoiselle? Or are you just happy to see me?"

Mademoiselle? Lance's conversation always seemed from a different time, a bygone era of gentlemen and romance, mixed with the modern metrosexual lady-killer.

That wasn't helpful. My face was now deepest plum,

clashing with the ocher in my mother's Pendleton coat. Lance saw my discomfort and quickly changed the subject. "You have the look of a woman on a mission." Those dangerously twinkling eyes sparked brighter.

So, I filled him in on my little situation and set him out to hunt down the many different UK and American editions of Dorothy L. Sayers's work. With luck he'd score me some images of covers too. He would no doubt come up with a whole bunch of details that I didn't even know I didn't know. His fingers were snapping away at the keyboard seconds later. I could have spent a whole day watching Lance do "his thing," flipping his sand-colored hair absently as he pulled facts and figures from cyberspace and dusty volumes of reference materials alike. But I was not the only one who found Lance to be a bit dreamy. Behind me a slightly miffed group of octogenarians had formed. I was certain they disapproved of my casually leaning on the counter and my slightly north of the knee miniskirt, so I corrected my posture. The group clucked, unimpressed.

Feeling the pressure to release Lance to his duties, I said a quick good-bye and dashed toward the revolving door.

"Have you heard from Tiff?" he called to me, over the mauve and silver heads now crowding in.

I felt a pang in the chest but smiled anyway, shook my head and gave a shrug as I spun on my heel. It had been far too long since I'd had any good face time with Tiffany Tibeault, my best friend in the world. Her latest adventure was a clean, sustainable water initiative in Africa. She'd saved a bundle working as a nurse on the Alberta pipeline, and now she could afford to go do something good, working for an NGO. There was no one on Earth with more focused energy to give than Tiff. These water people would not know what hit them. She would do fantastic things, and I was so proud of her, but it was hard not to touch base. There was an empty feeling where my iPhone should have been vibrating. I missed her.

A LITTLE UNCLE Kevin goes a long way, even if you're as fond of him as I was. After all, he'd been the one who showed me how to climb out a window using a rope, scamper up a tree to escape an imaginary bear or a real police officer and pinch Oreos from the package leaving no evidence. Not to mention the frogs in the closet, but the less said about that the better. Growing up as an only child, Uncle Kevin was the next best thing to a misbehaving brother who would get stuck with all the blame for joint escapades. Still, by the time we reached Burton, I was desperately trying to tune out the constant whistling, chat, squirming and drumming on the steering wheel. The Kia Sorrento was a good-sized vehicle, but I sure felt claustrophobic cooped up in it with Kevin.

On the other hand, I was very pleased with our new appearances. For once I was the redhead in the family, with a shoulder-length mane of glossy auburn. Uncle Kevin was jaunty with a silver mustache, fake tortoiseshell glasses and a herringbone fedora. He would have made an excellent companion if he'd been able to keep still. It was a challenge to convince him to take an orderly approach to our slow cruise of the streets of the older section of Burton. He preferred random and of course he liked speed, but he didn't do too badly, more or less. Anyway, the drive was beautiful.

Luckily, it wasn't hard to find a prime example of a Craftsman house in the older section of Burton, as it was small and compact. Unluckily, I found three. I hadn't asked

Karen for any distinguishing features of the home where she delivered the Sayers collection. I'd thought that Craftsman would say it all. So I was stuck with 4 Washington Avenue, 22 Madison Street and 87 Lincoln Way.

All very presidential. This part of Burton was like a Norman Rockwell vision of small-town America. Golden oaks and bright maples punctuated wide lawns. There wasn't a house that had been built after the thirties. The place screamed "family." A number of families were getting an early start on Halloween with inflatable headstones on the grass and small ghosts floating in the trees. Old oak trees and wonderful gardens lined the streets. Even though I enjoyed my life at Van Alst House, I would have loved to reside here.

Daydreaming of a future in which I could spend *my* days tending roses, I looked forward to visiting our collector, maybe more than once. After all, I did a bit of work scouting for books on the side and I could always use a new buyer for anything that Vera didn't want. I reminded myself to stop dreaming and find the right house.

I thought I could dismiss 22 Madison Street because of the collection of Fisher Price toys, Tonka trucks and headless Barbie dolls dotting the front lawn. Just in case, I took a picture to show Karen. I also used my phone to take shots of 4 Washington Avenue. The property was a bit run-down, but still mouthwatering. My dream is to settle down in such a house and restore, restore, restore.

When we pulled up in front of 87 Lincoln Way, an older man was puttering around the property next door. He checked us out, radiating suspicion. I figured him for a widower, because no one with a wife would be allowed in front of the house in black socks, sandals, baggy shorts and a tartan cap. Even if he was dutifully raking the lawn. He probably thought we were casing the joint, which we were, sort of.

I waved. The last thing we needed was to attract a lot of attention, and it was important to put him at ease. And I didn't want to give the occupants any advance notice before returning with Karen. Or cause some neighborhood busy-body to notify the police about a suspicious car. Who knew what kind of provenance the Kia had?

"Stop the car," I said and hopped out. I approached the neighbor, smiling, my fabulous fake auburn hair blowing in the autumn breeze. I thought I was a good match for the red and gold leaves swirling around. I sniffed. Someone nearby was baking, apple pie if my nose was to be believed. The aroma made me smile, as did the neighbor's tartan cap, Royal Stewart, my favorite, maybe because the Queen of England leans toward it.

"Hello," I said, extending my hand and continuing to smile brightly at the cap. "We were just looking for an American Craftsman house in this area and we spotted this little beauty. I can't tell you how exciting this is. A thrill." I gestured grandly toward Number 87 with its gabled roof and tapered columns supporting the roof over the wide veranda, with the deliciously exposed rafter beams. Trust me, I had done my homework. This one had it all: it was what they called a foursquare and had what looked like the original multipaned windows and the partially paned door that all real examples sport. I loved the earthy color of the house and the contrasting brick-red trim. The red door picked up the colors of the surrounding sugar maple trees. I wasn't exaggerating about the thrill. In my childhood dreams of having a real home with a real mother and father—instead of the ever-changing parade of lovable uncles—I always imagined us being happy in a house like this. Other kids collected My Little Ponies. I collected photos of Craftsman houses and kept them in an album. I realized that the dream of the mother and father was lost, but someday, I told myself, I'd have a house like this. Somewhere safe and legal, a place to love and be loved. I did hope no one would ever be casing my house in a Kia and a red wig.

Maybe I'd add a secret passage or two.

The neighbor's suspicious look persisted. He held on to his rake and ignored my outstretched hand. "You're just driving around looking for a certain house? Why would you do that?"

I let my hand drop but kept the smile plastered to my face. I realized I must have seemed slightly deranged, but it was too late to conjure up another faux personality. "I have a client who is very interested in a Craftsman house in Burton. And as I said, this is such a lovely example. We'd love to get inside, but the owners don't seem to be around." I pointed to the red front door and tried for a fetching little pout. This wig was starting to mess with my personality.

Never mind. It seemed to do the trick. I suppose it was the not-too-subtle suggestion that I was a real estate agent—without coming right out and saying it—but surely the pout counted for something too.

"They keep to themselves," he said. I thought I noted a wistful tone.

"Do they?"

"Very standoffish. Never have a word to say. They certainly don't add anything to the neighborhood."

"Hmm."

"And as you can see, they have let the property go. The foundation plantings have been chopped down and there's nothing left of the garden at all."

"Oh. What a shame."

"Scandalous. It was pristine when they bought it."

"When was that?"

"Just less than three years now."

I glanced back at the car, where Uncle Kevin was watching with interest. I hoped he wasn't getting any fashion ideas from this gentleman. Uncle Kevin is far too easily influenced. I would have liked to take a picture of the house, but I debated whether that seemed too suspicious. On the other hand, this neighbor didn't look all that tech savvy. If I used my phone to snap a photo of the house to show Karen, would he even know what I was doing? I decided to assume that you can't assume much about people and appearances can be deceiving. Certainly I was proof of that. The neighbor seemed to find this new redheaded me quite fascinating, a nuisance for sure.

Why is it that there is not a single person to be seen in the middle of the day on the average street in our area, yet whenever I need to snoop, there's practically a neighborhood committee meeting?

"Are the owners out now?" I asked. There was no car in the driveway and no sign of lights on inside on this gloomy day, so it was a good bet.

"You just missed them. They drove off in their fancy car, not ten minutes ago."

"Darn. That's inconvenient. Not my lucky day, I guess."

"Guess not," he commiserated. I felt his attitude begin to thaw.

"Fancy car, you say?"

He nodded, disapprovingly. He was sort of a cute old geezer with that tartan cap. Just needed a wife to establish a few guidelines about pants.

"Hmm," I said producing the smile yet again. "I suppose I should just leave a note. Do you know their names? I like to personalize these things." The neighbor looked very interested at that.

"Adams," he said. "I don't know their first names. As I said, they're not that friendly. They've never introduced themselves to me."

I resisted the urge to blame that on his cap.

I was disappointed to hear the confirmation that they weren't friendly. If this was the place, I was hoping for warmhearted souls who could be convinced to swap the Sayers collection for something else, thus saving my job, apartment and financial neck plus freeing Karen from her burden of guilt.

"That's fine. I'll leave a note for Mr. and Mrs. Adams then. Thank you ever so much."

Ever so much? Wow, I was really getting into this role-playing thing.

"Don't you have a card?" he asked. "Usually real estate agents just leave their cards in the mailbox. Brochures too. And information sheets with photos of properties that they have sold in the area. When I think of real estate agents, I think of lots and lots of teeth."

"Of course, I do have all that kind of promotion," I said, showing my teeth and pretending to reach into my shoulder bag for my nonexistent cards, brochures and information sheets.

He frowned thoughtfully. "But, of course I always throw that bumpf straight into the recycling bin. Waste of good trees. If I want an agent, I'll just call one."

"Exactly, and *I'm* eco-friendly. Plus I think a note would be better. More personal, as this is a very personal quest for my client."

"On the other hand, a card might be good. I wouldn't mind getting one in case I decide to sell. Maybe your client would be interested in my house."

"Indeed," I said, a bright smile glued to my face. Was he

trying to jerk my chain? Whatever, I hoped a steady stream
of information would distract him. "The client is obsessed
with American Craftsman style. I could never deflect her
from that. She has money, the kind of money that nobody
says no to, if you get my point." I could see that his interest
was waning. "I think I might not have too much trouble
finding someone interested in a unique Victorian like yours."
By unique, I meant marred by a couple of really bad remod-
els. I wondered who had stripped the gingerbread from the
house and what he or she had been thinking. Some folks
have no appreciation for history.

He said, "Maybe I should sign you up right now."

This definitely called for a diversion. No point in going
any further down the faux Realtor road. I pointed to the low,
neatly manicured boxwood hedge that separated the two
properties. "By the way, I am very interested in this green-
ery. Mine never seems to do well. My, um, husband does all
our gardening. Would you mind telling him your secret? It
seems so . . . luxurious, yet controlled."

Kevin was probably at the point of death by boredom by
this time, and he perked up immediately and leapt from the
car. He managed to insert himself between the nosy neighbor and me and bent over to examine the hedge.

"Remarkable. What's your secret?" he asked. "Bonemeal?"

Bonemeal? Really? I almost fell off my stiletto heels.
Who knew that Kevin had any idea at all about gardening?
Where in the world would he have picked up that skill? Was
it some special parole program that he'd never mentioned
to us? Of course, Uncle Kev was nothing if not mysterious.

Panicking that he wasn't going to wander down the "garden path" with Kev, I continued my weird flirting offensive
and reached out to touch the man's forearm, a move that

Lance and Tiff could pull off, but it just felt wrong to me. No more of that, I told myself.

He said, "I don't think I have a secret. It's just a row of boxwood." But the look in his eyes added, "Why is this weird woman touching me?"

Kev was beaming. "It's glorious! Do you feed it?"

"Feed it? No, I just trim it." The neighbor turned to his boxwood with new interest and respect.

Kev leaned toward him. "I bet you talk to it. Makes all the difference."

Kevin actually seemed to be taking care of the problem, for once. That's what it took to really thaw this neighbor. He leaned the rake against the bushes and stuck out his hand. "Harry Yerxa."

"Billy Bishop," Kevin said. "Glad to meet you." The World War One flying ace was a hero of his, but I worried that it was just a matter of time until someone recognized the name.

"The flying ace!" Harry Yerxa said.

"Yup. Named for him. My father was a big admirer." Kev knew well enough, as we all did, not to elaborate too much. It's the details that can trap us. I hoped he wasn't going to blow our cover.

Still, I was impressed despite myself. Although he was probably one of the world's best improvisers, he sounded like he knew a thing or two. He may have had the neighbor fooled, but I'd kind of fallen for it too.

While he was being his distracting best, I used my iPhone to take a couple of good shots of the Adams house from the sidewalk. It was not only heartbreakingly beautiful, it was also very photogenic. Then, leaving Harry Yerxa to fend for himself, I dashed up the path to the front door and pretended to leave a note. Actually, I was checking out the place in

case I needed to have an "informal" and unauthorized visit
at a later date. I was surprised to spot two separate dead
bolts on the door. What a shame to see them marring that
wonderful red front door. I rang the doorbell, just in case. I
heard the bell echoing from the inside. I waited and then
glanced around surreptitiously before peering through the
small panes in the top third of the door. I couldn't see a
thing. Next I knocked loudly and long. Finally I tried peek-
ing in the windows. I noticed that the windows were alarmed
as well. Out of the corner of my eye, I observed a wall-
mounted camera and then another tucked behind the exterior
light. That's a good trick. Amateurs disable the first camera
and don't realize that there are more. I wasn't likely to fall
for that, but I would be clearly visible on both of them. I was
very glad I had the wig and hoped that my features wouldn't
be identifiable on the recording of my visit. I pulled a piece
of paper and a pen from my bag and pretended to attempt
to write a note. I thought I simulated the frustration of having my pen run out of ink. "Darn," I said loudly. "My pen's
not working. Honeee!"

I headed down the walk and interrupted Uncle Kevin and
Mr. Yerxa, who were in a deep and meaningful discussion
about the spectacular specimen of burning bush on the front
lawn. I said, "So sorry to interrupt, but I just realized we
are very late for our appointment with the lawyer. And you
know what? My stupid pen ran dry so I couldn't leave a note
for the Adamses." I smiled winningly at Mr. Yerxa. "Would
you be kind enough to mention to the Adamses that we were
here? Thank you so much. Must run! I'll drop off a card
later."

Kevin responded instantly, and within a second we were
in the Kia and around the corner.

CHAPTER THREE

❧❧❧

"T HAT *WAS* A good hedge. I like boxwood," Uncle Kev said. "What's our hurry?"

"Crazy security there. I didn't want to be too identifiable on the camera. So I hope he really does mention that some Realtor was here."

"What kind of security? Cameras?"

"Yup. And not just one, plus double dead bolts. Not to mention connections on the windows and who knows what else. They'd even removed the foundation plantings. No one could hide there to gain access through a window."

"They had a murder in the neighborhood, Harry told me."

"A murder? In Burton?"

"Yeah. Some guy got himself stabbed not a block from here."

"That's terrible. Was it a robbery? A domestic assault?"

Kev said, "Doesn't look like it. Harry thinks it was some drifter. I figure more like a falling-out between gangs, but I kept my opinion to myself. The neighborhood's spooked."

"I'm not surprised. So maybe that's what the Adamses are worried about. But something tells me they also have stuff they don't want stolen, such as a collection of first editions that includes some pristine Sayers first editions. I hope the cameras didn't pick up me taking a shot of the house earlier."

Kevin grinned. "So should we come back looking very different?" As his mustache was half flopping off, the answer was easy.

"Yes. Different. But first I'll have to try the address, the name Adams and show the picture of the house to Karen, to see if any of it strikes a chord. I am betting that they have that security for some good reason. Did you find out anything about them during your gardening chat?"

"Don't knock the gardening, Jordan. People melt when they talk about their gardens. You can get anything out of them."

"And did you?"

"There are three people in the family, an older man who is either the husband or the father of a very pretty woman, and an adolescent who is either the son or grandchild of the older man. The woman is definitely the mother, as the kid calls her 'Mama.'"

"The older man sounds right, and Karen remembers a woman when she delivered the books. Anything else?"

"They've lived there about three years and they did a lot of interior remodeling when they first moved in. Harry says they're well-off, driving an Audi, and he thinks they sunk a ton of money into the inside of that house, even though they have pretty well destroyed the landscaping and the foundation plantings. I gotta say I agree with him on that. And he suggests that you warn your client they will probably expect to recoup their investment when they sell."

"I'll keep that in mind. My imaginary client thanks you."

"Anything I can do to help, just ask," Kevin said, stepping

on the gas. It would have been a perfect getaway if we hadn't passed a police cruiser idling by the curb as we shot by. I tensed, waiting for sirens and flashing lights before my brain processed the visual information. We were in the town of Burton. So what possible reason could there be for a Harrison Falls police officer to be—and there is only one way to describe it—lurking around so far from home.

Sure enough. Kevin pulled over. But only after giving me his well-known "Should we make a break for it?" look.

"There won't be any way to trace this Kia, will there?" he said.

"It's a valuable asset to Uncle Mick and Uncle Lucky. I'm pretty sure the documents will be in order," I said. "And for the record, we haven't done anything wrong."

"Impersonating a real estate agent."

"Not sure that's a felony," I said. We both jumped at the knock on the window. Uncle Kevin turned the color of boiled rice.

What do you know? The tall, slightly pudgy yet adorable Officer Tyler Dekker smiled his innocent smile as a serious blush raced from his neck to the top of his wavy blond hair.

"Did you take a wrong turn, Officer?" I said.

"Just taking a drive for my break," he said. "You?"

"Funny thing, I had the same idea. Just drive around. See the sights."

He nodded. "Nice way to try out the new hairdo." That smile of his with the small chip in the left incisor always gets me.

"What?"

"Of course, I did like you as a brunette. A lot." His ears were practically glowing at this point.

"Thank you. It's just a wig. I thought I'd try it before making a drastic color switch."

"Good thinking. And will you keep it?"

"The wig?"

"The red."

This wig had cost me some serious dollars and I hated the idea that I'd have to get rid of it because the law was onto me. On the other hand, I hadn't done anything wrong. But talking to cops is something that no one in my family is comfortable with. Especially Uncle Kevin. I figured he was near death sitting next to me. I didn't dare look at him, and I certainly didn't intend to introduce him to Officer Smiley.

He leaned in. "So, who's your friend?"

Even though I knew CPR, I hoped Uncle Kevin didn't have an undiagnosed heart condition.

"Friend?"

He pointed to Uncle Kevin.

"The one in the driver's seat."

"Oh. Right. He's an old acquaintance visiting from Denmark."

Officer Smiley blinked.

Uncle Kevin was quivering like an aspen.

I said, "Yes, he's visiting and just wanted to see the sights."

"Guten Tag," Kevin said.

Dekker blinked.

"Um, he has been touring. Most recently Germany, as you can hear. And now it's time to get him back to catch his plane."

I smiled and rolled up the window before Kevin said "Arrivederci" or something even more Kevin-like.

Really, it might have been better to have simply said that I was searching for a house of a collector who may have bought some of Vera's missing books from Karen Smith. What would have been wrong with that? If it had just been me, I would have done it. I've developed a soft spot for Officer Smiley, but there was the matter of Uncle Kevin. If his business acquaintances were interested in getting their mitts on him, the forces of law and order were even more so. And according to Uncle Mick, cops are the biggest gossips on the planet.

I waved as I drove away. Maybe the wave was a bit too frenetic. But the coincidence of Tyler Dekker showing up on that exact street did bother me just the tiniest bit.

I CHECKED MY iPhone as soon as Officer Smiley was a dot in the rearview. Dead. It's not like me to forget to charge it, but I was a bit off my game worrying about these missing Sayers books and feeling lonely without a word from Tiff and getting saddled with Kev and all the dangers that could present. I felt almost naked without my phone, so I weighed the pros and cons, pun intended, of bringing Uncle Kevin back to my flowery garret while I recharged the phone, instead of ditching him with Mick. The anxiety of not having the world at my fingertips was too great. I don't like to drive alone without it. I have my reasons. Kevin gunned it and headed for the Van Alst House, chirping away at my side as he drove.

Boy, could he chatter. He could have talked for the US of A in the Olympics.

I tried not to think of the disastrous implications of my uncle and Vera coming face-to-face.

When Kevin volunteered to remain in the car, I felt relief at getting away from the constant conversation. The relief was mixed with anxiety that he might get restless, leave the vehicle and encounter the signora or, worse, Vera.

As fast as my little legs would carry me, I was up the stairs and through the door into my cabbage rose–clad garret, the very best perk of this job. It was a bit messy at the moment, which I truly tried to avoid at all costs, lest there be some sort of impromptu inspection by the boss. And yes,

I'm sure she could manage to find a way around the lack of wheelchair accessibility. All witches can fly, right?

After a desperate scan of my morning chaos, I spotted the car charger. It was sitting on top of four very nice New English Library reissues of Sayers books on my Lucite coffee table. I loved the cover designs. I gracefully dodged piles of my favorite vintage summer clothes, on the way to winter storage. The inheritance of my mother's stunning wardrobe had started my love of all things vintage. Her clothing—in pristine condition—had been saved until I grew into it, another of the many reasons I felt so grateful to Uncle Mick and Uncle Lucky. Seeing the stacks of bright summer wear on every surface in my sitting room lit a flame of pride in me. But there was no time to fondle my treasures. I practically tumbled down the narrow back stairs to get myself outside before Uncle Kev got on the loose. To my utter, breathless amazement, Kevin sat, round eyed and expectant, still belted in the car. He was hardly even chatty on the way home. That was a relief after the ongoing verbiage of the drive over, but I didn't pay much attention to the change in one-sided conversation. I was delighted to have my recharged phone buzz with a text message from Lance.

> *Would the lovely lady like to join me for dinner, dancing and dishing? Say 6 o'clock at the Hudson Café?*

I texted back.

> *Well, I'm up for dishing, but over coffee! Dinner, drinking and dancing some other time. Lol. See you at 6.*

I decided my day might still turn around. Being at a dead end with work and on the hook for Uncle Kevin must have settled some Karmic debt. An evening with Lance would keep me from missing Tiffany too much and could actually pan out as far as a lead on these swindled books. I got to hang out with an oh-so-good-looking friend who loved to flirt like a devil. Or an angel. Something.

I was still smiling when I arrived at Uncle Mick's. I happily regained my former identity, abandoned Uncle Kev to park the Kia, took a deep breath, reclaimed the Saab and was off.

KAREN'S APARTMENT WAS beyond stuffed when I arrived at the Cozy Corpse and hustled up the stairs. The presence of Uncle Lucky was key to that. As you have probably figured out, he's a man who fills any room. And Walter added to the general chaos of the place. Karen was lounging in her brown corduroy chair, her eyes sparkling and her cheeks red. Walter was busy cavorting and knocking over stacks of books, happy to be home again. Uncle Lucky was perched on a nearby dining chair, one of one. He made me think of a lovesick moose.

Uncle Lucky keeps his thoughts to himself, but Karen couldn't keep her eyes off him. I really needed her to pay attention to me so that I could talk to her about the Adams residence and the possibility that these people were the clients.

After picking up seven toppled stacks of books, I gave Uncle Lucky a meaningful look. "Walter looks like he needs to go out. I'll keep Karen company if you don't mind doing that."

"He's fine, just a bit excited," Karen said, with a girlish giggle.

I shot Uncle Lucky an even more meaningful look and he located a plastic bag and lumbered to the stairs with Walter. The Kellys know how to take a hint.

Karen gazed at Lucky the way a teenage girl stares at Justin Bieber. At any moment I expected her to declare him dreamy.

I said, "Watch out for Walter and the neighbors' lawn. They're ready to go to war." I took over his chair, leaned forward and said, "Karen, I think I found the house. Does the address 87 Lincoln Way mean anything to you?"

She frowned, concentrating.

Please, please, remember, I thought.

"How about the name Adams for the clients?"

She bit her lip.

I hated that sinking feeling.

I held up my iPhone and showed her the shot of the house.

It was hard to keep breathing while I waited.

Finally, Karen's smile was back. "You know, I think that *is* the house. At least I'm pretty sure. Well, it might be."

"And, as I said, the name is Adams." My voice shot up an octave, showing my near desperation.

She shrugged.

I tried to stay optimistic. "Well, we'll go with what we have. We need to get over there and find out if we can get those books back without alerting this Mr. Adams—if indeed he is the client—to the fact that Vera wants them back and is beside herself over their loss."

Karen looked up. "Oh yes, I had forgotten why we were doing this. We have to get the books back. Are you sure I should go?"

"Absolutely. You need to produce something that you think he'll want for his collection. Something absolutely tantalizing. Worth trading. I'll coach you and we'll tell them that I'm . . ."

"Thinking of buying my business?" She beamed at the idea.

"What? Oh, right. That's a great idea. So that would explain my presence. I'm shadowing you. That will work. But I need you to make the contact. Tell them you might have to go to hospital again or something and want to see him as soon as possible, as there's other interest in whatever we're dangling in front of him."

All of sudden, Karen lit up. "I do remember! It was Randolph Adams. Of course. Let me see if I have the number." She fumbled through her client files. Finally, she squealed with joy. I squealed with her.

Karen made the call to the Adams number and I hovered. I was happy to see that she hadn't lost her touch.

"I remembered we talked about Edith Wharton among other writers during my visit. I have acquired two very fine Edith Wharton firsts that I thought you would like to have a look at. I have some other people who will be interested too, so feel no pressure. I thought as you had been so pleased with the Sayers books, you should be my first call."

Just as Uncle Lucky and Walter shook the walls thundering back up the stairs, Karen gave the thumbs-up to me. "That's wonderful, Mr. Adams. See you tomorrow morning at ten. I look forward to it."

We were set.

LANCE THE MAGNIFICENT had come up with information about several series of Sayers reprints and bibliographies listing each series. This was good. He also wanted to talk in great detail about the one thing I was trying to avoid: Tiff. This was not good.

"Yes, I miss her terribly. Things are in a mess now because of the Sayers collection. Tiff always kept me grounded. It's hard when your best friend drops out of your life. So, moving on, back to the books. You say there was nothing? Not even a teeny, tiny shred of something for me to go on?"

Lance was wearing his "I feel for you" face. It ranked far below his "I am devouring you with my eyes" face. Lance kept talking, but I zoned out on his sweet concerned look and missed every word.

"You know, you remind me of her. It's eerie almost." For a split second his charming twinkle returned. "I would totally have fallen for that dame."

"Wait, what? Who? Tiff?" Just as I'd always suspected. We were three friends but she was more than a friend to—

"Not Tiff. I'm talking about Harriet Vane. I didn't even need to do any research on her. I've read all the Sayers books more than once. And she is *so* you, Jordan."

I tried to suppress a goofy grin.

He said, "She's strong, self-made and lost both her parents early on. She falls into bizarre mysteries and gets herself quite the notorious reputation. Brilliant and dangerous all at once." Twinkle, twinkle, sparkle.

Brilliant and dangerous? I've been described with far less generosity.

"You are like someone from another time, Jordan, and not just the clothes." He locked his eyes with mine. "Wimsey and I share impeccable taste."

I did my best to get through the rest of our get-together. Pretty sure this is why people say men and women can't be friends; sometimes one of them blushes to death.

CHAPTER FOUR

❧❀❧

HARRY YERXA WAS busily clipping his boxwood hedge as I drove up to 87 Lincoln Way with Karen. At this rate I figured the hedge would be no more than six inches high at the end of the week. Thousands of bright leaves swirled around the lawn. He had chosen to dress for hedge clipping in yet another version of tartan. I wasn't 100 percent sure, but this one looked like Clanranald. Whatever the tartan, someone should have been kind enough to tell him that tartan shorts do not do the wearer any favors, no matter what his age is. At least he'd changed his cap. This one was a subdued tweed affair, but not subdued enough to save a person's eyes from the shorts.

Karen didn't even notice. She was happy to be able to remember the client and the house. She clutched her large tapestry handbag in excitement. "This is it! I'm sure of it. This is wonderful, Jordan. We shouldn't have any problem. I remember Mr. Adams as a lovely older gentleman with lots of interests, from Wilkie Collins to George Pelecanos and lots of authors in between, although usually he liked the boys rather than the girls, with the exception of Edith Wharton, for some reason. That could help us get the Dorothies back. He didn't confine himself to mysteries either. I seem to recall a fascination with Hemingway."

I was also happy. A glossy Audi sedan in an icy shade of silver was parked just in front of the garage. The Adams family was home! We were getting closer to finding the Sayers collection, and I felt optimistic about getting the books back.

"Maybe I'll regain my old life after all," Karen mused.

"Absolutely. I know you will."

As I helped Karen from the Cozy Corpse van and set up her walker, Harry Yerxa looked up from his boxwood shaping and squinted at us suspiciously. I had to remind myself that Jordan Bingham hadn't actually ever met him.

I tried to make eye contact rather than stare at the shorts or the knobby knees that should have been under cover.

"Hello," I chirped as we made our slow way up the walk.

He frowned and stared at me with an unwelcome flicker of recognition. "Have we met?"

I paused and pretended to consider that. "I don't think so. I am taking my friend to see Mr. Adams." I deliberately left my name out of the conversation.

He sputtered, "What happened to the good old days when funeral homes were quiet and dignified? Everything in this world doesn't have to be a joke."

Karen and I exchanged stunned glances. I was surprised that my jaw didn't smack the sidewalk.

"I'm sorry?" I said. Had someone died and we missed it?

He pointed to the van we'd just emerged from. "The Cozy Corpse? What kind of business is that? Did someone die?"

It took every muscle in my face to keep from laughing out loud.

"It's a reference to mystery books. I have a business specializing in used and rare crime fiction," Karen said gently. "See the smaller print?"

We left him peering at the van's lettering and tried not to collapse howling as we got to the door. The security cameras must have captured the hilarity. I hoped the neighbor didn't hear. I didn't want to burn any bridges with Harry. He was observant and he took himself and life very seriously. It was a safe bet that he'd be a person who was a very good source of information.

Stairs were still a challenge for Karen, and I did my best to help as she struggled up the six steps to the front entrance of the Adams house. Despite the struggle, we were still smothering our grins when we reached the red front door.

The door opened with a slow creak, and the song lyrics—"the Addams Famileeeeeee"—vibrated in my brain. I half expected to see Lurch answering, but a tall, slender woman faced us instead. She was elegant and entirely without angles, seemingly almost boneless, with a pale face and translucent skin with an otherworldly glow. Her ankle-length jersey outfit, a faded taupe, seemed to have been chosen to not draw attention from that face. Her long straight hair was a paler shiny shade of the same taupe color, and she wore it parted in the middle and rippling down past her shoulders. This was the long hair Karen had mentioned. I could not remember when I had come face-to-face with a more beautiful woman. This wasn't the beauty of a supermodel, but rather the stuff of romantic Arthurian legends and tragic ballads. But she was not wearing an expression of ethereal bliss. In fact, if looks could kill, Karen and I both would have been dead and long buried. When she shot a glance in my direction, I flinched and Karen stood speechless.

A flaming paper bag filled with doggie doo-doo couldn't have received a worse reception at that entrance. At least she didn't stamp on us.

Maybe not that far off from Morticia after all. I extended my hand and said, "So nice of you to have us, Mrs. Adams. I am Karen's friend."

She didn't deny the Mrs. Adams bit, but she scowled at Karen, who gripped the handles of her walker to steady herself. Mrs. Adams appeared to be blocking the door. "You didn't tell us you were bringing anyone," she said in the tone of a DA bringing a charge. Her voice was strong and bitter, a strange contrast with her lovely face and willowy body.

I said in my most harmless tone, "You may not be aware that Karen has been in the hospital for quite a while and is recovering from a head injury." I left out the details of the attacks and the memory loss. "I am just here as friend and chauffeur. I also pack, carry and unpack boxes as required." I smiled to show how harmless I was. I also decided not to tell this woman that I was thinking of buying Karen's business. One less lie.

Karen interjected along with her lopsided grin, "I could get addicted to this service. I'm not sure how I'll survive without staff. I'm spoiled rotten now."

The smile, the grin, the little jokes fell flat. From the look on this woman's lovely face, we were as unwelcome as a pair of skunks at a garden party. It takes more than that of course to derail anyone with Kelly genes. My experience may have been limited, but I was old enough to know that this kind of stalling was usually because someone had something to hide.

I stepped into the doorway, causing her to have to step

back into the house. Before she could regain her door-blocking spot, I turned and gave Karen a hand to get over the threshold. I kept babbling about how much I loved Craftsman designs, and Karen made an effort to make her way farther into the house. "We just need to speak to Mr. Adams for a couple of minutes," Karen said, moving steadily toward what would be the living room.

"He is not at all well," the woman said, now attempting to insert herself between us and the figure in the leather chair by the fireplace where a warm fire beckoned. "He shouldn't be disturbed."

"We won't be a sec."

"Delilah, my sweet," came a mellifluous voice from the leather chair in front of the flickering fire. "You must make our guests feel welcome. Stop worrying. I am just fine. More than fine."

I thought she swayed at the sound of the voice. At that moment she seemed like a pale, beautiful ghost, a shimmering reminder of a long-ago tragedy.

Karen took advantage of the moment to press forward and grasp the hands of the man in the chair. "Thank you so much for seeing us. I know it may not be the best of times."

I tried to concentrate on the conversation rather than drooling over the interior of the house, which was indeed quite drool-worthy with all that fabulous woodwork. The living room had three luxurious cognac-leather chairs and a matching tufted sofa that could swallow you whole while you cried out with pleasure. Not the type you got as a set from a bargain furniture store, but original pieces that were custom-built for thousands of dollars each.

The modern art on the walls contrasted nicely with the traditional Craftsman interior. Two large canvases in the living room had punches of red, streaked with what looked like thin gold leaf swirls in abstract patterns. Not a style I recognized and not my taste, but masterful and obviously investment pieces. A third one was visible through the arch to the large dining room, as were the floor-to-ceiling custom wine racks. Like the books, the wine would have been better in a controlled climate.

Although it partly explained the security, all the art and fine wine did seem wasted on these Adamses. Despite everything, 87 Lincoln Way seemed anything but homey. They hadn't even completely unpacked, although the nosy neighbor had mentioned they'd been there for nearly three years. I counted five boxes stacked outside the dining room. I reminded myself to be a bit kinder, as it couldn't be easy for Delilah looking after Randolph and having an adolescent son to boot.

Randolph was gazing into Karen's eyes as if she were the only woman in the world, never mind the room. "It is indeed the best of times. What else could it be when books are involved? Anything to do with books is always right and always timely."

"Exactly," I said. This was a relief. The man in the chair by the fireplace was as lively and cheerful as Delilah was pale and bitter. His longish wavy silver hair and chiseled features could have won him any role calling for a handsome, elegant older man. The startlingly blue eyes sparkled with good humor. His navy cashmere V-neck fitted well and probably accentuated those remarkable eyes.

"You must forgive Delilah. She only wants the best for me. But I don't need to be protected from life. Remind me of your name, dear lady," he said, twinkling at Karen. "My memory is not what it was."

"Tell me about it," Karen said. "I barely remember who *I* am most days."

"And she is Karen Smith," I said, "the owner of the Cozy Corpse and the most mysterious woman in these parts."

"Oh, of course!" He clapped his hands together. "I think my medications are making me quite stupid. I'd like to toss them all away, but my family makes sure I don't get to do that."

A look flickered across Delilah's face. I guessed that Randolph's condition was a source of deep pain to her, and making sure he took his meds over his protests just added to her troubles.

Karen said, "Don't worry. But even if you don't remember me, you probably do recall the Sayers first editions I sold you."

"I remember you perfectly, well now that your young friend . . ."

"Jordan." I filled in that blank.

"Jordan, of course. Yes indeed, the Sayers firsts were and continue to be unforgettably gorgeous." He gestured absent-mindedly toward the staircase for some reason. My gaze turned toward the two glass-fronted bookcases that flanked the fireplace. The shelves were full of fat volumes, leather bound and embossed in gold. Classics.

I didn't see any sign of the Sayers collection. That was a relief, as the fire was glowing and the heat from it wouldn't do that collection any favors. Vera would pass out at the thought.

I took another look at the stairs and noticed that a chair-lift had been attached to the wall portion, no doubt to let Randolph get to the second floor and the collection easily. His bedroom too, I supposed.

Randolph said, "Delilah, my precious, should we not have some hot tea for our guests? Miss Smith and Miss . . . ?"

I was ambivalent about giving my real name in case I needed to try a few extralegal tricks to repatriate Vera's books. However, I didn't want to make Karen part of anything like that, and anyway we'd both been captured by the numerous cameras and could probably be identified easily even if we used false names. So I bit the bullet. "Jordan Bingham. I am here as Karen's friend."

"Jordan has been a lifesaver," Karen said. "And I would love, love, love some hot tea. It's my drug of choice lately. And it's *such* a chilly fall day today." She gave a charming little shiver. Delilah might have been beautiful, but Karen could melt a man's heart.

"I'm pleased to meet you, Mr. Adams," I said, extending my hand.

"Please, call me Randolph," he said. "Don't make me feel any older than I am. Delilah?" It came out as a question, but there was no doubt it was an order.

Delilah stood her ground, although I couldn't help but notice she was quivering. I realized that she was unwilling to leave our new friend Randolph alone with us. Why was that? Karen and I were only interested in books and the ambiance of the house. It was hard to imagine what the danger could be. Whatever imaginary risks there were, Randolph Adams seemed blissfully unaware. I decided we'd follow his lead. At least until the front door slammed and we all jumped, except Randolph, who just kept beaming at Karen and occasionally at me.

A younger male slunk soundlessly into the room. He was a good-looking kid, with high cheekbones and a smoldering-anger thing going on. His royal moodiness was wearing 7 For All Mankind jeans, a faux distressed T-shirt and Blundstone boots. I thought it must be nice to be able to afford a two-hundred-dollar pair of pants before you could even vote. Delilah brightened at the sight of him, so I guess my opinion wasn't universal.

"How was school today, Mason?"

"Okay," he said, without much enthusiasm.

"Well, I'm glad you're home," Delilah said, in the unmistakable tone used by mothers everywhere. "Now I want you to keep an eye on things, while I make tea for these people."

These people. Ouch.

Without an argument, Mason sank into a chair and sat observing Karen and me. I guess we were the things that an eye needed to be kept on.

Mason's reaction was a surprise. He didn't even put up a pale show of resistance. What kind of teenager was this? But it was also a relief. At least she hadn't asked him to make the tea while she stood guard. I couldn't imagine drinking anything prepared by Mason.

Karen leaned forward and focused on Randolph. As he appeared not to remember anything of their previous meeting, she started from the beginning. "How are you enjoying the Sayers firsts?"

He blinked, then sat thinking. And thinking.

"You really like them, Gramps," Mason said. "You've been groping them every night." Mason's voice came as a shock. It was silky and rich, a voice for an old-time matinee idol, rather than a contemporary teen. I guess he got Gramps's vocal genes rather than his mother's.

Randolph looked surprised, then pleased. "I do. I love them. Did you get them for me, Mason?"

What were we dealing with here? Severe memory loss? Some kind of brain disease? Whatever was going on with Randolph, it did explain Delilah's concern. Maybe she was worried we would try to exploit him. Of course, that was exactly what we had in mind: getting the Sayers firsts back from him by whatever means necessary. Preferably but not necessarily legally in my case.

I wondered what kind of meds were so necessary that serious memory loss was a tolerable side effect.

"I am glad," Karen purred, leaning forward and giving me the full wattage of her charming smile. "Because I have something even more appealing."

I listened with admiration. She was transformed from the damaged, nervous invalid she'd become into a dealer using all the snake-charming skill at her disposal. Randolph Adams wasn't much of a cobra, but he was staring at her, entranced.

"What is it?" he breathed.

"Something rare and valuable."

His eyes glittered.

Karen said, "It has just come available, but the owner doesn't want it on the open market."

"Why not?" The smooth, seductive voice of Mason caused us to turn our heads. I was more surprised by the undercurrent of suspicion in his voice than by the question.

Karen is used to questions from left field. She didn't miss a beat. "The usual. He is overly invested emotionally in his entire collection."

"Then why sell?" Mason wasn't giving up.

Karen turned on her charming smile. "Because there is something he wants more, of course."

Randolph interrupted. "Oh dear, I've already forgotten what he's selling. My memory isn't what it used to be."

Mason said, "It's not you, Gramps. She hasn't said what he's selling. And she hasn't said why she's telling you this either. But don't worry. I've got your back."

Randolph twinkled. "You are a dear boy, Mason, and I thank you, but I don't think we have anything to worry about with these ladies."

"You don't," Karen twinkled back.

What a pair of flirts. I decided to watch Mason. At least he wasn't flirting, which would have been beyond creepy. I hoped he'd keep my mind off the interior of the house and on our mission. But it was all I could do to keep my eyes away from the glossy wooden staircase with the fine example of Craftsman banister. There was not a spot (aside from Mason and Randolph) that my glance could reach that didn't spawn house lust. The exposed brick fireplace was not only flanked by a pair of polished bookcases, which were topped by Art Deco windows. Sigh. But back to Mason and not a moment too soon.

"And so what is it?" Mason said. He was leaning back in the leather armchair, languid and relaxed on the surface, but I could sense the tension underneath. Had Randolph been ripped off by unscrupulous—not that I would know anything about that—dealers in the past? Or was something else at work?

"What would you say to Wilkie Collins?"

I shot a glance at Randolph. Would his memory loss extend to this pioneer of the mystery world? But no, Randolph licked his lips. "Wilkie Collins. Tell me more."

Karen's eyes were shining. "A complete collection, short stories and all."

"Really?"

"But only for the right person."

"What makes the right person?" Mason broke in. "Gramps doesn't have that much money."

I doubted that, given the house, the high-end furnishings and the new Audi in the driveway, not to mention Mason's wardrobe.

Karen said, "But he has the right attitude. He'd never break up the collection. He'd care for it and give it the respect it's due."

"That's true," Randolph said. "I love my books."

"But what's the catch?" Mason had a way of cutting to the most important point. I had to hand it to him. He might be creepy and unsettling, but he was sharp.

"There isn't a catch, really," Karen shot back. "The collector has something he wants in exchange."

"What's that?" breathed Randolph.

"Something I know you have. And something that we can all benefit from." Karen gazed with affection into Randolph's eyes. I loved watching the seductiveness of the encounter.

"Let me guess," said Mason. "The Sayers collection?"

Karen barely managed to keep her lovely, seductive expression. This Mason was making it tricky to reel in Randolph.

"Not the Sayers!" Randolph said. "I love them. You just said so, Mason. And I remember."

"Well," Karen said. "I was trying to break it to you, gently. But you're right. It is the Sayers. He's been looking for just such a collection for years and just missed the chance to buy this one. He wants to make it worth your while."

I heard a clattering sound from the kitchen and rose to see if I could help Delilah. I stuck my nose in and offered.

Before Delilah could answer me, Mason was right behind me. I could practically feel his breath on my neck.

Delilah's eyes widened. "I'm fine," she said abruptly.

"If you need help, I'm here," Mason said, making him the weirdest adolescent in the world in my opinion.

I was convinced that Delilah's hands were shaking as she picked up the tray containing an Art Deco silver teapot and white china cups with a black Greek key design.

Awkward didn't quite cover how I felt scurrying before her to take my seat again.

Karen was saying, "And the Collins collection really is delicious."

Mason snapped, "What's in it for Gramps? He already has what he wants."

The room went quiet.

Delilah poured the tea with grace and concentration, and the gesture seemed to relax her, just a bit. Karen and I both accepted our tea, milk in first, just the way we take it. Just for a moment, it felt like we were among friends. That moment didn't extend to Mason.

"Yes," Mason said, "and if the Collins collection is so great, why is this client of yours so happy to let it go?"

If this was Mason at eighteen or so, I couldn't imagine him at forty. Look out.

Karen was ready for him. She placed her cup on the saucer on the table in front of her and said, "Because he has all the Collinses and multiples of most, and he's more interested in having the complete Sayers than having two of each of the Collinses. You're a collector, Randolph. You understand that."

"I do," he said. "But I like my Sayers. I like the way the characters speak and the life they lead. England. Wonderful!"

"I can certainly help you find them again. Easily. They're lovely but not all that rare," Karen said. "I'll enjoy that hunt. You'd be ahead at the end of it. And please keep in mind that this deal helps everyone."

"Speaking of finding, how did you find us?" Mason said.

Karen said, "How could I forget Randolph? I delivered the Sayers collection to this house in the spring. Delilah was here, but I suppose you must have been at school at the time."

Mason shot a glance at his mother, who was now standing by. She wasn't quite wringing her pale, limp hands, but I felt certain that she wanted to.

"I was here when they were delivered. Gramps managed to find his way to a book fair over in Grandville. He took a taxi," she said. Mason scowled. I got the impression that Delilah had fallen down on the job and was going to get an earful when we left, even though Randolph's escapade at the book fair was ancient history.

Delilah added, "He encountered this lady and one thing led to another."

Karen laughed out loud. "It sounds a lot racier than it was. I was very happy to meet this new customer and even happier to find the Sayers collection and deliver it. I understand Randolph had been looking for a long time."

Randolph chortled. Delilah looked horrified at this turn in the conversation. Mason seemed just as suspicious as ever. "You mean he just gave her the address?"

Delilah nodded. "He had it written down for the cab."

You'd have thought that Karen had wheedled Randolph's bank information out of him. It was just a street address. Pretty straightforward when you had a name.

What was wrong with these people?

I said, "Karen is a very reputable dealer. She's been in business for many years and she's well regarded by everyone. You don't have anything to worry about. If you are concerned, please check around the book-collecting community."

Randolph said, "Nothing to worry about at all. Don't mind Delilah and Mason. They worry about everything and get their exercise leaping at shadows. I'm very glad you did find us. Now what were we talking about?" His handsome face was lit with excitement.

"Exchanging the Sayers collection for this amazing find," Karen said quickly. "Before the opportunity evaporates."

"What's in it for you?" Mason interrupted.

"Mason. Manners!" Randolph said.

Karen took it in her stride. "Good question. What's in it for me, besides the joy of connecting people with books they want and love? Well, course, I'd be lying if I didn't mention there's a small profit for me. I can't eat books." Her luminous smile softened the words.

"You shouldn't have to, my dear." Randolph reached out and squeezed her hand. "Bookselling is a time-honored profession. You deserve to have a comfortable living. I am filled with admiration." I figured Karen would melt at the gesture and the words. This was one courtly old dude. I'd probably have stammered and blushed too if he'd squeezed my hand.

Karen pressed her advantage, as Randolph still held her hand. There was a bright pink spot on each of her cheeks. "So, can I tell my client it's a deal? He's eager to have his books find the right home."

"Of course, my dear. Of course. It sounds like a splendid arrangement. Does it not, Delilah darling?"

Delilah had been biting her lip. "We need to think about it, don't you agree, Gramps?" Now that I was sitting close to her and she wasn't towering over me in her willowy way, I noticed the dark shadows under her eyes and the fine lines between her eyebrows and along her mouth. A fairy princess, yes, but one with a few problems.

There was just the hint of warning in Randolph's lovely baritone. "I have already thought about it, my sweet."

Mason just had to butt in. "She means think about it without all this pressure."

Karen managed to look so hurt I wondered if she might have missed a career on the stage. I sat up and attempted to radiate the appearance of injured integrity.

Randolph said, "I don't feel the slightest bit of pressure with these lovely ladies. So I say, let's do it."

Mason sneered. "It won't be the first time you've been fooled, Gramps. But I hope it will be the last."

Delilah straightened and seemed to find strength somewhere. "You love those Sayers. And you've never been interested in Wilkie Collins."

A bit of confusion settled on Randolph's handsome face. He sagged in his chair and let go of Karen's hand. "I haven't been interested in Collins?"

"Not in the least, and I advise you to decline, Gramps."

"That's true," Mason said. "It's not like it's Hemingway."

Delilah shot him a warning look.

"Hemingway!" Randolph perked up again.

Karen leaned in and picked up his hand. "Hemingway? I didn't realize that was also an interest. Have I got a deal for you! The same dealer is hoping to find the perfect home for a pristine hardback copy of *The Old Man and the Sea*. There is even a signed postcard tipped in. This is a once-in-a-lifetime opportunity."

It was a great save, but just a moment too late. Randolph didn't rebound as I'd expected. Instead, he seemed to deflate. He sat, staring at the wall in front of him. "I don't know what to do."

Delilah got to her feet, stepped forward and enveloped him in a hug. "You need to rest. Tell these ladies that you will think about it and get back to them."

"But isn't it urgent?"

"Urgent? I don't think so."

"But Delilah, my darling, it's a once-in-a-lifetime opportunity."

She said gently, "Gramps, you should know that that's the oldest trick in the book."

"It is?"

Karen said, "But it truly is quite a unique opportunity. Perhaps not once in a lifetime, but it will work beautifully for everyone. Please don't think we're trying to pressure you to get a quick sale. This collector is very skittish and inclined to change his mind. He'll assume that any delay is a sign that the purchaser doesn't care enough. If this is something you've been wanting, I'd suggest that you not take too long."

She took a breath and I took that opportunity to jump in. "Why don't you stay here and finish your tea with Randolph and I'll just dash to the shop and get the Hemingway. That way you can socialize and I'll be back in no time."

Karen bit her lip. "Great idea, except you'll never find it. It's the most valuable item in my possession and I have it stashed in a place you'll never be able to locate." She smiled ruefully at Randolph. "After you have a couple of break-ins you learn to be really cautious."

Mason got to his feet. "Here's my idea. Time to hit the road. Don't call us. We'll call you. Gramps, they're going. Say good-bye."

Randolph merely slumped in his chair, fingering his lap blanket and muttering confused and nonsensical sounds.

No help there.

SECONDS LATER WE were standing on the walkway. Worse, we were now even further away from repatriating the Sayers collection than we had been.

"What was that all about?" Karen said.

"You got me. Those were very strange people."

"They certainly were secretive."

"Very secretive." I knew all about secretive. As a Kelly relative, I grew up steeped in it. No little friends invited home. No sleepovers. No birthday guests who weren't uncles. My uncles might have been willing to wear party hats, bake birthday cakes with wax paper–wrapped dimes and put together highly unusual loot bags, but they were definitely paranoid. We lived by the old line, just because you're paranoid doesn't mean they're not out to get you. That I understood and accepted. They had their reasons. I felt that same vibe there in the beautiful Craftsman house, a gorgeous home, but without the heartwarming eccentricity of my uncles. Despite three generations of attractive people, it had felt stark and unloved. I told myself I was just being silly and my reasons probably had more to do with house envy than fact. But still, I was pretty sure the Adams family had secrets they wanted to keep from us. But what could they be?

"And poor Randolph is obviously starting to lose his marbles," Karen said, a thoughtful expression on her face. "Not that I'm anyone to talk."

"Did he seem worse to you than when you first met him?"

"Yes. Well, of course, you are asking me." She tapped her head and grimaced.

I had an idea. And it wasn't a nice one. "Randolph is obviously a man of means."

Her eyes opened wide. "Are you thinking what I'm thinking?"

"Well, the mother and the son are very defensive. Do you think there's any chance they're controlling him for his money?"

"Something was wrong," Karen agreed.

"Maybe Randolph's not really the grandfather. It wouldn't be the first time some sharp operators got control over a vulnerable and well-off older person. They certainly want to keep him from meeting people and from talking to us. Did you notice that he became much more docile after the tea was served? Then lapsed into . . . whatever that was."

She nodded. "I did notice."

"Perhaps there was some kind of sedative in his tea."

"Wouldn't we have gotten it too? Oh, right, there could have been something in his cup. Delilah set up the cups in the kitchen and then managed who got what. I think you're right, Jordan."

"And you know what else? I'm beginning to wonder if maybe the security is to keep Randolph in just as much as it is to keep other people out."

Karen nodded. "I have to agree. And I must say I've had warmer welcomes in my life. I can see why no one visits this house."

"Exactly. There's something going on. Even so, we have to find a way to get back there with the Hemingway. We should do that as soon as possible."

"You're right, of course. I wish I could have convinced them to swap for the Wilkie Collins. I think I'd make a bit more on the Hemingway."

"It doesn't seem right that you have to trade something that valuable for this, Karen. After all, you didn't *steal* the Sayers."

"To tell the truth, I got a real deal on the Collins and the Hemingway. They came from one of those estate sales where no one in the family realized the value of any of the books. They couldn't wait to sell Dad's junky old novels to the sucker. They thought they were taking this little old lady to the cleaners when they demanded twenty-five dollars, practically laughing up their sleeves. The Hemingway's worth about eight thousand. It was all I could do to keep a straight face. I hit the jackpot."

"Even so, that's your livelihood and—"

She held up her hand. "I don't want to argue about it, Jordan. I need to trade something of value to Randolph because I have finally admitted to myself that I must have known at some level that those Sayers were too good to be true."

"How could you have known?"

"Dealers have a sixth sense. Don't tell me you never get a hunch about a guy that proves right."

I rolled my eyes. "Are you kidding? My track record with guys and hunches is really dismal. My last boyfriend maxed out my credit cards and cleaned out my bank account, which is why I am working for Vera instead of finishing grad school. So never count on me for that kind of insight. But back to my point, I'd like to find a way to ensure you're not out of pocket on this exchange."

Karen raised her small pointed chin and fixed me with a firm glance. "I have to contribute. I think it's Karma for me in a way. You know I was playing a little too fast and loose with the provenance of some of the volumes that came to me from Vera's collection. There's nothing like a brush with death to make you rethink that kind of activity. From now on, it's by the book all the way."

"So to speak," I said with a grin.

Even though Karen's income was precarious after her devastating injury, it all made sense. I could understand the desire to make amends. It worked to my advantage, as I needed to get the Sayers volumes back for Vera if I was to keep my job—I couldn't steal them and remain the only member of my family to go straight—and Karen's donation to the cause was going to make all the difference.

Still, it seemed to me that we had just struck out with our best shot at getting them back. And to make matters worse, while we had been standing and talking on the sidewalk, it had started to pour rain. As I fumbled with the key to the Cozy Corpse van, I imagined Delilah and Mason enjoying us getting that drowned-rat look that suits so few people.

"So how did that go?"

As Karen eased herself into the passenger seat, I whirled to face the neighbor, Harry Yerxa. He was holding a large plaid umbrella.

"I thought you might get wet, so I'll walk you to your side of the van." He leaned in to say to Karen, "I'm sorry I wasn't a bit faster. You both look half drowned."

"We are very wet," I said, "and it went horribly if you must know."

"I'm not at all surprised," he said with a self-satisfied smirk. "I told you they were very odd people."

I felt like snapping at him, but he was accompanying me to my side of the van and that umbrella kept me from drowning. I looked down and mourned my lovely pointy-toed black patent stilettos that had finally come back in style. I hoped I could save them. Harry had taken the time to get the umbrella but not to change his footwear. The socks in his sandals were sodden.

I said, "Thank you. I'm sorry you're getting soaked on our account. We appreciate it."

"Just being neighborly," Harry said. Of course he could hardly have said, "Just being nosy."

"The Adams family could take lessons. I hope they're a bit more receptive to other visitors."

"What other visitors?"

"Anyone who comes by."

Harry shook his tweed-topped head. "There are no other visitors. You're the first people I've ever seen here since they first moved in. And not much gets by me."

There was no arguing with that.

"None? Nobody at all? Really?" He had missed Karen's delivery of the Sayers collection. And what else?

"That's right. You're the first. In two years and eleven months."

"What?"

"Two years, eleven months and seventeen days actually. I was thinking about that, and they moved in on my wife's birthday exactly one year after she died. At the time, I thought it was a bit of good luck to have new neighbors and a man about my own age. But they never even answered the door when I brought them some cookies. I've given up. I was surprised you got through the door to tell the truth."

I didn't mention that wouldn't have happened without the old foot-in-the-door trick.

"We'll see you in a bit," I said. "We're coming back with something for Randolph."

"And you think you'll get back in again."

"Sure hope so," I said as I left the shelter of the umbrella and hopped into the van. I didn't mention that we'd been as good as booted out. I just wished I felt as confident as I sounded.

FIVE MINUTES LATER, we were idling at a crosswalk as a gazillion high school students ambled across the street. I must have stared at them a bit too long, because Karen patted my shoulder.

"We're not giving up. Don't let him intimidate you."

Who was intimidated? Kellys don't get intimidated. Even when they should.

"Looking at these kids reminds me that something about that Mason is really bugging me."

"What?"

"Something kind of weird about him, not in a nerdy way, but just . . . off."

"Off? Well, a lot of kids seem off to me. School is so much for them now. I don't know how they can manage those packs. I bet some of them weigh seventy pounds."

"Wait! That's it."

"What?"

"A backpack. Mason didn't have one. And he had no laptop, no phone, no gaming stuff."

"Right. Well, maybe not every kid has that stuff."

"But every kid has some kind of stuff. Kids today have accessory overload. Face it. He was wearing expensive clothing and two-hundred-dollar boots, so it's not a lack of money."

"Well, maybe he wasn't coming from school. Maybe he had an appointment or something. Oh. You're right. He said that it went okay. I don't know why I'm arguing with you, Jordan."

"They wanted us to think he'd come from school. Delilah asked how school was. So why wouldn't he be in school?"

"Playing hooky," Karen said. "Don't tell me you never did that, Jordan."

"Not me. You couldn't keep me from school. I loved it. But maybe Mason doesn't go to school."

"You mean he's homeschooled? Lots of people do that now. And he did seem kind of different."

"Well, it could explain that weird, 'I was not socialized properly' vibe I got from him, but I doubt it. I think he'd be much better behaved if he was homeschooled. And the parents who homeschool their kids are proud of it. They don't pretend their children go to regular schools."

"Well, he's old enough that he could drop out, I suppose. Maybe she's ashamed?"

"Something's wrong and we'd better swap that Hemingway for the Sayers on the double. I'm not going to let Mason scare us off. But I bet they'll try to keep Randolph away from us. And it might take more than a foot in the door to get in this time."

She said, "Do you think Randolph's in danger?"

"I have a strong feeling about it."

Karen hesitated. "But he came to the book fair. Does that make sense if they were keeping him prisoner?"

It was my turn to hesitate. "You heard what Delilah told Mason. He got away. It wasn't planned or authorized. We have to get to the bottom of it," I said as we pulled the van into the driveway of the Cozy Corpse.

"Agreed. Well, we're here now. I'll get the Hemingway."

"Let me go inside first and get you an umbrella."

"Are you kidding? I'm already drenched! No point in you getting any wetter."

"I'm wet too. Harry's umbrella was too little too late."

"However, I can change clothing."

"Don't you need a hand?"

"No," Karen said. "Once I have my walker, I do not. But thanks."

"But the stairs . . ."

"I have to start taking care of myself," she said firmly.

I sat in the van and shivered despite the heat blasting from the vents. Minutes later, I saw a sliver of light show on the edges of the small basement window on the side of the old brick building.

At least I knew where Karen most likely hid her more valuable items. She probably figured that most thieves wouldn't get past the spiders, mice and general air of horror movie in the basement. Too much like work for the average crook, even with the key forgotten in the dead bolt. I thought back to the shelves where I got the logs and matches and the lack of dust in that area. A smart crook might figure out it was worth checking that out. As long as he wasn't spooked by spiders.

While I waited for Karen, I used the time to call my uncles to engage a new accomplice for our Sayers recovery project. Uncle Mick was thrilled at the idea of having Uncle Kevin out of the house.

"Are you sure it's no trouble?" I teased. "We could ask Uncle Lucky instead."

"No! No trouble at all, my girl!"

"Really. Kevin must be tired."

"He's not. He'll be thrilled." I could just imagine Mick's face getting fire-engine red. I really shouldn't have been tormenting him. But cold, wet clothes bring out the worst in me.

"I hate to bother him."

"Please, bother him. Lord knows he has it comin'."

"Oh, fine. We need him to watch a house for us. There's something very fishy about the family. I'm worried about the older man. We were threatened by the son and we were in the Cozy Corpse van, so it would be easy for that kid to find out where Karen lives. I don't want to put Karen in any danger, but we need to make an important trade to get Vera's Sayers books back."

Uncle Mick's voice dropped to a whisper. "Karen's in danger?"

Uncle Lucky must have been in the room.

I said, "Oh, probably not. But there's something a bit weird there and there's no point in taking a chance."

Uncle Mick said, "Huh."

I took his point, because everyone in my family loves taking chances, including me.

"It would be better if we had some idea what they're up to. I'd be able to cook up some plan to deal with them."

Uncle Mick whispered, so I figured Lucky couldn't be far off. "Maybe you shouldn't be dealing with them. Have you thought of that?"

"We're so close to recapturing those pilfered Sayers books. I'd like to hang on to my job and continue to save to get back to grad school. You know that." I didn't bother to threaten to move back into my space with my uncles. Uncle Kev was parked in my girlish quarters with no sign of moving on anytime soon, and Mick and Lucky would be thrilled to trade him for me. No questions asked.

"Don't worry, Uncle Mick. Kev's just for insurance. If for any reason we get in trouble, Kev can call out the cavalry. That would be you and Lucky."

"Humph."

"The sooner he gets there, the sooner we're done. Thanks, Mick. Now do you know where he is?"

"Oh, I know where he is, all right." I figured that meant too close for comfort and wearing out his welcome. Oh, Kev. When will you learn? Lucky and Mick are probably your last chance. Don't burn that bridge.

"Great. Tell him to get back over to 87 Lincoln Way in Burton. He has to stay out of sight and watch for us to arrive. If we're not out of the house in a half hour, he needs to do something dramatic."

"Do you think I'm insane, my girl?"

"Right. Don't tell him that. That could go very wrong.

Hair set on fire. Bombs detonated. Okay, just tell him to call you. He respects you. He'll listen."

"I'll make sure he follows instructions. You be careful, Jordan."

I jumped when Karen knocked on the van window. She was holding an umbrella over her head and smiling.

She said, "I am so sorry, Jordan. I changed out of my wet clothes. I was just trying to be independent and I only now realized that you are sitting there, still soaking and probably freezing."

"Both true, but for a good cause," I said, trying to grin, although my teeth were chattering. My theory was that Karen hadn't invited me in because she wanted to retrieve the Hemingway from its basement hiding place. We Kellys are not all that trusting either.

"Come on in. I have some warm, dry clothes for you. I don't know why I didn't think of it earlier. You'll look like your own grandmother in them, of course, instead of your normal beautiful self, but you'll be comfortable. And it's not like you care about impressing that crowd."

"You got that right. Let's get this over with."

What could go wrong?

CHAPTER FIVE

❧❦❧

"ONCE MORE INTO the breach," Karen muttered as we parked in front of the Adamses' house. At least we were no longer looking like drowned rodents, although my hair gave me a hamsterish look I wasn't proud of. The Hemingway was wrapped in so many layers it could have sunk to the bottom of Lake George without getting wet. Under the worn brown slicker I had borrowed from Karen, I was wearing her tweed wool cardigan, paired with a cream turtleneck and a pair of brown pants that didn't quite reach my ankles. Karen has red hair and brown suits her. It makes me look like I need medical attention, but even so, I was grateful to be warm and dry, and felt a bit guilty, as she was the one who needed taking care of.

We rang the bell and banged on the door of the house until our knuckles stung. There was no silver Audi in sight, although it could have been tucked in the garage. Worse, there was no answer. I observed light behind the drawn blinds and what sounded like low voices in conversation, but that could have been a television set.

I felt like smoking them out. My resolve to lead an honest life was very inconvenient at that moment. Fortunately, the civilized side of my nature prevailed and we gave up. We headed down the walkway and almost straight into Harry Yerxa. He said, "I see that they're in there and they won't answer the door. Now you know how I felt for nearly three years."

At the same moment, an idea blossomed. "We do. It's a horrible way to treat people." I lowered my voice. "We think if we could just talk to the grandfather, things would be better. They seem to be sedating him or something."

Harry's jaw dropped. His eyes bugged. And I had him exactly where I wanted him.

"You mean they're drugging him? But why?" For Harry, this would be better than watching *CSI* or *Law & Order*. His eyes glittered behind the oversized glasses.

You know that moment when you should just walk away from a bad situation? I had a keen sense for it, and this was that moment. But I didn't walk away. It wasn't only my recent obsession with Wimsey and his sleuthing or that my job and home depended on figuring out what was going on. There was also this little bit of Tiffany that had rubbed off on me. Randolph needed help, and you never turn your back on someone who needs help. Even if they triple bolt the door and turn the surveillance cameras on you.

Figuring that honesty might actually be the best policy and having nothing to lose, I blurted it out.

"Our best guess is that this mother and her son may have latched onto a suitable victim, maybe one with no close relatives to get suspicious and a fair amount of loot. They could be plundering his possessions and probably clearing out his bank accounts and investments while they're at it."

He nodded. "I've heard of that kind of thing." His umbrella

tipped as he turned to stare at the house. As he turned back, rivulets of water ran down his face and his tweed cap sagged damply. "But what makes you think that's what's happening?"

You would never know that Karen had suffered a brain injury the way she seamlessly entered the conversation. "We tried to exchange a very valuable book for a moderately valuable collection that we know he has. As he is one of my clients, I am aware that he normally would prefer the more valuable book. He could always put together the other collection. I'd be happy to help him."

Harry nodded. "But—"

Karen ploughed on. "But Delilah and Mason wouldn't hear of it."

"Mostly Mason," I added.

"Delilah and Mason? Those are their names?"

"What? Oh, right. You've never met them."

"Not for lack of trying. But I gave up on them. I'm not desperate, you know."

"Of course not."

"But I don't understand, if they're after the money and all, why they wouldn't take you up on that deal."

Karen said, "That's the thing. It doesn't add up. It's possible they've sold the collection and Randolph doesn't know a thing about it. He's having memory problems, most likely because he's drugged, so they're getting away with it. In fact, I'd put money on it."

Harry sputtered, "That is simply despicable."

I said, "There were boxes in the foyer. When I saw them first, I thought perhaps they hadn't unpacked yet. Now I'm wondering if they were selling off Randolph's possessions."

Harry said, "That would explain a few things. Should we call the police?"

I flinched at the *P* word. And I'd been hoping he wanted to play amateur sleuth with us.

Karen cut in, "Um, the police will want evidence and what we have is a hunch."

"A solid hunch," I added.

"Oh, very solid," Karen agreed.

"Of course." Harry nodded. "The police need evidence."

"But we need to get that evidence *before* we involve the police," I said. "This will probably mean the FBI, if he's been kidnapped." Of course, I was making it up as we went along. A little TV goes a long way.

The wet cap bobbed. "The FBI? Yes, that sounds right."

Okay, now that he was in, I could almost hear the *Criminal Minds* theme song coming out of his ears.

"So will you help us?"

"Will I help you? Of course, ladies. Of course, but how? What can I do?"

I shook his hand to seal the deal. "What you've been doing. Keeping a neighborly eye on the place. And then let us know if Delilah and Mason leave. If we can get to Randolph, I think we can turn the tables on them."

"Brilliant! I'm your man." Harry beamed and we did too, although by this point we all looked like drowned rats yet again. Karen's slicker was good to a point, except that the neck was too wide. Icy water was now running down the back of my neck and soaking into the tweed sweater.

"Excellent. We'll give you Karen's number at the Cozy Corpse. It's her cell number too."

"You don't need to give it to me. I already have it."

We both blinked at him. I didn't remember Karen giving him her number.

Karen said, "What do you mean?"

"I have it."

"How did you get it?" Something about that creeped me out.

He started to laugh. I wasn't sure it was a laughing matter.

"If you don't want people to get your number, maybe you shouldn't be driving around with it clearly painted on your van."

That was a relief. "Sorry," I said. "I think I'm just freaked out by these people. Didn't mean to offend you."

"Me neither," Karen said. "And I'm freaked too. We've been imagining the worst and it's taking a toll."

"No offense taken, ladies. I'll let you know the minute I see those two reptiles head out and I'll do my best to keep an eye on—what's his name?—Randolph?"

"Yes. Don't put yourself in a compromising position though."

"Don't worry about me," he said, brandishing the clippers.

I said, "Right. I suppose we'd better get your number too."

"Thought you'd never ask." He couldn't seem to stop chuckling. I realized that for the first time in a long time, Harry Yerxa was having fun. I was glad we could help with that. I wrote out my number and hoped it wouldn't be too soggy to read if he needed it.

Harry fished a small notebook from his pocket, scribbled his number, ripped out the sheet and handed it to me. I dropped it into my bag.

He wasn't the most typical ally, but I was quite sure that Lord Peter Wimsey would have enlisted Harry too had the shoe been on his aristocratic foot. Now, if we could just figure out where Kevin was hiding out. I knew that my uncles would have made sure he was there to ensure our well-being. Even though Harry and Kevin seemed to have hit it off earlier, I didn't want Kev to connect with him. My most chaotic uncle was quite capable of getting poor Harry

Yerxa into a tight spot. Kev loves tight spots. He thrives on them and often creates them for others.

By the time we got into the van, Karen and I were almost cheerful, having gained Harry as an ally. We didn't spot Mason approaching until he pounded against Karen's window. That got our attention.

Under the black hoodie, his face was grim. He thumped his hands on the glass again, and our whole vehicle shook. I pressed the automatic locks but the key lock gave my frozen, wet fingers some trouble.

Delilah scurried behind him, her flowy garment whipping in the wind. "Please come in the house, baby," she pleaded.

"I told you two scam artists to stay away!" He banged the window again to punctuate his rage. He pointed at Karen. It was only a finger, but a weapon couldn't have been scarier.

"I don't know what the hell your problem is, lady, but if you come here again, you will regret it." Karen and I watched, stunned, as he stormed through the rain to his house. Delilah followed, her long hair drenched, hands stretched out to him.

"Motherhood. I may be glad I missed out," Karen said with a wobble in her voice.

"I hear you."

"Do the kids still say WTF?" This time she managed a grin, though we were both breathing heavily in the now fogged-up car.

I laughed. She sure had spirit. Even so, she was fragile and I needed to get her home before she caught a chill or we were accosted again.

I was also way too soggy and I needed a chance to think. Uncle Kev should have been watching the Adams house as we drove off. With luck, he'd keep me posted and wouldn't get himself or anyone else into trouble.

I just had to have faith.

Usually, when things got weird or worrying, I would get in touch with Tiffany, and she'd give me some perspective. Occasionally she has brought to my attention such things as respecting boundaries and some of the more subtle points of the law, such as: locks aren't always for picking and normal law abiding citizens don't run around in wigs snooping on their friend's clients. I guess some other part of Tiff had rubbed off.

I seemed to be sabotaging my own goal of being the first person in my family to go straight. Tiff would have plenty to say about that. If she were still in contact.

My Spidey Sense warned me that something was wrong. I just couldn't quite put my finger on what was going on. Randolph hadn't seemed unhappy and wasn't entirely under their control. Could it be some sort of Stockholm syndrome? Or was he maybe just going in and out of senility, unable to recognize his abusers, so he treats them well, because he's a gentleman. It all felt wrong and it was making me even more anxious about my task for Vera. I needed to get those books to keep my job and home. Would I be able to with Mason standing guard?

Karen said nothing for the rest of the way. I knew she was troubled too. This time she let me help her.

"We'll get through it," I promised her.

"Alive, I hope," she said.

AS I CRUISED down the long Van Alst driveway toward the back entrance, a sad figure caught my attention. I'd recognize him under any circumstances, even drenched. It was our letter carrier, Eddie, who had carried an unwavering torch for Vera since they were young. He was raking up piles of wet leaves. I paused and rolled down my window. "Eddie?"

"Jordan!" He waved, and then looked down at his slippery pile. Pointing at the amber glow in the window, he said, "She hates the leaves."

"Do you want me to get you a proper raincoat?"

"It's too late for that, but I'm almost finished. Thanks."

I left Eddie toiling in the downpour. I had to hand it to Vera; she sure knew how to keep a guy interested and desperate. He didn't even work for her and he was probably delighted to have been summoned to toil for Her Highness.

I did work for her, but on this particular day, I preferred to dodge her and her instructions.

My garret was deliciously warm. The signora had left me a gift of hot lemon "tea." It was mostly rum and honey, but if that was what Italians wanted to call tea, who was I to argue? I still hadn't figured out how she knew exactly when I would be home, but the "tea" was piping hot and had a good three fingers of rum in it. I gulped it down even before I ditched my sodden clothes.

Good Cat rolled on my bed playfully. Purrs and chirps filled the quiet room. "I have to freshen up for dinner. No time for cuddles." I headed to the claw-foot tub. The clothes I had borrowed from Karen splatted in a wet heap on the floor. Cradled in the tub with the luxurious lavender suds, and a second cup of "tea," I let my mind go.

A few thoughts bubbled to the surface. First, it was nagging at me that we'd run into Tyler Dekker on our first visit to Burton. What was he doing there? Was Tyler also following a hunch about something in Burton? What were the chances that those two things were the same? Why had he pulled us over even though he was out of his jurisdiction? And he said he liked the wig. I hoped he was flirting with me and wasn't going to turn into some sort of horrible pervert with a bad hairpiece fetish.

I let the lavender bubbles slowly wash away Officer Smiley's image. There were other things bothering me. That Mason kid. He had really spooked us. I'd seen confidence and calm beyond his years. That urged me to believe his threats.

"Teenagers can be right little psychos," Mick had exclaimed watching the news one night, about two weeks earlier. Maybe this was one of those times. Was Mason a psycho? If so, what did that mean for Randolph or for us if we went back?

Perhaps it was the rum in the "tea" that caused me to doze off in the tub. There was Lance in the moonlight, doing his Lord Peter impersonation. I loved the character for who he was, but also for his unrelenting romantic pursuit of Harriet Vane, no matter what. As the dream drifted, I found myself dressed as Vane and Lance as Wimsey ready for a fancy-dress Halloween ball, not that anyone in Harrison Falls but Vera would know who they were. Still, we looked very glam, me in a drapey velvet gown and Lance with a monocle. And just as we were about to touch lips, my eyes popped open.

"Kevin." I sat upright sloshing water and "tea" onto the floor. My most aggravating and talkative uncle was alone with a cell phone and no one to chat with. Yet, I had not even had a text.

Unnerving.

No time for worrying though. I was going to be late for dinner.

CHAPTER SIX

❦

DINNER HOUR WAS eight p.m. at the Van Alst residence. Early on, I had learned not to be late and to give
the signora plenty of notice if I was not going to be there.
Vera insisted on it, and I had a theory that was so she didn't
end up having all that food thrust at her. I am a dinner diversion of a different kind.

I hustled downstairs and raced along the endless corridors, hoping to make it before I turned into a pumpkin. I'd
barely had time to work my wet hair into a French twist and
slip into the full-skirted, three-quarter-sleeved vintage royal
blue wool dress with a belt and a peplum waist. I'd laid it
out before I left for our Adams misadventure. Except for my
elegant black leather dress boots and traces of Siamese hairs,
it was all very Christian Dior "New Look." I can't believe
the treasures that people donate to church bazaars. The wool
dress was warm too, something to be treasured in my new
home, as Vera was stunningly cheap with the heat. I'd have
been grateful if someone set my socks on fire, as I still

needed to shake the chill of our wet afternoon. My mother's
lapis earrings and her cocktail ring could dress up a paper
bag, but with this dress, they looked divine. I'd run out of
time for makeup, but in my little satin clutch I kept an emergency tube of Dior red. Not that it mattered, as Vera couldn't
have cared less what I looked like, as long as I was dressed
for dinner, arrived on time and had some information on
the missing Sayers books.

She glanced at her watch as I waltzed into the dining
room. I slid into my regular chair at the opposite end of the
Sheraton table from Vera and smiled, showing off my Dior
smile, a bargain at our local discount store, BTW. I was still
close enough to see that Vera had found yet another gruel-
colored sweater, this one missing two buttons but only one
elbow. Where did she get her wardrobe? Most respectable
charity shops or church bazaar volunteers would toss those
items into the trash as soon as they spotted them. However,
this was a mystery for another time, as I had more than
enough on my mind between Fort Adams and getting my
mitts on the Sayers collection.

Before Vera could grill me on the missing books, the
signora arrived with her giant tray containing a tureen of
my favorite soup, homemade chicken broth with lovely little
pasta stars, and a large bowl of what looked like freshly
grated Parmesan. She ladled the soup into my Crown Derby
soup bowl and said, "Cheese? Yes? Yes, yes, cheese."

"That's fine thanks, Signora," I said as the fragrant Parmesan cheese kept coming. From the sideboard, one of the
Siamese gave me an evil look. Bad Cat. Identical to Good
Cat, except in temperament and behavior. I met its eye,
curled my lip and pointed at my boots.

"Cheese," the signora insisted, not liking my diversion.

"Stop now, Fiammetta, for heaven's sake. Listen to what people are telling you," Vera bellowed.

That stopped the cheese talk but sent the signora scuttling with the tray to Vera's end of the table.

"Soup, Vera. Very good for you. Eat!"

Vera looked at her soup with a total lack of interest. As usual she'd probably have three tablespoons while I would probably have three bowls. At least that would be the signora's plan. There'd be no point in fighting. Luckily, I think that hot homemade soup is the perfect fall food and the best way to get over getting drenched and disappointed. And it's a terrific warm-up for the main course. The sound of rain slashing against the windows and the shriek of the wind couldn't dim the magic of the signora's soup.

"So," Vera said, "when will my Sayers collection be coming back?"

The moment of truth. Of course, for one raised in the Kelly tradition, the truth does not come easily. I could always bluff. However, Vera had a sixth sense about that kind of thing. I gazed around the dining room before I spoke. If I got fired, I'd miss this amazing room where Vera's grandfather Van Alst entertained captains of industry, governors and the upper crust of the region. Lord Peter Wimsey would have felt at home in this room, I was sure of that. I would particularly miss the Sheraton table and chairs and the silver candelabra on the priceless carved–black walnut sideboard with the dragon's head knobs. It seemed to me there was a bit less silver sitting on it than there had been. Disappearing valuables were part of life in Van Alst House. Vera had to keep going somehow, and there was no way she'd part with her rare book collection. Better to auction off the candlesticks great-grandfather Van Alst gave his bride than mess with the books. But of course, the books had been messed with. That was the point.

"In my lifetime, Miss Bingham." She loved saying that.

"Sorry."

Vera waited, drumming her fingers on the table.

"And?"

Nothing to do but bite the bullet.

"We've had a setback."

Silence.

Even the imaginary Lord Peter Wimsey winking at me over the flickering candles on the table couldn't make that silence pleasant.

"We have found the person that Karen sold them to."

"So what's the setback? Doesn't he want to sell them? Is it a he?"

"He is a he and he is willing to trade them."

"For what?"

"For a pristine signed first edition of *The Old Man and the Sea*."

"The fool."

"I'm sorry?"

"Can't stand Hemingway. Never could. Pretentious, drunken oaf."

"Oh. Well, the collector, a man called Randolph Adams, is itching to get it and seems happy to trade."

"As I said, a fool."

"However—"

"Why do I think that I won't care for the direction this story is about to take?"

"You won't," I said.

"Out with it. What is the obstacle? Money?"

"No. Karen feels terrible about selling your books with-

out checking the provenance adequately, so she is willing
to give the Hemingway."

"Humph."

"I think it's very decent of her."

"If you say so."

Sometimes you just have to take a stand. Even against
Vera. "I *do* say so. She's trying to make amends for something that really wasn't her fault."

"Carelessness. Sloppy business practices."

"Perhaps. But if I may say, she wasn't the only one fooled
by the perpetrator. I was and you were too."

That hit home.

I added. "She's trying to do the decent thing."

"Big deal."

I took a deep breath. I kept my voice even. But I felt I had
to defend Karen. "It *is* a big deal. She's having a tough time
with her business and her health. This was not her fault."

Vera waved her hand. "Whatever. What's the holdup with
the Sayers firsts?"

"A crime in progress as far as I can tell."

"What? Book theft?"

"I don't know."

"What *do* you know, Miss Bingham?"

"Well, I know that Randolph Adams bought the collection in good faith from Karen." I paused and held up a hand
to stop Vera's inevitable interruption. "As I have mentioned
several times, Karen did not know the books had been stolen. Randolph's family seems to keep him drugged, more
or less a prisoner in his home. They don't want us to do the
trade, so that makes me wonder if they've sold the Sayers."

Vera scowled. The signora swooped in from the kitchen
with a platter of chicken cacciatore, another Italian dish

perfect for this wicked weather. I like it when she serves it with orzo, and that's what she'd done. My mouth watered.

The food and earlier "tea" and bath strengthened my resistance to Vera's perpetual negativity and lack of faith in me. I have learned not to resist when the signora gives me a plate that's enough for twin truck drivers. It really does keep up my strength.

As usual Vera paid no attention to the food. "And if they have sold the Sayers books?"

"Then I have another challenge."

"Yes, you do, Miss Bingham."

"First I have to find out if the collection is there."

"How do you intend to do that?"

"We have enlisted the help of the neighbor to let us know if the daughter and grandson go out. He'll call if they do, and Karen and I will head over and try to get in to see Randolph."

"And . . . ?"

"And we have someone else keeping an eye on the place." Just as well not to mention that it was my most felonious uncle, the one with a tendency to distraction and impulsiveness.

Vera raised an eyebrow. "You are missing something, Miss Bingham."

"What?"

"Eat," the signora cajoled.

"Sure thing," I said. "It looks wonderful. Smells great too."

As she advanced yet again toward Vera, Vera said, "What is this?"

"Cacciatore! Chicken! Very good."

"What's that green stuff? Is it zucchini? You know how I feel about zucchini. What's it doing in the chicken cacciatore? That's one of the few things I like to eat. How many times have I told you I won't have zucchini in the house? Let alone contaminating my food."

Chunks of zukes were clearly visible in the savory dish, but the signora brazened it out. "You eat. No zuccy in. Chicken is good. You too thin, Vera. Eat."

There was love in the signora's helicoptering ways. And it was one of the things I enjoyed most about dinner. The signora knew how to handle Vera. She was an Italian ninja, never in the same place for more than a second. It even flustered Vera into submission. Sometimes.

"Oh never mind. So Miss Bingham, are the police not missing from this scenario?"

"Uh yes, yes, they are."

"And why would that be, since you believe these people to be committing crimes?"

Well, let's see now, first of all, because Kellys and Binghams avoid the police at all costs for very practical reasons. Secondly, because Uncle Kevin was now involved in our plan to get the Sayers books back and Uncle Kevin was what people called a "heat score." As Uncle Mick had once explained it to me: "Your Uncle Kevin is like a nineteen-year-old kid, in a bright yellow sports car, doing sixty-five in a school zone, blasting his music, wearing his cap backward. The cops can spot him from miles away, and they know at the very least he's guilty of being an idiot." Those were two good reasons. Best not to bring them to Vera's attention, especially when my stock was low enough with her. I tossed out a better explanation.

"We thought of that and gave it quite a bit of consideration—"

"Get to the point, Miss Bingham."

"Yes. Well, the main point is your Sayers collection, if it's there. We are afraid that if the, um, authorities get involved and the Adams relatives put up a good argument, the Sayers collection may actually be considered evidentiary material and then who knows when you'd get access to it. Could be years the way trials play out these days, and that's if they ever find the scoundrels."

Okay, so that was a stretch.

Vera said, "Humph."

I held my breath. I'd been expecting to be fired for days now. I had been hoping to finish this delicious meal before that happened. I made up my mind that if Vera pulled the plug on my job, I would finish my dinner before I left. I said, "We'll be back there in a flash if we hear from our . . . operatives." Operatives, would she buy that?

"And if you don't?"

I picked up my fork. I was going to get a few mouthfuls soon. The return to my uncle Mick's cooking, or worse, my own, didn't even bear thinking about.

"I am sure that we will."

"What if you can't gain access to the house? What if Randolph doesn't let you in? Where does that leave my collection?"

Gone. *Pfft.* Up in smoke.

I said, with the confident manner I'd been brought up with, "I'm certain that you'll have your books back in the near future."

"To reiterate, what if you fail, Miss Bingham?"

"Then I will find a way to rebuild that collection for you at my own expense." Yikes! Where did that come from?

Vera's eyebrow shot up again. No comment from her though. Not an "Oh no, you can't afford that, Miss Bingham" or an "It wasn't your fault." Zip.

"I value my job. I care about it. Although the loss of the

Sayers books was not my doing, I want that collection back as much as you do, and you can count on me."

"I hope so, Miss Bingham. I certainly hope so."

There was no doubt in my mind that Vera meant it.

Somewhere in that moment I made the decision that if perfectly legal but sneaky approaches didn't work, I was prepared to be resourceful and use the skills of those less concerned with the law. No point in making Vera a co-conspirator. Not yet, anyway.

I felt a great sense of relief, which I celebrated shortly after with the signora's amazing rustic Italian prune plum cake and gelato. I felt more than a little entitled, as I was about to venture out again into the dismal fall night in Vera's service. To accentuate that point, the dining room windows rattled and the driving rain beat against them. I had seconds of the cake. This made the signora very happy and me even happier.

I barely managed not to burp loudly when the bad cat plopped into my lap. The second dessert did, however, test the stitching on the blue dress.

I WASN'T SO sure about Harriet Vane, but I figured Lord Peter Wimsey would manage to be witty and urbane in any kind of weather. He seemed like the right sort of role model as well as fictional heartthrob. A guy you could count on to be perfectly dressed for any occasion 100 percent of the time. Of course, it helped to have a valet who never seemed to sleep. This reminded me of Uncle Kev—the anti-Wimsey—a guy you could count on about 40 percent of the time if you were lucky. For instance, for the last couple of hours, he hadn't answered his phone. And I knew that even if he couldn't talk, he could almost certainly have texted me to say he was on the job and things were okay.

I decided to give Karen a break on this part of my plan. She needed to warm up and rest, and she didn't need to take any chances with the law. Anyway, there was no point in everyone being miserable. I wished fervently that my wardrobe included some wet-weather gear that wasn't just for style. But it didn't. Jeans, fleece and hooded jacket were the best I had.

I headed back to Uncle Mick's to see if Mick or Lucky had heard anything about how Kevin was making out. I tried his phone again a couple of times with no more luck.

In the short distance from the Saab to Uncle Mick's kitchen my umbrella blew inside out. Uncle Mick looked up from the stove where he'd just finished heating up the contents of two cans of Alphagetti. It's always been a favorite rainy night dinner at the Kellys'. Usually followed by a bouquet of Tootsie Rolls.

"Late dinner?"

"Business. I got a little project going. Your uncle Lucky's got one of his own."

I glanced at Uncle Lucky, who beamed mysteriously.

Mick wiggled his ginger eyebrows. "It's keeping us busy. Got to go when the fish are biting."

I knew better than to ask which fish and tried not to worry about what that could mean.

"Any word from Kevin?"

"Kev? He left to go to Burton for you. He hasn't been back here. Can't say I mind. The project's a bit harder with Kev underfoot."

I understood. Uncle Kevin could derail any activity. He just needed to be within a one-block radius to do that. And Uncle Mick's and Uncle Lucky's pet projects always seemed to involve split-second timing and complete discretion. Neither was Kev's best thing.

"Well, that's not so good, because I haven't heard from him either." I decided this was the right time to fill the uncles in on the details. They listened without interrupting. I was pretty sure that scenarios of all the trouble Kev could get into were playing in their heads.

"Oh boy," Mick said. "This won't end well."

"What's he driving?"

"He's in the Kia." He sighed. "I loved that car."

Full-blown disaster seemed a foregone conclusion. With Kev you never just assume a flat tire.

Uncle Lucky glowered. He loved that Kia too.

Walter snuffled from his chair. He didn't care about cars. Mostly he just loved his dinner, and that didn't seem to be getting to his dish.

"I hope the neighbor doesn't recognize it. I'm going back to check on him. I'll take the Saab. No one there has seen it in that neighborhood."

Mick shook his head. "They could find out who you are from the license plate if they've got any brains at all."

"I'm not sure that they do, actually."

"No point in taking the chance. Lucky can take you in the Navigator. Right after dinner. You hungry? I know you love Alphagetti."

Ah. Yet another moment of truth. "Sorry, I'm feeling just a bit queasy. Probably because I'm worried about Kevin. It will pass."

Was it my imagination or did Walter look relieved?

The back room of Michael Kelly's Fine Antiques was always full of wonderful finds. The yellow sou'wester and jacket were an unexpected bonus. They didn't fit, but you can't have everything, and bigger was definitely better in this weather. I'd stopped worrying about my appearance, as it was a lost cause today. I was surprised to learn that Walter had his own little bright yellow slicker and boots, the latest gift from the newly crazy pet-owning uncles. Walter was yet another plus.

I asked for and received one of the burner phones that my uncles always have tucked around their living quarters. Safety first, and all that.

I left the Saab at Uncle Mick's and joined Uncle Lucky in the Navigator.

Time to head out.

CHAPTER SEVEN

꩜

WITH LUCKY AT the wheel and Walter quivering with excitement, we soon arrived back at 87 Lincoln Way and parked two doors down. Lucky became invisible in the car, a trick I would like to master someday. I mean, how does he do that? Instead of being warm, dry and invisible, Walter and I went for a walk. Apparently, Walter wanted walks in any weather. Our yellow slickers—and my sou'wester— were the opposite of invisible. They were in-your-face visible. They were "you cannot unsee me" visible. They were "we cannot possibly be up to anything while dressed like this" visible. I figured there were worse strategies. And I stayed dry.

It's easy to meander if you have a dog with you. Chances are that dog is not going anywhere in a hurry, unless there's a squirrel involved. As it was too wet for any self-respecting squirrel, we meandered. That meant I could keep an eye on Number 87 without appearing to. Walter ogled the bushes for all the wrong reasons. As we walked and I occasionally stooped to do my civic duty with the attractive plastic bags provided by Lucky, I could see movement behind some of the curtains in the Adams house. Lights went on in rooms. Went off in rooms. Went on in different rooms. It was hard to make out who was in which one, but I figured the slender shadow was Delilah and the taller one had to be Mason. There was no shadow corresponding to the courtly Mr. Randolph Adams. I didn't know what the shadows were doing, but they were certainly busy and purposeful.

Next door there was only one light in the front room downstairs, which I took to be the living room. A television flickered and I could clearly make out Harry Yerxa sitting in front of it. So much for being our operative. I do despise a quitter. Walter, now, was no quitter. Amble. Amble. Amble.

At least we could be fairly sure that all the Adamses were firmly tucked in their well-protected home. But where was Kev? Walter was not just another pretty face. He was there to see if Uncle Kev could be located.

Of course, there were two purposes to this trip.

"Find Kev, Walter. There's a treat in it for you if you make it snappy."

Walter was well aware that my pockets were full of treats. I had made sure of that.

I unhooked his leash and gave him a little push. "Find Kev, Walter, and, as Vera would say, 'in my lifetime.'"

He waddled forward and I splashed after him. His curly stub of a tail reverberated with excitement. Nice that someone was having a good time. Up to the end of the block and then down to the opposite end we went. I was beginning to think Walter was stringing me along. Worse, there was another dog walker, almost certainly one of the neighbors. Since nobody in their right mind would bring a dog to someone else's neighborhood on a night like this, I thought he or she might be suspicious of us. We kept our distance, only giving a falsely cheerful wave once. The other dog walker waved back, but kept his head down. His (or was it her?) dog was a large shambling creature, of no recognizable breed, although that may have been the effect of the rain on its fur.

I kept my face averted as we passed a black Impala parked outside Number 89, next to the Adamses. I tried to keep my mind on the two most important men: Randolph Adams—of course there wasn't much I could do for him at the moment—and Uncle Kev, who I had begun to really worry about. Why wasn't he answering his cell? Was he lying injured somewhere, having fallen out of a tree? Or was he possibly reduced to a pile of smoldering ashes, having grabbed onto a live wire to steady himself in some hiding place? Or he had already drowned in a backyard pond that he failed to notice in the dark and was now being nibbled by koi, which would mean a closed casket and it would be all my fault and . . .

You see, this is the impact that Kevin has on people. "Being around him can make you question your hold on sanity itself," to quote Uncle Mick.

"And Kev has treats too," I whispered. Walter's wild eyes bulged with excitement, but he didn't move. I gave him just enough of a nudge to get him to trot down the side yard of the house on the far side of the Adams home. I squished after him, waving my arms and calling "come back" and other commands that Walter would never obey. No danger of that.

The fake runaway dog routine allowed us to wander through that backyard looking for Kev. We found no bodies with broken necks and expressions of frozen horror on their handsome faces. We found no smoldering corpses. No floaters surrounded by malevolent koi. We found sweet bubkes. Well, Walter located a couple of items that were too disgusting to mention, but that was the extent of it. I found that my

shiny black rubber galoshes had filled with very cold water.
I also found that we were not alone.

From the back corner of Number 89, I took a quick peek
out onto the street. To my surprise, I could see the Impala
was still parked, its interior dark and apparently unoccupied.
There was something wrong about the car. I crept forward
toward the street, hugging the side of the house and desperately hoping that no one chose that moment to peer out the
windows of the Adams house. The car was not unoccupied
after all. I could tell from the way the glass was fogged.
Someone was slouched down in there, and that someone
could have taken a few invisibility lessons from Uncle Lucky.

Who was he?

Why was he there?

Was he a he?

Could this be a potential buyer for the loot that Delilah and
Mason were plundering from Randolph? Or a confederate?

Too many questions.

Not a single answer.

But if he was watching the Adamses—and seriously, who
else could he possibly have been watching—then he must
have been watching me too. And most likely seeing right
through my ridiculous ploy. What would Wimsey do? Use
the truth with just an element of deception? I thought so.
Perhaps that's why I had what was not my best idea ever,
maybe even one that Wimsey would have warned against.

I don't know what came over me. I tossed a handful of
treats toward Walter, which sent him off to the furthest end
of the yard. Then I dashed forward and ran down the sidewalk, waving my arms and yelling, "Walter! Where are you?"

Not quite as dangerous as it would have been without
Uncle Lucky, parked nearby as a fail-safe and a witness.
Speaking of witnesses, the other dog walker was now slowly

making his or her way down the opposite side of the street with the large, shaggy pooch. I decided the dog walker was a man, as he was on the tall side for a woman.

I walked up to the car with the fog on the windows and pressed my face close to the window. I knocked. The man inside could clearly see me and could just as clearly see me see him. He stared. I knocked again. And smiled. Slowly the window lowered.

"Can you help me?" I whimpered. "I've lost my little pug, Walter. He's my fur baby and he was just here with me and he ran behind these houses, but he's not there now and I don't know where he got to. Have you seen him? Did he run out of the yard and down the street? I just need to know what direction he ran in if so. And I saw you here and I wondered . . ."

My uncles have taught me to be observant. I took careful note of the man inside the car. He had a narrow, lean face, chiseled cheekbones and a jawline that should have made him handsome but just made him look fox-like. His dark eyes glittered at me. Maybe he was bitter because someone somewhere had broken his nose more than once. Possibly the same person who'd left the scar that cut his forehead and eyebrow, and even his cheek. He was fortunate he hadn't lost an eye.

A snuffling sound at my ankles somewhat detracted from my story. If that wasn't enough, Walter uttered a sharp pair of barks.

"There you are, Walter," I squealed. "Thank heavens."

The foxy-faced guy leaned forward, squinted down at Walter and back at me. Thanks to the sou'wester I wouldn't be that easy to identify. The window rose, the engine started and the Impala peeled off down the road, spewing Walter and me with muddy water. Maybe that was the same mud that made the license plate impossible to read, unless I was one of those brainless people Mick mentioned earlier.

I hoped that Uncle Lucky had picked up on the car and
the driver and had found something to ID him. One thing
for sure, solid citizens don't behave that way.

"Thanks a lot, Walter," I said. "You're a perfect sidekick."

Walter wagged his tail and took off into the inky night.
I chased after him into the backyard of a plain brown house
two doors to the right of the Adams residence. Calling for
Walter was part of my cover story. I figured on such a vile
night, people wouldn't pay too close attention and certainly
no one would step outside to help me. I was counting on it.

"Come on, Walter, we have to go get in the car with
Lucky. Walter? Walter?" Really, what was I doing trying to
reason with a dog, a spoiled dog at that? Walter stayed just
out of my reach. "What's the matter with you? Wouldn't you
like to be warm and dry? Aw, come on, Walter."

But Walter was hiding. This hiding place had nothing to
recommend it. You couldn't see Number 87 from here. You
couldn't really see anything. It was as if Walter hadn't listened
to the plan at all. Number 89 was in total darkness, something
I don't advise for homeowners who don't want to get burgled.
Just sayin'. Dark house equals not home. Not home equals
opportunity for housebreaking. In these days of automated
timers, there was no excuse for it. Not only was it dark, it was
dangerous. Kids' toys and garden tools were strewn across
the side and backyard. I tripped over a bicycle, swore and kept
going. I imagined Walter wheezing with laughter.

"You can have my Alphagetti any time you want it. Let's
go, Walter."

I tried being tougher. "You want to walk home by yourself? Good luck with that, Walter."

I could see the spoiled little fiend dancing just out of my
reach.

"Fine. You're on your own. I'm going to the car to eat a treat with Lucky."

I felt a powerful push on my shoulders. I staggered forward, tripping over a rake and splooshing into the cold, slippery and treacherous mud. Walter barked in approval. I couldn't respond as the breath had been knocked out of me.

Something licked my ear and panted. A dog? What dog? Of course, it could only be the large, shaggy pooch that pokey dog walker had been idling with.

"Nice doggy," I said, trying not to inhale the reek of wet dog hair.

"You shouldn't have mentioned that treat," a male voice said.

I managed to twist my head and look up. A man with a beanie *and* a hoodie was staring down at me. That might have been less intimidating if I hadn't been lying belly-down in the mud in this forlorn and dark yard. With a dog more or less standing on my back.

"I hope you really do have a treat," the hoodie guy said.

"Oh, sure. Call off the Hound of the Baskervilles and I'll get it out of my pocket. Is this dog dangerous?"

"No more dangerous than Walter," he said.

"How do you know Walter's name?" I narrowed my eyes.

"Well, aside from the fact that you have been bellowing it for about half an hour, Walter and I are old friends."

He moved around to face me and took his hand out of his pocket and leaned toward me. I managed to get my hand into my pocket and reach for a treat. I sloshed in the mud and struggled to my feet, but my galoshes slipped and I was down again.

The guy grabbed for me. The dog barked loudly. Walter yipped. Just as I had managed to grip the treat, he spoke again. "Give me your hand before you drown in this mud, Jordan."

Jordan?

He knew my name too?

I stared. I attempted to struggle to my feet.

"Who the hell are you?" I sputtered and slipped again.

"What do you mean? You mean you don't recognize me?"

In my cartoon life a light would have gone on over my head at that moment. But of course, this was real life and all I could think of was, "What the hell are you doing here?"

"Same as you. Walking the dog."

"You don't have a dog, Tyler Dekker."

"I do now. But *you* don't have one, Jordan Bingham."

"Walter is Karen's dog, as if you didn't know that. I'm just helping walk him."

He extended his hand to help me up. Beggars can't be choosers, as my uncle Mick likes to say, and people lying in the mud can't be too choosy either in my opinion. I reached out for his hand and pushed forward.

"Mud becomes you," he said. "Who would have thought it?"

I scowled at him and then stared behind him where another figure was looming. This one was brandishing a shovel.

"Oh no!" I shouted.

"Yes, it does," he chuckled. "Not every woman can claim that."

"No, don't!" I yelled, lurching forward. "Put that shovel down!"

"Just kidding," he said. "But really, it would take more— What? Put what shovel down?"

The shovel put an end to that when it smacked his head with a thunk. Officer Tyler Dekker sank with a splat in the mud. The large shaggy dog howled. Walter whined. I screamed. "Uncle Kev, are you out of your mind? What have you done?"

I dropped to my knees to help. A person could drown in this mud.

Kev let his hurt feelings show. "What do you mean? This creep was going for you."

"This creep as you call him is a police officer."

"A cop? That's even worse."

"Kev, you don't know what you're talking about. He is the closest thing to a friend on the force that any Kelly or Bingham has ever had."

"Jeez."

"What are we going to do? He's out cold."

"Well, how was I to know?"

"I told you to put the shovel down." Of course, I'd been talking to Uncle Kev. Part man, part vortex of destruction.

"I thought you were yelling at your attacker."

"I didn't have an attacker. I was *talking* to a friend who did not have a shovel. I told *you* to put it down."

"An easy mistake to make," Uncle Kev said peevishly.

"Not really. You had a shovel and he didn't."

"In the heat of the moment, things got confused."

"No kidding," I said, digging in my slicker pocket for the burner phone I'd taken from Uncle Mick's. I prayed it wasn't full of mud.

"What are you doing?" Kev said. "Let's get out of here."

"I'm calling 911, and you definitely better take your own advice and hightail it before the cops show up."

"But . . ."

"No buts. Hit the road, Uncle Kev. We'll catch up later." I pressed 911.

"A man has been attacked behind a house on Lincoln Way! Number 89 or 91. What? I don't know if it's north or south. It's to the right. It's a mud-brown house with a muddy lawn. You may hear dogs barking."

Uncle Kev stood staring and listening to the one-sided conversation.

"Send an ambulance.

"He's been hit on the head.

"With a shovel.

"I don't know who hit him.

"I didn't see the person's face.

"Okay. Male. At least I think male. Between five-five and six-two, I think. Give or take.

"I didn't see what color his skin was. It was dark. No, the area was dark, not the skin. I don't know what color. I didn't see his hair. I don't even know if he had any. He may have been wearing a hat."

Uncle Kev headed past me into the dark, slippery back-yard and vanished into the gloom.

I shook Tyler Dekker's shoulder. "Tyler. Tyler. Are you all right?"

He groaned, and that was a good thing.

"The ambulance is on the way. And probably the police are too. Are you on police business? Tyler? You don't live anywhere near here."

Another groan, followed by a moan and whispered words. I leaned forward. "What did you say?"

"No police."

"What do you mean no police?"

"No police."

"But Tyler, you are the police."

He pushed himself up to a standing position. It looked slow and very painful. He leaned against the side of the house. "Not here I'm not and not tonight especially." He closed his eyes and swayed.

"What is that supposed to mean?"

"Call them back. Tell them . . . No, they'll come anyway."

"Yes, they will, and you need to go to the hospital and be seen to. You took a real slam with that shovel."

He met my eyes. "Who slammed me?"

Okay, I just couldn't rat out my uncle any more than I could abandon Tyler. "I don't know. Some guy whose face I couldn't see beaned you with a shovel."

"Why?"

"I don't know."

"But you yelled at him. I heard you."

"I saw him raise the shovel and I said no and I told him to put the shovel down."

"And he beaned me?"

"Yes."

He raised his hand, touched his head and winced.

"There's blood on your hand," I said. "I think. But it could be mud. Let me see." I reached over and touched his head.

"I'm getting out of here."

"What? No. Wait until the paramedics get here."

"No can do. Gotta go. Take care of the dog."

"The *dog*? Really? Oh, come on."

As I stood there openmouthed, Tyler Dekker disappeared into the yard as well. I thought he turned in the opposite direction from where Uncle Kev had vanished. That was the only good thing. I turned and followed but found no sign of either one as I peered blearily around.

There was nothing to do but leash up Walter. The other large, shaggy dog seemed just as mystified as I was. Was this Tyler Dekker's dog? If so, why would he have left it behind? Was he in worse shape than I thought?

"Can't you find him?" I asked. "What's the use of all you dogs if you can't even locate an injured man?"

I heard sirens approaching and made a quick call to Uncle Lucky to tell him I was okay. He'd make himself scarce when the cops showed, as is the Kelly policy, unless he thought I needed help. I assured him I didn't.

A siren whooped behind me on the street. I made my way to the sidewalk to meet the paramedics and, lucky me, the police.

A tall, heavyset police officer got out of a Town of Burton police cruiser. He did a double take as he spotted me, covered in mud, including my face and hair. All very *Night of the Living Dead*.

"Did you call in a disturbance, ma'am?" he said.

Another officer, who I took to be his partner, also approached and walked toward the back of the house. This one was short and on the skinny side.

"No," I said.

"What happened to you?" He seemed to have a bit of trouble keeping a straight face.

"My dog ran off and I fell in the mud behind this house." I pointed toward the brown house, which I had come to hate. "I don't know if you can call that a disturbance."

"And you didn't make a 911 call?"

"It's nothing a shower and shampoo won't fix, Officer," I said. "You might want to warn your partner that it's slippery back there. I almost killed myself getting up once I fell in that mud."

He looked as though he wasn't entirely convinced. "We got a call that a man was attacked."

"Attacked? Really?" I said.

"Did you see anything, ma'am?"

"Did the attack happen around here?"

"We got a call saying there was an attack at this address."

I glanced around in alarm. "Now that's scary."

"The caller was a woman. She said that a man was attacking another man with a shovel in back of this house here."

I said, "But I was just there."

"Yes, ma'am. And did you see anything?"

"Just my dog being amused when I did the backstroke in the mud." To reinforce my story, Walter panted wheezily, and as usual it sounded like the wickedest kind of laugh. The ridiculously shaggy dog that Tyler Dekker had left behind sidled up and looked sympathetic. He leaned in against my thigh. The cop snorted. Highly unprofessional in my opinion.

"No guys running by?"

"No."

"No one—"

"Nothing, Officer."

"Did you hear anything?"

"No. Well, *splat.*"

"Nothing else suspicious?"

"Nope. In fact, I . . . Oh, wait, you know, I yelled when I fell. I might have even cursed and swore a bit. And I grabbed at something to get myself out of the mud. I wonder if someone saw me and thought that I was a guy getting attacked."

The cop scratched his cheek. "Hard to say."

"It is possible. I thought I saw someone on the street, but they didn't come near me. Maybe they called it in just to be on the safe side."

"Guy would have to be pretty chicken for that."

"I don't think it was a guy. Looked more like a woman, although the visibility was really poor, especially from the mud puddle."

"No details that you recall?"

What the heck? The man wanted details, so I decided to give him some. This was in direct conflict with the Kelly motto not to complicate things with unnecessary whoppers that can trip you up. "Well, I could be wrong, but I thought she had an umbrella with polka dots. Or it could have been some other repeating design. As I said, visibility was poor."

"Anything else?" This guy was the reason my family didn't like cops.

"No. I didn't see anything else. I didn't hear anything else. I'd really like to go home and take that shower now, if you don't mind. And if I think of anything, I'll be sure to call you, Officer."

The other officer emerged from the back of the house and glowered. Unless I was mistaken, his knees were very muddy. He shook his head. "Nothing back there."

I turned to leave when the first cop asked for my name. "Carly Jenkins," I said, plucking the moniker from nowhere. "I'm staying with my cousin, over at 4 Madison." I mumbled the four, just in case he followed up. It could always look like a mistake.

For the second time, I turned and began to limp off. No one tried to stop me.

Of course, Uncle Lucky was nowhere to be seen. Even though I'd told him to go, I felt abandoned. Every man I knew was vanishing that night. Except, of course, for the cop who insisted on doing his job instead of thoughtfully disappearing.

"You need a lift, ma'am? You're limping."

I turned back and flashed him my best smile. I can't imagine how grotesque that looked in my mud-spattered face.

"No, thanks. It's not far and I need to blow off steam. I don't want to take this mood out on my cousin."

He shrugged and turned to flash his light into the muddy yard. The other one said, "I'm telling you there's nothing and nobody there." They both seemed disappointed. I think "my" cop had liked the story about the woman with the umbrella who'd gotten all mixed up.

I glanced around as I made my way to the corner. My teeth were beginning to chatter and I felt a chill. There wasn't much I could do in that state. Not the right time to try to get into the Adams house. The same went for speaking to Harry Yerxa. For the second time in the same day, I needed a hot tub and a signora special and I needed get out of the rain.

As soon as I got around the corner, I whipped out the cell and called Uncle Lucky. I knew he wouldn't be far.

"Come and get me," I chattered. "And your darling Walter. I'm on Jefferson Circle, just off Lincoln Way." I didn't mention that I was royally ticked off at Walter. After all, I was just about to make a mess of my uncle's second favorite car. While I waited, I wiped off the burner phone and dropped it down the sewer. Just in case.

Uncle Lucky raised an eyebrow when I clambered into the Navigator with Walter. The eyebrow rose higher when the additional muddy dog hopped in.

"Long story," I said. "Please get me somewhere warm and dry and away from this neighborhood full of mud, cops and crazy people."

At that moment I couldn't have cared less about the Adams family or Vera's stupid collection.

Uncle Lucky turned on the heat, probably because he could hear my teeth chatter.

When I warmed up marginally, I said, "So, about Uncle Kev. Just so you know, he bashed Tyler Dekker on the head with a shovel and then he took off. You have met Tyler Dekker and so you are aware that he is a police officer, even though he's not in this jurisdiction and he was not only in plain clothes but also definitely disguised. So you may want to think about working up some kind of alibi for Kev. I don't know what Dekker was doing there. He wandered off too, but not in the same direction that Kev did. I think he was okay. I hope so. It's sure been a crazy night."

Lucky was quiet all the way to the Van Alst House.

"I appreciate this," I said in a gentle tone. Uncle Lucky has always been a rock for me. "I know I've been a real nuisance, and I am really sorry about your car. I can get it detailed for you." Uncle Lucky raised a substantial ginger eyebrow and gave me a look to indicate what he thought of that idea.

For the rest of the drive, even though the heat was on in the Navigator, I couldn't shake the chill. Of course, none of the icy waves I felt were coming from my uncle. He was kind enough to keep both dogs with his usual lack of recrimination or any kind of comment.

"You're the best, Uncle Lucky. Just want you to know that."

He shrugged modestly. What a guy. I hated to push my luck, but I had no choice.

"Do you think someone could drop the Saab off in the morning? I'm going to have to get back to the Sayers biz tomorrow and I'll be stuck at home without wheels."

I did borrow Uncle Lucky's phone to call Tyler Dekker. Long story how I knew his number. Mostly I wanted to know if he was alive and coherent.

No answer.

"Call me when you get this message. I'll be home in fifteen minutes. Leave a message if I don't pick up. I need to know that you're all right. I have your dog, if it is your dog, and I'll return whatever its name is tomorrow."

To be on the safe side, I texted him twice.

CHAPTER EIGHT

❧❦❧

SOON I WAS scrambling up the back stairs of the Van Alst House to my cozy flowered garret and the old-fashioned claw-foot tub. I did not encounter Vera or, sadly, the ever-vigilant Signora Panetone with "tea."

I stripped off the second I was in the door. Even my underwear was oozing mud. I stuffed my filthy clothing into a plastic garbage bag. I wasn't even certain any of it could be saved, but I sure didn't want to spread the mud around my perfect little home. I put the sou'wester and the raincoat into a separate garbage bag. With luck we could salvage them in the shop shower at Michael Kelly's Fine Antiques. I mopped up my dirty trail on the floor while I ran my second bath of the day. I felt thankful there was no shortage of hot water in the Van Alst House. This time, I didn't linger in the tub. I toweled off then slipped into a pair of flannel pajamas that Tiff had given me for Christmas. They had Professor Frink from the Simpsons on them, Tiff's little joke that I was a nerd at heart. I added thick gray woolen socks and climbed under the flowered comforter. I could have used Good Cat to snuggle up with, but for some reason there was not so much as a whisker to be seen.

Figures.

I was asleep in seconds. I think I heard myself snoring.

The phone did not ring, which was good in one way and not so good in another.

I made it through the night, but Tyler Dekker might not have. And of course, I'd misplaced Uncle flippin' Kevin.

MY EYES POPPED open. Judging by the stinging light it was still before seven a.m. I had slept in fits, punctuated by stress dreams like this: Lord Peter Wimsey rising from his knee, saying, "I have changed my mind, dear Jordan. I prefer a woman with some modesty and humility."

Lance stood, arms crossed, watching this exchange, his head shaking in disapproval. "To think I actually wanted to date you." As he pouted attractively, a throng of blue-haired women with bifocals suddenly appeared and whisked him off into the ether.

Then Officer Smiley and his soggy, shaggy dog sashayed past, both sneering. "Tsk, tsk, Jordan." Followed by a heavy thunk.

Uncle Kevin stood triumphant over Officer Smiley, waving a bloody shovel and grinning like a homicidal idiot. On his shoulder a Siamese cat caressed his round face with a silky brown tail. "Hey Jordie! Took care of this little problem for ya . . . but you should really think about putting some clothes on before you catch your death."

I would have screamed but there was mud in my mouth.

For the next few minutes, I lay on my bed and gazed up at the cabbage rose wallpaper. The previous night had been pretty stressful, not only because of the events on Lincoln Way and the Adams debacle. I was no closer to the Sayers collection but much closer to the wrath of Vera Van Alst. I was a bit too groggy to get up, but I didn't dare fall back to sleep and miss breakfast.

I reached for my iPhone and called Uncle Mick. He was always up at five.

"What time did Uncle Kev get home last night? Or this morning?"

Uncle Mick sighed heavily. I thought of that as his Uncle Kev sigh. "Not home yet."

"What? Maybe he went up to his room and conked out and didn't tell anyone."

"Lucky has already checked."

"He could have crashed in the shop."

"Crossed our minds too, but he's not there either."

"This will sound nuts but it's Uncle Kev, so possibly he slept outside in the backyard or in the shed."

"Even though it was pouring rain, we also scoured Lucky's unit and mine, the rest of the property, the shed and the garages. All of them. And before you ask, Jordan, yes, we did look inside the cars. All of them including yours. Front seats, back seats and trunks where applicable. No sign of our Kevin."

"Well, that's not good."

"No. It isn't. I have to go now. Both dogs need to be fed."

I tried Tyler Dekker again. I left a message asking him to call me. Said I was worried about something. I didn't give my name. He'd know who I was.

Once again, I asked myself what Lord Peter Wimsey would do. Maybe he wasn't the perfect sleuth to take cues from, as the disaster last night might suggest. But I was in the mood to speculate, especially as it would postpone actually getting up.

I wondered how His Lordship would feel about this space. Would it remind him of the servants' quarters in what he called the ancestral pile where he'd grown up as the son of the Duke of Devon? I always figured that his childhood home would be like Downton Abbey. But he'd never have said anything to remind me of the difference in status. As far as I could tell from my reading, Lord Peter Wimsey was always witty and agreeable, and occasionally silly. I hoped he wouldn't mind that at any given time a cat might swish a tail in his face, even if he was relaxing on my little striped love seat in my tiny sitting area with the sloping walls. Where would I have stayed in the ancestral pile if I'd accompanied him to meet his mother, the dowager duchess? That was something I would just love. Along with meeting the delightful duchess—the amazingly named Honoria Lucasta, not that anyone ever called her that—I would get to *really* dress for dinner. Or would my background and nationality have worked against me? It was bad enough that Harriet Vane was always elegant and cool. How could an ordinary girl from the former colonies compete? Never mind. I was taking my investigation cues from Wimsey, not Harriet. Wimsey was always audacious and unexpected. He also usually had someone to help out. Too bad Uncle Kev would never measure up to Bunter, Wimsey's valet. Bunter never gave anyone grief. Ever. And that put an end to a perfectly good fantasy.

It was time to face the world.

AFTER MY ROUGH night, I was even less thrilled than usual about the obligatory breakfast with Vera. For some reason, I was even a few minutes early. This should have earned me a gracious welcome, but Vera was no Dowager Duchess of Denver. That was not the role that she was going for.

Not knowing about Uncle Kev and Tyler Dekker brought a bit of extra gloom to the conservatory. It had stopped raining at last, but the sky was dark and threatening.

Today, the coffeepot was on the table, and I reached for it, the way a drowning woman reaches for a life preserver.

I was surprised to catch a glimpse of a small TV that was blasting the morning news in the kitchen. For some reason I'd believed televisions had been banished from Van Alst House. Even from the conservatory, I could see that the signora had stopped with her platter in her hand and was staring at the screen. I even thought I caught a whiff of something burnt, although surely that wasn't possible. Vera had her head in the *Times* and she waved away my attempts to say good morning. I think she was trying to dodge her breakfast. But it took more than a wall of newsprint to derail the signora. First she swooped by me and deposited a small mountain of pancakes on my plate. She pointed to the pitcher of syrup on the table and made a strategic approach to Vera.

"Pancakes, Vera. You eat. Very good. Syrup too. Eat, eat!"

The paper lowered somewhat. "What kind of pancakes are these, Fiammetta?"

"Pancakes. Very good. Eat, Vera!" The signora plunked the platter of pancakes on the table next to Vera. Was she actually flustered? "Must eat."

Vera slammed the newspaper on the table, if newspaper can be said to slam. "What's that green stuff in those so-called pancakes, Fiammetta?"

From the sidelines, the pair of Siamese watched the back-and-forth with thinly veiled contempt. Cats are not interested in green stuff.

I, on the other hand, watched, fascinated, my fork suspended. I admit I was curious about the green stuff. Green and breakfast never go well together in my book. I was with the cats on that one.

"No green stuff. Good. Very good. You eat."

"Is that zucchini?"

"No, no, no zucchini. Good pancakes. Wonderful pancakes!"

Oh, zucchini. Well, that was all right then.

"How many times do I have to tell you? I refuse to have zucchini sneaked into my food."

I popped the first tasty bite into my mouth as Vera and the signora bickered. I have learned to tune out the vigorous zucchini wars, and as mentioned previously, this day I wasn't really at my best.

From the kitchen I heard the foghorn voice of the morning news announcer. He trumpeted (if foghorns could trumpet) local events.

There is shock across Williams County this morning as police have confirmed that the body of an unidentified white male was found in an upscale residential area of the town of Burton. This is the second suspicious death within the week. A still unidentified white male was found stabbed to death just last week. Anyone with any information about either case is urged to come forward or call the Williams County tip line.

The sweat prickled at the roots of my hairline again. I shivered and my fork clattered on the plate. I got up from my chair and walked toward the kitchen, knees shaking. On the screen a body bag was being carried on a gurney, between two familiar houses on Lincoln Way, the Adams home and Harry Yerxa's. I felt more than a little lightheaded. Oh, Uncle Kevin.

"What is going on?" I muttered under my breath. Could Kev have finished off Tyler? Kev was a lot of things, but he wasn't violent, although his presence seemed to bring it out in others. Tyler Dekker had been there too. Was it possible he'd retaliated against Kev for bashing him on the head? That seemed equally unlikely. I found it hard to believe that a third person could have been wandering around the area though. Who? Lucky and I were safe. The dogs were safe. No one else had been around except the sharp-faced driver of the Impala, and he had shot out of there after I spoke to him. Had he dispatched a victim before he left? It seemed unlikely, as I had been mucking around in the backyard and might have seen or heard something.

Who was in that body bag? Was that dead person Kevin? Or Tyler?

I swallowed hard, but that did nothing to get rid of the lump in my throat.

"Miss Bingham!"

I snapped back to here and now.

"Yes?"

"What are you gawking at?"

"The local TV news. There's been a murder over in Burton."

"I didn't hear the newscaster say a murder. I distinctly heard a *body*."

"A second body. They found another man last week." My voice rose like an escaped balloon. I'd heard about that, but there had been no further speculation until now.

Vera snapped, "Well, it's nothing to do with us. Don't let your imagination run riot. It must be those Irish genes, and after all, it's not like you are Dorothy L. Sayers, and that reminds me, when are my books being returned? The clock is ticking."

The clock might have been ticking for my job, but time had stopped for somebody. I hoped not Kev or Tyler, but whoever, it made the missing books seem much less important.

"I'm going back today. There was a lot of strange stuff happening on that street last night. Made it impossible to get in to see Randolph Adams. Don't worry. It's all under control."

Too bad that wasn't true.

IF MY UNCLES had a clue I'd be knocking on a cop's door, they never would have returned the Saab that morning. Good thing they headed back home to get the Navigator detailed. I had offered to take care of that for them. After all, it was my mud.

"Lucky says you've been through enough. You leave all that to us, my girl. We'll get a deal," Mick insisted.

Fifteen minutes later, I hammered on Officer Smiley's door, on the eastern edge of Harrison Falls. Of course, there was no answer. I hammered and banged. Nothing. No one. Too bad. Very worrisome. I had taken the time to dress nicely too. My autumn-toned cotton gypsy peasant dress had a corset waist. I liked the look with my fitted denim jacket and my vintage deep-orange purse, just large enough to tote a fridge. Knee-high boots, matching cable-knit tights and huge hoop earrings completed my "boho radical" look. The outfit made me feel very Jane Fonda at a Black Panthers' meeting.

I really didn't want Tyler having recurring nightmares about my creature-of-the-mud outfit last night. There was no car in the driveway of the tiny brick ranch house he was renting. Nothing on that property had changed since 1964, as far as I could tell. It was every contemporary decorator's nightmare "BEFORE" picture. So of course, I loved it. There wasn't so much as a twitch of the checkered café curtains in the kitchen. I walked around and managed to peer into the windows. No one in the living room. In the bedroom, the bed was made. Everything was very neat. No Officer Smiley marred the neatness. The little house was empty. Just to be sure, I knocked on every window as I peered in. No response. Even the bathroom door stood open. No Smiley there that I could see.

The news announcer's voice kept echoing in my head: body of an unidentified white male. It was enough to make my heart race. Was it possible? No information had been released about the body. Just an unidentified white male. I felt sick. I couldn't imagine never seeing that chipped incisor again. It was what made Officer Smiley's grins so contagious. Or so irritating, depending on the circumstances. Five minutes later I had concluded that there were no unlocked windows or doors in the house. No sound came from it.

Across the street, a silver-haired woman somewhere on the high side of seventy was standing outside, inspecting her oak trees. Or at least pretending to. I knew she was watching me.

I crossed the street and made myself smile.

"Hello. I'm looking for my friend. I thought we were supposed to meet here this morning, but I seem to have missed him. Did you see him head out?"

"What's his name?"

"Sorry?"

"Your friend. What's his name?"

"Tyler. Tyler Dekker. Why do you ask?"

"Just checking. For all I know you may be a burglar casing the joint."

I needed a bit of a chuckle. "I could be, but I'm not."

She put her hands on her hips and gave me a stern glance. "That's what they do, you know. They ask the neighbors when they'll be back and then they use that information to get in and clear everything out."

"Not my plan. For one thing, there's very little to steal inside that house, and for a second, Tyler is a police officer, so that's a terrible target for housebreakers. I think they mostly prefer things the easy way."

"Suppose you're right."

"Can you tell me what time he left? It's very important. Don't give me his schedule or anything like that."

"I wouldn't even if you did ask me."

We continued our verbal wrangling for several minutes, before she stalked back toward her house and out of my reach.

You win some. You lose some. My uncles taught me that early. I wasn't happy that I'd lost this one.

I HEADED FOR the Harrison Falls police station and smiled at the desk sergeant.

"Dekker booked off sick," he said, giving me a curious glance. "Can someone else help you?"

"What? Oh no, it's just a social call. I was in the area and thought I'd say hi. I'll give him a call. Thank you." I brought out my most innocent smile and flashed it. "Can you tell him Jordan says 'hi'? Never mind. I'll just text him." I felt like a teenage girl talking to the mother of the guy I had a crush on.

That smile wasn't easy to produce or sustain, given this latest news. Dekker wasn't in and he wasn't at home. The icy feeling of the cold mud the previous night was nothing compared to the way I felt now. Was he really sick? If so, where was he? Not home for sure. Waiting somewhere? In an emergency room?

My hands wouldn't stop shaking. Was Tyler dead? Had the blow from Uncle Kev killed him before he got home? I had to get more information. I really couldn't let the desk sergeant in on it.

And there was only one place to get it.

I headed out to the Saab to make the trip to Burton.

LINCOLN WAY WAS a hive of activity. Police vehicles, news vans, you name it. I had to park three blocks away.

As I walked back toward the Adams place, I stared at everything with surprise and interest. I'd been practicing that look, as I didn't want the sick feeling to show on my face. I didn't want anyone else to know what I feared.

I headed straight for Harry Yerxa's place.

No answer.

Wasn't anyone home today?

In Harry's case it seemed very odd, as he was such an inquisitive person. How could he resist the drama on his own street? Perhaps he was just out annoying the police. It would be just like him. As much as I would have enjoyed watching that, I didn't want to come nose-to-nose with any investigators.

I walked down his walkway and up to the front door of the Adamses. No sign of the Audi. It could have been parked in the garage or it could have departed. No way to know.

Of course, I never expected anyone to answer, but I had to knock. I issued a little wave to the cameras and gave the front door a good bang. I almost toppled over when it swung inward.

"Hello," I called. "Randolph?" I didn't really believe that Delilah and Mason would have left Randolph on his own, but nothing ventured, nothing gained. I glanced around. The cameras were on, trained on a middle-aged woman who kept shaking her head and trying to escape back to her house. Harry Yerxa was missing out on his fifteen minutes of fame. No one seemed to be watching me. I could almost hear those Sayers books. Lord Peter whispered in my ear, "It's easier to get forgiveness than permission, my dear." Well, he might have if he'd been real. It's actually easier to get arrested, whispered the voice of reason.

"Hello?"

I stepped inside and glanced around.

What had happened here? The Adamses' neat living room was a scene of chaos: a chair tipped over, dishes abandoned and books lying on the floor. The boxes that had been piled by the door were gone. The books from the built-in bookcases were also gone, and the wine racks in the dining room were half empty. I could understand moving out and taking valuables. But why was there such a mess? Had Randolph decided to fight back? Would that explain it?

"Randolph?"

I stood at the foot of the stairs and glanced up. No movement. Not a sound. I didn't think there was much chance that either Mason or Delilah would have let me get this far if they were on the premises. On the other hand, I had no legal reason to be in that house. As a rule, this is not enough to stop anyone in my extended family, but I was trying for a different lifestyle. But on the *other* other hand, if the Sayers volumes were there, then I could simply pick them up and . . . what? I was already inside. I could always say that Randolph had agreed to trade for the Hemingway and then I could come back with that. No. I shook my head. This intriguing idea wasn't consistent with my plan to lead an exemplary life and work toward my PhD. It was consistent with my plan to keep my current job, which was intended to rebuild my bank balance and let me resume my normal life.

I was quite paralyzed by the pending decision.

I heard a noise behind me and whirled. A police officer, a female this time, was lumbering around the side of the house and up the stairs. I rushed out to meet her. "Officer, would you be able to help me with something? I am looking for Randolph Adams, an elderly man who lives here. I'm a friend. He isn't usually left alone in the house, but he should be here now." Okay, so I wasn't completely truthful. "The door was left open. Open, not just unlocked. I'd like to check, but, you know, that would be trespassing. I am sure you understand my problem. I'm very worried. I heard on the news they found a man murdered in the neighborhood, and there is no answer on the phone. What if it was Randolph?" My voice was shaking and I didn't even have to fake it. I did play up my distress. It hadn't occurred to me until this moment that the body could be Randolph's. I'd been too worried about Uncle Kev and Tyler Dekker.

The officer was burly and tough looking, and that Kevlar vest wasn't doing her any favors. She had badly overbleached hair in a long ponytail and fierce black eyebrows that looked like they'd been shaped by a pro. One tough cookie, chewing gum. So I was relieved when she smiled kindly at me. She had a gap between her front teeth. It added to the smile.

I blurted out, "You have to go inside! What if he's fallen and can't get up? I don't think he has one of those security buttons!"

She snapped her gum. "We're dealing with a crime scene outside. I don't—"

"You're right. It's more likely he's the murdered man over there." I pointed toward the rear of the house. To tell the truth I wasn't faking the tears stinging my eyes. How did I suddenly have three missing men on my hands?

"How old is he?" The officer pushed the door open a little farther with the edge of her notebook. There was no expression on her face, but I could see her start to take interest.

"Randolph? He must be in his seventies."

"Then I can tell you he's not the man whose body was found."

Her smile returned. I felt a mix of relief and panic.

"Guy was younger," she confided. "Twenties or thirties. Early forties tops. I shouldn't be saying anything."

I gulped. Chances were that body was either Tyler's or Uncle Kev's. That was enough to make me sick.

She nodded. "It can't hurt to check on this guy." She proceeded to the foot of the stairs. "Sir?" she called out.

"Mr. Adams," I offered. "Randolph."

"Mr. Adams, are you up there?"

Nothing.

"Randolph?" she tried. I followed her up the lovely wooden stairs to the second floor. She peeked in each of the bedrooms. I followed her. Not surprising. The chairlift had been on the bottom of the stairs. Now no Randolph. No anyone.

Even though I didn't think he was in the house, I said, "Should we check the bathrooms? I think sometimes older people . . . fall."

Three bedrooms and two bathrooms later, no Randolph.

"I guess I was worried for nothing," I said. "No one here."

"Looks like they went on a trip," she said, glancing around. The entire second floor was in chaos, clothes tossed and discarded, more books tumbled, drawers opened. The beds were unmade and towels lay on the floor. Somehow this didn't mesh with my idea of Delilah, pale and elegant.

"Maybe."

She looked at me sharply. She was after all a cop. "Is there something you're not telling me?"

I shook my head. "I don't know. I tried to do some business with Randolph, but his daughter and grandson kept running interference. I thought perhaps there was some kind of elder abuse, fraud."

"Do you have any evidence?"

"No. Just a strong feeling."

"What kind of business?"

"Books."

"Books?"

"Yes. He was a collector and I am working with a dealer. He was interested in a Hemingway first edition, but his family has been making it difficult to see him. It felt to me like he was being controlled by them." I didn't mention the Sayers, or Vera, or even Karen's name. Just being cautious. I had begun to realize that I was unwise to be in this house at all. Something wasn't right. It really had nothing to do with me, and yet there I was sticking my nose in and attracting the attention of the cops. I could just imagine Uncle Mick's reaction.

"Well, if they were supporting him and they didn't want him wasting his money on books . . ." The cop shrugged.

I must have looked horrified, because she quickly added. "I'm just saying, that's how they might have been looking at it. I mean, I like books as much as the next person."

Before heading out, we both looked around again. She was keeping an eye out for something to indicate there'd been a crime, and I was searching for the Sayers books, while trying to give the impression I wasn't looking for anything. That was quite a challenge when I spotted some of the titles. I stared. Sure enough there was *Murder Must Advertise* lying on the floor in front of a low built-in bookshelf under the window in the central hallway. A window! Vera would have a fit if she thought they'd been exposed that way. All it would take was one absentminded moment, a window left open, a sudden rainstorm. It occurred to me that I had spent way too much time around Vera. On the shelf lay *Gaudy Night* and *Five Red Herrings*. Partway across the room *The Nine Tailors* lay open, spine up. I shuddered. I glanced around and located *Busman's Honeymoon*, *Unnatural Death* and *Whose Body?*

By the time I found *Strong Poison,* I was breathing heavily. I barely managed to keep myself from reaching out and scooping them up, holding the volumes close to my chest and racing off, cackling maniacally.

The cop was regarding me strangely. "All good there, miss? Don't worry. We'll ask around about your friend. I'm sure he's fine. You know, I wouldn't be surprised if they left because it's pretty scary having a murder in your backyard."

"I guess so." It didn't account for the state of the house.

"You'll see." She gave me a pat on the arm. She was being very sweet for a police officer, considering all officers were sworn enemies of Kellys and Binghams. But then she didn't know who I was.

"Thank you, Officer."

"Candy," she said with a surprising twinkle in her eye. "Candy Mortakis. And don't you worry. We don't want anything happening to a fragile old man. I'll keep an eye on the house too. Personally."

"Oh, I am probably just overreacting, um, Candy, but thanks. That's very helpful."

Great, now I had arranged for a cop to be watching the house I probably needed to break into.

What was this about? First, I was tripping over Officer Tyler "Smiley" Dekker and now this woman. What was I? Some kind of cop magnet? I had merely wanted to take advantage of her official presence, not become her new BFF. *Get me out of here!* I screamed, but inwardly of course.

She said, "I see there are stairs up to the third floor. It doesn't look like it's finished space up there, but I suppose I should check that out. We find a lot of stuff in attics."

I watched her wide, square rear ascend and veer out of sight. I felt confident that Randolph wasn't up there, at least not if he was still breathing. I had trouble imagining how he could get to the second floor without the chair lift, never mind the third floor.

I waited. I fought the urge. Unsuccessfully. Then before she could descend, shaking spider webs from her cop's hat, I did the deed. I grabbed every Sayers book I could spot and dropped them into my deep-orange bag. Luckily, it was not only deep orange, but also deep. I draped my fitted denim blazer over it. It was a crazy thing to do, and I have never lifted anything, not from a shop, nothing. My form of rebellion was going straight, and yet here I was, giving myself the five-finger discount, swiping books. I couldn't believe myself.

But the one thing I was sure of was that this Adams house was in some way a crime scene. It was just a matter of time until the cops figured that out and wrapped it in crime-scene tape. Just a matter of time until the books and everything in the house was evidence. Of what, I didn't know. That collection would disappear forever. I figured I would make it up somehow. If Delilah and Mason came back and saw the books missing, they'd know it was me or Karen right away. But I knew they weren't coming back. Even if the interior hadn't been plundered, it was obvious. The house was empty. Soulless.

"Nothing up there," Officer Candy said, clumping down the stairs and, as expected, brushing spider webs from her cap.

I hoped she hadn't noticed my guilty start at the first clump.

"You're jumpy," she said with a cheerful gappy grin.

"Yeah," I agreed. "I keep thinking of Randolph. But he's obviously not here. I wonder when they'll be back." Of course, I knew in my bones he wasn't coming back. Just didn't know why.

She gave the place a speculative glance. The kind that made me think she might make detective one of these days. "You might be right to worry. Something tells me they won't be back."

"That's what I think," I said, trying not to tilt over with the weight of the books in my bag. "But I don't know why."

"Well, I've seen a number of sites where people left town with no forwarding for very compelling if not valid reasons. They all look a bit like this. Clothes strewn, papers all around, safe's empty."

"What?" I said.

"Safe's empty," she said, happily.

"What safe? I didn't see one."

"Over here." I followed her into what must have been the master bedroom, with lovely sheets strewn around and drawers pulled out. In the walk-in closet was an open wall safe. I had been too busy coveting the Sayers stash to see that the first trip around.

"First of all," she said, "who has a wall safe?"

"Oh."

"Exactly. Do you?"

"Me? No, of course not. What would I keep in it?"

She shrugged. "That's my point. Most people don't have one because they don't have the right stuff to put in it. Do you even know anybody with a wall safe?"

I shook my head.

Not strictly true, of course. Wall safes were only some of the hiding places my uncles had, although they'd never be so obvious as to hide one in a bedroom closet. Vera too had a couple of wall safes, one hidden behind the portrait of her most hideous ancestor and one behind the mirror in an upstairs bathroom.

She said, "But these people did. Why is that?"

"I have no idea."

"It will be something, for sure."

Hard to argue with that.

"Right. Something for sure. Important documents maybe?"

"Like what?"

"Wills. Powers of attorney. Deeds. I don't know. A treasure map?" I grinned foolishly.

She chuckled. "We'll clear this up."

"I suppose. I just hope that Randolph is all right. His family was acting so weird when my friend and I came by. I think they realized we could see they were taking advantage of an old man. And the younger guy was downright aggressive."

"Hmmm, could be."

"What if that's what made them pack up and go in such a hurry? Dragging poor Randolph with them. Maybe that caused them to bolt."

She gave me a kind but pitying look. "I doubt that you and your friend with your raised eyebrows were enough to set them running."

"They were edgy, very edgy."

"Apparently. But was anything said? I'm still betting you weren't the cause."

If not, what had been, I wondered. My gut told me that their departure was connected to our visit, but I still wasn't sure why.

"I'd better get back," she said. "I'll call this in and see what they make of it at the station. Guess I'd better get your name and coordinates."

Oh boy.

I made the split-second decision to give a police officer my real name, the address of the Van Alst House and my iPhone number. This was not the smartest thing I've ever done and it certainly was one of the most unsettling. Still, I figured an inside track on what was going on in Burton was worth a bit of discomfort.

"I'll call you," she said as we made our way out the door. She was grinning. I was not.

"Great," I said with a sinking heart.

THE LOCAL RADIO station was playing up the murder with energy and pizzazz: "The Body in the Mud," "The Man No One Knew" and "Murderville."

No name had been released. No age. No details.

I turned off my car radio.

Officer Chatty Candy had told me that it was a man in his twenties, thirties or early forties. That could easily have been Uncle Kev or Tyler Dekker. I needed to find out.

I drove off, conscious of the guilt from the load of Sayers books in my bag. Two blocks away, when I figured no cops were coming after me, I pulled over and sat in the Saab, my hands shaking, and fretted over all I didn't know and what I had just done.

Something was nagging at me. If Tyler Dekker was dead, he could hardly have called in sick that morning. Unless, someone had killed him and knew enough about him to call the station pretending to be him. Uncle Kev didn't know enough about Tyler to do that. Anyway, that was just too convoluted. No, Officer Smiley wasn't dead. Therefore, Uncle Kev hadn't killed him. I breathed a sigh of relief.

The relief didn't last long. Tyler Dekker had been up to something underhanded and more than just playing hooky from work. He didn't work for the Burton force, so he could hardly have been undercover there. Whatever it was, it wasn't on the up-and-up.

So then I had to ask myself, if Uncle Kev hadn't killed Officer Smiley, had it been the other way around?

CHAPTER NINE

⟡

THE MAJOR MEDICAL facility in our area is Grandville General Hospital. Any trauma, that's where they
take you. It was a few minutes out of my way, but I needed
to check.

At the information desk, I asked for Tyler Dekker, possibly admitted suffering a concussion last night or today.

The attendant checked and shook her head. "No one here
by that name."

Of course, I wasn't relieved. What if he was unconscious?
What if he had no identification on him? What if he wasn't
there but was somewhere else, unconscious and alone?

It occurred to me that Uncle Kev might also have been
injured and admitted. It went without saying that he wouldn't
have ID.

I said, "It's just that my uncle didn't come home last
night. I am very worried about him. And he hit his head
earlier in the day. He's about five foot eleven with reddish
hair, very fit and has ginger eyebrows and very blue eyes.

The nurses will love him until he rearranges all the furniture and medical equipment and—"

"We have no notes about an unidentified patient," she said, flustered. "Usually they tell us when that happens. Tyler Dekker, you said?"

"Um, sometimes when he hits his head he may call himself something else. Kevin, maybe."

"Is this some kind of joke?" She glanced around and over my shoulder, looking for cameras, I supposed.

"No joke. Just a worried niece. I'll be glad if he didn't end up needing medical care."

So there was that. No Tyler Dekker. No Uncle Kev and apparently no unidentified males lying in emergency or ICU.

That was either very good or very bad.

I TOOK A minute to send yet another text to Smiley. There was nothing smiley about that text though. Then as I was in Grandville, I popped over to see if Karen needed anything. I wanted to unburden myself about the books I'd taken too. I found Uncle Lucky's Navigator parked in the driveway, a collection of boxes in the rear storage. He had some kind of project going and I would have to find out all about it when this nightmare was over.

The male neighbor gave me the stink-eye as I made my way to the back of the building and Karen's door. I waved. Upstairs, Karen was having a nap and the spare dog had joined her on the bed. Walter was keeping Lucky company in the living room.

Lucky had a notebook and pen, and was fiddling with notes for some project. He declined to share the info with me. Walter also had a project: a rawhide chew.

There was no reason to wake Karen and disturb her. I

imagined it would take a day or so to recover from our adventures. She was in good hands with Lucky, Walter and whoever that new dog would turn out to be.

I had nothing much to do but go home and worry.

TO SAY THAT dinner was tense was an understatement. Vera was feeling very hard done by without her complete collection and continued to badger me about it. The signora was a bit quieter than usual, and even the cats were keeping a low profile. I spotted one tail swish into the kitchen and then another vanish into the corridor.

I could not bring myself to tell her that I had located some of the books. The fact I only had eight might have sent her over the edge, but that was only part of it.

I didn't know what to do. Yes, Vera's books had been stolen, but Randolph hadn't stolen them. I had stolen them from him. A direct violation of my principles, not to mention my plan to go straight.

She grumbled at one end of the long table while I ruminated at the other. The signora shook things up a bit when she arrived with polpette con funghi—which I now know means meatballs with mushrooms. She served the meatballs in tomato sauce over rice. Heaven. Of course, that wasn't all.

"Is that green, Fiammetta?" Vera thundered.

"What? I no hear you, Vera. Eat! Eat!"

"Green. Is that zucchini is these meatballs?"

"Parsley! Is parsley! Eat!"

I ate. I was perfectly happy that there was zucchini in the meatballs. A lovely taste sensation and one that took the heat off me, for the time being anyway.

At the end, when Vera seemed to mellow a bit and forget about the zucchini takeover, I bit the bullet.

"I need to ask you to do something for me."

I didn't say favor. I didn't beg. I didn't even say please. This was Vera, after all.

"I know you are still on the board of Grandville General Hospital."

She nodded gravely. I was aware that she hated being on the board, but felt it was the duty of a Van Alst.

"I need to know if there was an unidentified man admitted to emergency either last night or sometime today.

"At the risk of being painfully obvious, Miss Bingham, I suggest that you make inquiries at the hospital."

"They were immune to my charms, I'm afraid."

Vera actually smiled at that one and then snapped back to her stern self.

"And who might I be inquiring about?"

I took a deep breath. "One of two people. Officer Dekker seems to be missing and was seen near the scene of the murder. He may be injured. He has not been at work. His dog was left behind."

"What about the police?"

"They say he called in sick. I don't want to make trouble for him. I think he's working on something on his own."

"Fair enough. And the other man."

"Tall, nice looking, red hair, bright blue eyes, engaging manner."

"A relative, I take it?"

I nodded.

"Anything else I should know?"

"It's complicated. And very important."

That's the thing about Vera. Just when you think she couldn't be any more self-focused and obsessed, she'd turn around and do the right thing.

"Thank you," I said, just as the signora started another round.

She was disappointed that I turned down coffee and dessert, as I planned to meet Lance to talk about my troubles.

LANCE AND I took a booth at the back of Café Hudson, a place where we had a long history. We each had ridiculously large cups of coffee with "coffee art" on top. Apparently they had been "handcrafted," making me wonder how else you could make coffee. Footcrafted?

I checked my iPhone again nervously while nibbling a chocolate croissant. The ringer was on: no new texts, no news.

"Expecting a call?" Lance scootched closer on the banquette. I could smell his cologne, shampoo and what I think was Gain detergent. I caught myself before I actually huffed his neck.

"I am expecting many calls. All of them involve Uncle Kevin and/or the police."

Lance winced, but I spotted the glint in his eyes. Here was a man only too happy to jump into an adventure. I hesitated to get him too involved. I wouldn't want him to vanish like Randolph, Tyler and Kev.

"Tell me," he whispered.

I stood the menu on end as a screen and pulled the books from my bag. Then taking a deep breath, I started my twisted tale of suspicion and light burglary. Lance listened intently. Dying to get to his role in the drama.

"I need you to hang on to these, just for a little while. I know it's asking a lot, considering that I basically stole them." I sighed. "But if I keep them at my place, the signora might find them and tell Vera. I need them kept safe, with someone I trust."

"Say no more. You're doing the right thing as usual, Jordan." He put his hand on mine on the books.

"I'm not really, but it was the only thing I could think of. So thank you so much for saying that."

Lance locked eyes with me for a long moment. My pulse pounded in my temples. Why did he smell so good?

"One thing though," Lance said.

"What?" I squeaked, very much aware of the sweat forming on my lip.

"I get to read them!" he said with glee, patted my hand and swept the books into his satchel.

"They're collectors' items. Pristine. They're not for casual reading. And you work in the library. You could borrow books anytime. And didn't you say you'd already read them all? Anyway, I think I have to go now."

"Always the heartbreaker, Jordan."

Ouch. Well, never mind. I had no time to make out, or deal with the messy consequences of fooling around with a good friend. A very good-looking friend. A very nice-smelling, good-looking and flirtatious friend.

"I'll take care of them. And I promise not to read them. Why do you have to go?"

"Unfinished business. Don't let anything happen to the books. My life is in your hands."

"What are friends for?"

CANDY TOOK ME by surprise. First of all, she walked up behind me and tapped on my shoulder as I was unlocking the back door to the Van Alst House. I shrieked and shot about a foot off the ground.

"Sorry," she said.

She didn't look all that sorry.

"It's me. Remember? Candy Mortakis, from over in Burton? Guilty conscience?"

Oh, for heaven's sake. Taking a cop out of uniform is the same as putting her in a disguise. Candy looked like a normal person, although this was hardly a normal thing to do.

As I was gasping for breath, the back door opened and the signora peered out, brandishing a rolling pin. *Va via! Ladra! Ladra!*"

"Get out of here, thief," was the gist of the signora's hollering.

"What the hell?" Candy said.

By the time I could speak, an upstairs window opened and Vera said, "Get off these premises, whoever you are. I have phoned the authorities."

"Well, that puts me in my place. All that sweating through police academy wasted," Candy said with a snort. She seemed to think the whole situation was pretty funny.

Vera said, "Be off with you!"

Candy called up to Vera, "Good luck with that. I am the authorities, ma'am. Here to speak to Jordan Bingham about an incident in Burton."

Vera slammed down the window. I was glad Candy was "the authorities," because I knew Vera would have tossed me to the wind if I'd been arrested.

Candy was grinning, even if I wasn't. "What is this place? You live in some kind of Shakespeare play? Gotta love the way these people talk."

"On a good day, it's Shakespearean," I said. "On a bad day more like something from Dante's nine circles."

She stared at me and smacked her gum.

I changed the subject. "What are you doing here?"

"Well, you know. We seemed to hit it off and I'm new to this area and I don't know a lot of people and I thought we could maybe have a chat. Or maybe we could arrange a girls' day."

I decided I was probably having one of those weird

dreams I'd been troubled by lately. That would be about the only thing that would explain this visit.

Vera's window shot up again. "I demand to see your identification. Immediately."

"It's all right, Vera. This is the full force of the law right here on your back doorstep. There's nothing to worry about. Oh, unless you're here to arrest me, um, Officer Candy. Are you?"

She grinned wickedly. "Now why would I want to do that?"

The books! Shut the front door! my guilty conscience screamed.

From upstairs, Vera's gravelly voice asked, "And why, Miss Bingham, is the full force of the law making you jump like a scalded cat at ten thirty in the evening?"

I didn't think I'd shrieked. "Purely social, Vera."

The window slammed shut again.

The signora was still there, however, rolling pin raised. I figured she was prepared to use it.

I held up my hand. "Friend, Signora Panetone."

She narrowed her eyes. "You okay?"

"I'm okay. Thank you."

"Well that was all quite dramatic," Candy said, continuing to grin. "I knew you'd be fun to be around."

"And you probably also know why I prefer not to scream around my back door."

"Next time I'll just text."

The signora said. "You hungry? Yes. Yes."

Candy said, "No thanks, I—"

"Save it. Resistance is futile and I think you'll find you are hungry after all."

She shrugged and we stepped into the house. We ended up in the conservatory, which is not all that cozy on an autumn night, but this was the Van Alst House. Nothing was cozy except my apartment, and I wasn't about to invite this cop up there, no matter how cute her name was. She'd need a warrant for that.

The signora flitted and swooped about, bringing a vast tray with plum torte and whipped cream, almond cookies, delicious little anise-flavored *pizzelle* and a pot of tea.

"What are those?" Candy pointed.

"*Pizzelle*. They're little waffle cookies. She makes them with a special press. The others are almond cookies."

Candy said, "Huh." We sat staring at each other across the table and munching the delicate waffle cookies. Outside, in the blackness, trees waved and leaves swirled.

"Must be nice," Candy said, looking around.

"You should see the catacombs."

She snorted.

The signora crossed herself and said, "No catacombs. *Madonna santa! No!* You eat. Be nice, Jordan. Eat now!" I thought her vocabulary was improving and I grinned at her to show my approval. Her black eyes glittered. "You want fruit salad?"

"No thanks, this mountain of food is just fine." It occurred to me that all this food at bedtime might be contributing to my weird dreams too, especially when combined with the mayhem in my life.

"That sounds great," Candy said, smiling.

The little gap between her front teeth was kind of endearing if you liked that sort of look. I found myself wondering if all cops had some kind of tooth identifier. But that reminded me of Tyler Dekker, and my heart sank where no cookie could rescue it.

The signora scurried back to the kitchen. Candy leaned forward. "This is awesome. I want to live here. Can you adopt me?"

"It comes with a job that is not all tea and cookies and fruit salad, let me tell you."

"Just what is your job?"

"Before we chat too much, how about you tell me what you're really doing here?"

I really didn't want to talk about my job, which involved getting books for Vera from many sources, in case Candy got an inkling of what I had been up to at the Adams place.

"So," she said, "guess what?"

That was all I needed. Games.

"Not good at guessing."

"It's about your friends."

I blinked. "What friends?" Did she mean Tyler? Lance? Or Tiff? But how could she even know about them?

She gave me a skeptical glance. It might have made me nervous if she hadn't just popped an entire *pizzelle* into her mouth. Food is the great leveler.

I waited until she'd swallowed. "Duh," she said, scattering a few crumbs. "The Adams family."

My heart did a little flutter and I stood up. "What about them? Did something happen to Randolph? Did he turn up at the hospital after all?"

Why hadn't I looked for him when I was checking for Kev and Smiley? I felt desperately stupid.

"Nope. He didn't turn up."

"Did they?"

"Uh-uh." She shook her head and reached for a piece of plum cake.

"What, then?"

"Not what. Why."

It was the end of a long day and I had more than a few worries and I really didn't need these games. But I seemed to have no choice but to play along.

"Okay. Why?"

She beamed. "The Adams family didn't turn up because they don't exist."

I plunked back in my seat. "What?"

"They do not exist."

"But they do. I saw them. I met them. They were real."

"Well, I'm sure they were flesh and blood, Jordan. But there is no record of them anywhere before they moved to Burton. Wow, this cake is amazing. I don't suppose there's any more?"

There was the better part of a cake left, so that made me wonder what she had in mind. However, the signora practically levitated with joy at those words. "Yes! You eat. I give you one to take."

I waited until calm was restored.

"So," I said, "explain to me how you know this."

"Not so very hard to find out these things. I am the full force of the law, remember? And there has to be an upside besides getting free cake."

"No doubt. But again, how?"

"Well, I dug a little and these people—whoever they are—their cover is only skin-deep. If that."

"Huh. So I was right?"

"About what?"

I tried not to glare at her. "About Delilah and Mason being con artists out to fleece Randolph."

She grinned again.

"Afraid there's more to it than that."

"Can't you just come right out and tell me? It's getting to be past my bedtime here."

"Cute. Well, I suppose I could. But where's the fun in that?"

"I haven't actually been having fun. I've been worried about Randolph and what's happened to him."

"You think something happened to him?"

I fought a frisson of annoyance. "You know I do. He's not there and now his so-called family is not who they say they are. There was a murder in his backyard. So what else would I think?"

She shrugged. The signora distracted us by arriving with an entire plum cake quadruple-wrapped in plastic wrap and a container of fruit salad, ready to transport back to her cop cave, wherever in Burton that was. "You eat tomorrow!"

"You betcha."

"So," I said. "Randolph?"

"That's the thing. He's not who he claimed to be either."

I blinked. "Who is he?"

"You got me. The whole crowd of them didn't seem to exist before three years ago."

"Well, they must have existed."

"Sure, physically those three bodies were living and breathing, but their identities didn't. And after all that time, any trail leading to them is bound to be cold."

"The next-door neighbor said they moved in three years ago."

"Right, and prior to that: nothing."

"There must have been something. They bought a house. You need money for that. Bank accounts."

"About three years ago a lot, and I mean a *lot*, of money was deposited into an account in Randolph Adams's name from a bank in Trenton, New Jersey. Turns out that money was transferred from the Cayman Islands."

I searched for the right words. How much could a fairly new police officer in a small town in upstate New York find out about the Adamses in such a short time?

She must have read my mind. "I have friends. Connections in bigger places. I called around."

"But unauthorized searches of personal information are illegal, aren't they?"

"Absolutely. But you gave me a good reason when you were so worried about your friend Randolph. The word on the street is that a mob accountant named Randall Abrams was skimming from some high-level mobsters and the wise guys got wise. About three years ago he disappeared along with his wife, Dawna, and the young guy who was his assistant. The money went with Randall. These mob guys are not the kind of people who let things go. They want their money back and they want Randall Abrams and everyone with him dead. Doesn't matter if he's a sick old man. They can't be reasoned with. Hey, you don't seem all that happy about it."

"Of course I'm not happy to learn that he was a fraud too. I'm not surprised about Delilah and especially Mason. But I really believed Randolph was in danger."

She picked up her latest piece of cake. "Cheer up. Maybe he is."

I shot her a dirty look. "Not funny."

"Sorry." She couldn't resist a grin.

"It isn't a game."

"Somehow it feels a bit like a game." I swear she twinkled at me. "I feel there's something about you and those Adamses that I'm not getting."

"Tell you what I'm getting: a headache. Maybe that's what you're hoping for?"

She laughed out loud. She sure was a good laugher. "I'm just hoping for something interesting to happen in Burton."

"I guess you got it, what with a couple of murders and all."

"Yes. But they don't let the new kid do anything but the most boring footwork on those cases. The detectives are little kings. Tyrannical too. But the question remains, what does this thing with the disappearing Adams family mean?"

I shrugged, feeling suddenly deflated. "You got me."

Nothing could deflate Officer Candy. "This is the most fun I've had since I got here."

I said, "What brought you here in the first place?"

"I wanted to get some good experience. I thought with a small force I'd get closer to the action. When I grow up, I want to be one of those little kings."

"And is that working?"

"Not even a little bit. I'll have to make my own opportunities."

"Good luck with that."

I didn't like the idea of being part of Candy's opportunities, but anyway, I turned the discussion back to the missing Adams family and added some of my own speculations. "Could that money have come from Randolph himself? Could he have been convinced to leave his former life and go underground in Burton? Maybe he liquefied all his assets and faked his death or something. Could Delilah have tricked him? Or coerced him?"

"Anything is possible for people who don't exist. But you do have to ask yourself, if you had enough money to buy that house and to live for years without anyone apparently working and to collect books and art and nice wines, would you pick Burton? Wouldn't you go somewhere glamorous?"

I shrugged. "I really like it around here, but I take your point. Burton is hardly Paris or Rio."

Candy said, "And now that they've vanished and we don't know where or how, it will be almost impossible to find where they've gone. Especially if they get themselves new names and melt into another small town where they have no connections."

"We don't even know if Randolph is still alive," I said. "Sorry to introduce a serious element into the funfest."

She managed to look a bit chastened, although I wasn't entirely convinced it was sincere. She said, "Oh, right. This is serious and we already have a body, don't we?"

"Yes. We do. Do you know who that is?"

"No."

"Not an idea?"

"So far none."

"Fingerprints?"

She smiled again. "Now that's interesting too."

I waited.

She kept smiling.

"Come on," I said. "You're dying to tell me."

"I am actually."

"And . . ."

"He didn't have any."

"No fingerprints?"

Her grin was back. So much for being chastened. "Who would imagine such a thing?"

"Yeah. I didn't know that was possible." Not entirely true, because I did remember my uncles speaking about people with no prints in hushed voices tinged with respect and envy.

Candy tilted her head and dusted the crumbs off her sweater. "Leave the fingerprint issue aside for the moment and tell me, what do you do for fun around here?"

What was this about? The missing fingerprints were the only thing that mattered to me at that second. Fun? What did that have to do with anything?

"For fun? I read classic mysteries. I spend time with my friend Lance who's a local librarian. I go to flea markets and bazaars and garage sales, and I hang out with my family and the family dog." Okay, not entirely true, but that was my Kelly side coming out.

"Wow. You have got to get a life."

"I like my life. In fact, I love it." The strangest part of that statement was that it was true. A year ago, I wouldn't have imagined saying it. A lot had happened in that year.

"Yeah right you do."

"I do. I'm saving to get back to grad school. I can't swing it just yet, but I'm sure hoping for next year."

"I'll watch for you on TMZ."

"Maybe you'll make it first."

"I'm not nearly as interesting as you are."

I felt a flutter of nerves. I had just explained how totally devoid of interest my life was, leaving aside recent encounters with theft and murder. As they say, that was a story for another time. I did not want this police officer to find anything about me or my life interesting.

She continued, "That's why I followed up. I thought you might be a possible friend."

A possible friend? Was she kidding? Did she routinely interview for friends? "But you're a cop. Are you permitted to socialize with witnesses?"

Now I had all her attention. "Witnesses. Are you a witness? Witness to what?"

Oops. Think fast. "To Randolph's situation."

I reminded myself to remember to think first, speak second.

"Right. I thought you meant the murder."

I choked back a nervous giggle. "Hardly. But I am wondering who that guy was. No ID at all, you said. And no fingerprints. That sounds like someone who might be known to the police, as they say."

"Sure, it's a giveaway, especially no fingerprints. No idea is too bizarre to consider, especially as he had a wallet and cash on him. But his picture is circulating."

"Did he have a driver's license?"

"Yup."

"Well then—?" The rest of my comment was drowned out by her hoot of laughter.

"Fake! Pretty good job. But it turned out to belong to some dead guy."

"You mean he killed someone else?"

"Nah. We followed up. Looks like he just ripped off the identity to get new ID. No way to know who he was until the DNA gets analyzed, and that takes forever and a day. It's not like on TV."

It would have been pushing my luck to ask to see the photo of the dead man. I said, "I suppose you'll be showing a picture to people in the neighborhood to see if they recognize his face."

"Yup. We cops do that kind of thing even before our friends suggest it."

I was not thrilled at the idea of being her friend.

"Sorry. I'm getting a bit too into it. Of course, we can't ask the Adamses, as they're missing, but their next-door neighbor, Harry Yerxa, is pretty nosy. I'd go so far as to say he doesn't miss a trick."

She raised a cop-like eyebrow. "How do you know him?"

"He struck up a conversation every time we tried to get in to see Randolph."

"Every time?"

"Ah yes, well, um, they wouldn't answer the door."

"Uh-huh. And who is we?"

I made a strategic decision not to mention Uncle Kev. "Karen Smith, the dealer who sold the books to him."

She leaned forward and held my gaze. "And when was the last time you talked to him?"

"To Harry? Why are you asking?"

She made a little cop-like face, thought a bit and then said, "Because Harry Yerxa seems to be missing too."

My jaw dropped so fast I might have been a cartoon character. "Missing?" I squeaked. "Why would Harry be missing?"

"You tell me."

"But I have no idea. Are you sure he's missing?" I felt a surge of sadness tinged with panic. I had come to like Harry Yerxa, nosiness, bizarre wardrobe and all. He had spirit. And he hadn't been home when I'd tried his door.

"We're sure."

"I mean did you check everywhere in the house? Again, he's an older man. Maybe he slipped on the stairs. Maybe he fell in the bathtub. Maybe—"

She put a hand on my arm. "Just like you thought about Randolph? Everyone past the age of fifty doesn't fall over at the drop of a hat, you know. We did check the house."

"Oh. No. Could he have witnessed something?" Then an even more horrifying idea came to me. I gasped. "He wasn't the body, was he?"

I hated this idea.

"Definitely not. For one thing, he's too old, and for another, he is who he says he is. I imagine he has fingerprints too, although we won't know for sure until we find him."

"Wait a minute! Why did you check his house?"

"We got a call that something was happening on that street. An older person was injured."

"A call?"

"Yes."

"From?"

"Anonymous."

"But none of that makes any sense."

"Exactly. None of it makes any sense. Yet."

I blinked at her.

"You seem—how can I put it?—excessively concerned."

"I hardly knew him, but he was sweet, in a grandfatherly way. And full of energy. He did need someone to help him with his wardrobe."

"Back to making sense. Are you sure you can't add anything to help, Jordan?"

I was telling the absolute truth for once when I said that I couldn't.

"Why are you so pale?" she demanded.

I couldn't tell her that I was pale because I was worried the body would turn out to be Uncle Kev. It was entirely possible he wouldn't have fingerprints and almost 100 percent certain he'd have fake ID. Tyler Dekker had been creeping around with a fake dog, and he wouldn't have been carrying his ID either, as he was obviously up to something. But I doubted that a working cop would lack fingerprints. That was the only thing I could feel good about.

"I guess I am worried about Harry. I don't know him well but I liked him right off the bat. Are you 100 percent sure that Harry Yerxa is not the, um, corpse? You sure we're talking about the same guy? The older man with the passion for plaid. He lives to the left of the Adamses in that white Victorian-style house."

"I know who Harry Yerxa is. And trust me, he's not the victim. This guy was much younger. I already told you that."

"Sometimes it's hard to judge how old a person is." I was indeed stretching the truth when I said, "Well, Harry Yerxa had a young-looking face. Maybe . . . No that's ridiculous, isn't it? And he didn't have a young face. He was obviously a senior."

She squinted at me and then sighed deeply. "Fine. I suppose it couldn't do any harm. Come out to the car with me and I'll show you the ID photo that we got at the station. I think it's a real long shot that you'll recognize this guy."

She stood up and tugged at the waistband of her pants. Her clothes were all wrong for her body type and obviously the wrong size. Candy's hair was so damaged and frizzled, it hardly looked real. I actually heard it cry out for a hot oil treatment. She'd obviously tried to tame it with at least a dozen ill-placed bobby pins. Even if my relatives hadn't taken the opposite career path, I could never have been a police officer if they allowed themselves to be seen in public like this off duty. She should have been an attractive woman.

I had to resist the urge to drag her upstairs and give her a makeover.

CHAPTER TEN

━━◆◆◆━━

I FELT MY throat tighten as we got near Candy's navy-blue Tahoe. Especially as I was very, very worried that I would soon be gazing at the dead face of Uncle Kev.

"Something wrong?" Candy said, stopping and turning back to me in concern.

"Maybe I'm allergic to all the leaf mold in the air," I croaked.

She shrugged, walked over to the driver's side and unlocked the door of the Tahoe. "Get in," she ordered.

I climbed into the passenger seat, although it's very hard for anyone with my genes to sit in a car with a cop for any reason. I reminded myself she was just a junior officer in a small jurisdiction and she was off duty on my territory. Plus it was her own car. Nothing official. Still.

"I'm breaking a dozen rules here," Candy said. She flicked on the interior light and handed me the image the police were circulating of the victim.

I must have exhaled in relief to see that it was no one that I'd been worrying about.

Again with the cop eyebrow.

"Expecting someone?" she said.

"Just relieved it isn't Harry," I said, failing to mention Kev. "I am so glad. I hate the idea of really liking a corpse."

Candy rolled her eyes. I wished she wouldn't do that quite so often. She said, "I told you more than once it wasn't him. You'll have to learn to listen to me. I do know my job, even if I'm new here."

I barely heard her, as I'd leaned forward to get a better look at the victim. The face on the sheet of paper—once I got used to the idea that he was dead—was very familiar.

No question about it. This was the man in the car that had been parked outside the Adams house last night when I'd been walking Walter.

I must have gasped because Candy said, "What? You know this guy?"

I hesitated, which, of course, stimulated her cop senses. She watched me very closely as I sat silently. "And?"

I decided to go with the truth. "You know what? I'm pretty sure this guy was parked near the Adams house the other night."

"What?"

"He was parked near—"

"I heard you, but I can't believe what you're saying. You saw the vic?"

Had the truth been a bad idea? My uncles would have said so.

"I did see him. What's the problem?"

"How come you didn't mention it before? When was this?"

This was awkward. I would have regretted telling her, but she'd known right away that I recognized him. Note to self: learn not to react dramatically when surprised. Of course, she was going to interrogate me. She was a cop. I hadn't told my new best friend that I'd been fake dog-walking Walter the previous night, so I needed to leave out that bit.

"Whoa, whoa! What's with the interrogation? I see a lot of people every day. How was I supposed to know this guy would turn out to be important? 'Important' is not the right word, I guess. The fact is, I made several attempts to see Randolph Adams, as you know. And on one of the occasions this man, the victim, was parked there."

"And?"

My turn to shrug. "And what?"

"And what happened?"

I stared at her. "Nothing happened. He was just parked on the street."

"In front of the Adams house?"

"Well, no. In front of the next house down. Not Harry's. Number 89. The one to the right of the Adamses. I figured he was waiting to pick someone up. He didn't do anything to draw attention to himself."

I left out how I knew he was in the car and how he could have used some better training in being invisible.

"Then what?"

"Nothing. He drove off."

"But you noticed him."

"He was in an older model Impala. I noticed it as I walked by. I guess I glanced inside to see the driver. That's the person I saw."

"You thought it was suspicious at the time?"

"I really didn't. Just a guy in a parked car who drove

away. Of course, it was before the Adamses disappeared. And before there was a murder."

"You notice anything else?"

My uncles had long ago taught me how to move my eyes if I want a lie to look truthful. I looked to the right, as I always do when I'm telling the truth. I let myself appear to try to recall for a minute, then shrugged.

"He sped off right after I glanced at him, for what that's worth."

"Well, well. I guess you really are a witness." Candy gave me a penetrating look.

"Instead of . . . ?"

"To tell the truth, I thought you were just plain nosy. But I decided to show you this photo. What are friends for?"

"You knew I was really afraid it was Harry." Or Kev or Tyler.

"Yes, and I could see how relieved you were, so you're welcome. So he was outside the Adams residence?"

"Right. Not the best looking guy, was he?"

"Ugly as sin," she said.

"But I didn't really give him any thought at all. And I certainly didn't worry about him."

"No reason to."

"In retrospect, I suppose I should have worried about him."

She nodded. "Or worried about whoever killed him. There's something smelly for sure. We'll find out who he was. Fingerprints or not."

I hesitated. "Good. Will you let me know? I guess I am nosy. But I feel involved."

I was kicking myself by this point. As much as I had wanted to know who the victim was, I had made myself vulnerable to Candy. For a bit of reassurance. Candy was not only almost a stranger; she was a police officer with instincts.

She said, "Sure, why not. Unless I have a good reason not to."

In addition to all the worry about Uncle Kev and Tyler and the missing books, the stress of being around an edgy police officer who wanted to make a name for herself on the Burton police force was starting to wear on my nerves.

My head was throbbing. I couldn't wait to get away from Candy's intense presence and back to my soothing little attic.

After I said good night for the third time, Candy reached out and tentatively touched my arm. "Hey, I don't suppose you want to go to a movie this weekend? Or something?"

I smiled weakly.

AS SOON AS Officer Candy drove off, I locked the back door and headed up the dark, narrow stairs to my flowered bower.

A note under my door indicated that Vera wanted to talk at me.

I headed back down the narrow stairs to the first floor and then along the endless corridor in the east wing to get to the front foyer and the stairs to the second floor and Vera's suite. It's not a place I visited often, although it was good exercise getting there. I knocked on the door and waited until Vera rolled over and opened it.

"No," Vera said.

I blinked. "No what?"

"No unidentified injured males have showed up or been taken to Grandville General Hospital, last night or today. They've had heart attacks, strokes, gastrointestinal drama, premature babies, injured toddlers and teenagers as well as females hurt in collisions, all attended by relatives. No one of your descriptions, attended or unattended."

"That's good," I said.

"I certainly hope so, Miss Bingham, because I went out on a limb for your request, taking advantage of my position on the board and leaning on the chief of staff. I hope it was worth it."

I nodded. "I appreciate it."

"What now, Miss Bingham?"

I shook my head. "I have no idea."

"What about the body found in Burton?"

"No. That's one good thing. Officer Mortakis showed me a picture of the victim. It wasn't anyone I knew."

To my astonishment, Vera said, "I hope your friend and your relative are fine and there is some explanation for this that doesn't involve violence to them."

As she spoke, a Siamese whipped through her bedroom door and disappeared into her suite. I really hoped it was Good Cat.

"Thank y—"

But by then she had shut the door in my face. Still, I had to think that our relationship had just made a great leap forward.

I headed back to my room, feeling equal parts gratitude and surprise.

IT IS USUALLY wonderful to unwind in my attic space with the sloped ceilings and faded cabbage rose wallpaper, but usually I'm not worried about missing friends or relatives who may be lying unidentified in some lonely morgue. Uncle Mick and Uncle Lucky were not used to chasing after their little brother and were probably just relieved that he was out of their hair. They didn't seem to be bent out of shape by his absence. I didn't know if Tyler even had any relatives. For the first time in the five months since I'd first met him, I considered that I knew nothing about him at all. Not even whether his parents were alive. Perhaps he had a ton of relatives and had just never mentioned them. I couldn't imagine that. Maybe it was a guy thing. Could it be he'd ended up at the hospital and someone had come to take him home? But if that had happened, it hadn't been in our local hospital.

I was tired but too restless to sleep. I thought about the books I had pilfered from the Adams house. If these books could talk, what would they tell me? I wanted to know why one of them was actually flung at a wall hard enough to damage the spine. I couldn't imagine Randolph doing that under any circumstances. He loved these books enough to pay Karen well for eleven Sayers novels. Maybe he didn't care as much as Vera. She was infatuated with every book in her collection, but he cared and paid plenty. So why had those eight been left behind? Where were the rest of the books?

Of course, it had to have been Mason who had tossed the books. But again, why?

Was there anything to be learned from them? I lay on my flowered quilt, closed my eyes and thought about *Whose Body?* the first of the Wimsey novels. Coincidentally, the book dealt with someone who was not who he appeared to be. That was relevant to me: Mason wasn't who he appeared to be. None of the Adamses were who they appeared to be. Tyler Dekker was certainly not behaving like a cop. And Uncle Kev wasn't behaving at all. As for the victim, who knew for sure, but I bet he hadn't been what he appeared to be either.

I shook my head and tried to concentrate on the matter at hand and the books that were linked to this whole situation. At least that copy was pristine. I breathed a sigh of relief, even though *Whose Body?* was my least favorite of all the Sayers books, maybe because it's such a short book compared to the others. But then it was Sayers's first. Although you could always count on Lord Peter to be equal parts debonair, urbane, knowledgeable and silly, I felt that he improved with each book. It didn't take Sayers long to expand to more substantial novels and, of course, to bring in Harriet Vane to spice up the action, because an intelligent young woman can bring a lot to a book.

Harriet Vane—a successful author of detective stories, like her creator. I enjoyed thinking about Harriet and wondering whether I might have liked the kind of life she'd lived. It made a nice change from thinking about the missing and dead people I knew. Fictional dead folks I can handle.

Could I become a detective novelist? I knew plenty about crime and also knew not to be fooled by what you see on the surface. I was well aware that pleasant, ebullient and attractive men could have more interest in your sterling silver than in your heart, no names mentioned. I loved reading and researching, and I loved writing, but Lord Peter would find that a bit less than original. I was better off with the career I was having so much trouble hanging onto.

I wondered idly whether Vera also might have daydreams about the people in the books she collected. I shook my head. Who would Vera Van Alst aspire to be? I'd read a lot about Agatha Christie and Dorothy L. Sayers. Christie had a family and exotic travel. Dorothy L. Sayers had a lively, creative and productive life. She worked tirelessly; she was intellectual and she loved good food and partying with her friends. So not Vera, then. On the other hand, Sayers was passionate about her beliefs and she liked a good argument. As does you know who. Being housebound for so long and now set in her ways, Vera was more like Nero Wolfe, without the "charm."

I wondered if she'd always been like that or if a softer Vera had once roamed these grounds.

I shook my head to clear the competing thoughts. Time to get back to productive thinking. At the Adams house, I hadn't located Sayers's second book, *Clouds of Witness*. I had really enjoyed *Clouds of Witness* because it dealt with the crazy situations that one's nearest and dearest can drop on your doorstep. Or as my uncles would say, "Ya can pick your friends, but ya can't pick your relatives." This was usually in reference to Uncle Kev, no big surprise.

Clouds of Witness was definitely one of the stolen fine firsts. I knew that. Or did I? Was I wrong? So many strange things had happened, I could hardly trust my brain at this point. Eleven Dorothy L. Sayers first editions, that's what I needed to get back. All the Sayers novels had been pinched. None of her collaborative efforts had been taken, nor had the short story collections. I loved those short stories. Perhaps they would have been swiped next if the perpetrator hadn't been stopped. But they weren't missing now. I was sure of it. Or was I? I had brought back eight volumes. Were there only eight missing books? I knew the hamster in the wheel would never get a break if I didn't find out for sure.

Karen would be fast asleep, helped along by medications. Naturally, I was reluctant to ask Vera, since that kind of inquiry could easily blow up in my face. And I felt attached to that face. Mind you, it had a pretty dumb look on it right now. I should have been absolutely certain how many books were missing. It was too late to call Lance and check, so I closed my eyes and tried to recall the books. *The Unpleasantness at the Bellona Club* hadn't been there either. But *Unnatural Death* had been. I'd checked *Unnatural Death* gingerly and found it to be in excellent condition. At least it hadn't been damaged by the rough treatment in the Adams house. It would certainly pass the Vera test.

I clearly remembered picking up *Strong Poison*, where we readers first met the splendid Harriet Vane in the prisoner's dock, accused of murdering her lover. That's when Lord Peter first fell and fell hard. Lucky lady, except for the murder charge. Then I'd inspected *Five Red Herrings*, a classic puzzle mystery. Sayers said that every sentence in this book was important to the solution. So many of those sentences involved the minute details of railway schedules that it had failed to get my motor running. *Five Red Herrings* was Vera's favorite Sayers book, but then she adored puzzles.

I had moved on to *Murder Must Advertise*, in which Peter really shone, in my opinion, as he assumed another identity and went undercover in an advertising agency. I found that undercover thing exciting when it was happening on the page, but not so much when it was happening to me.

I hated to be out of my depth. Sayers lived and breathed advertising for years, and that's why *Murder Must Advertise* seemed so authentic.

Next I'd inspected *Gaudy Night*, where I really got to know Harriet Vane and started picturing myself living that scholarly way of life in the nineteen thirties. What would it have been like to be born in an earlier century and to have enjoyed the academic life in a women's college at Oxford in that era? I thought I'd look good in the billowing academic gown. But I mustn't digress. At any rate, I knew perfectly well, if Harriet Vane had been born in my circumstances she would be in graduate school right at that very moment, come hell or high water. Something to ponder. But for now back to my task of remembering: *Busman's Honeymoon* was right up there on my A-list too. And it had been one of the books I'd recovered.

But I was troubled by the missing books: *Clouds of Witness, Have His Carcase* and *The Unpleasantness at the Bellona Club.* I'd failed to find them.

Late or not, I called Lance. He was surprisingly agreeable, conisdering the hour. He was also willing to take a look at the books. He confirmed all eight of the titles were there and also verified that the other three were not.

"So I'm not crazy," I said.

"Not sure I'd go that far," he chuckled. "It is the middle of the night. I'm going back to sleep."

After Lance disconnected, I closed my eyes and thought back to the room at 87 Lincoln Way. Had I located every Sayers book on that section of the shelf and on the floor? Had Randolph chosen a few of his favorites to take on the Adams family trip to wherever? Or did I manage to miss those three in the chaos of the Adams house? I'd been in a minor panic because, at any moment, Officer Candy could have thumped down the stairs from the attic and caught me. Perhaps I just hadn't realized what they were in the midst of the debris. Or maybe the three books had landed under a piece of furniture. A dozen possible scenarios flashed through my mind.

What if there was a miracle and it turned out that they'd never been stolen at all?

I got out of bed and headed downstairs to check the library. Hammy the hamster and I wouldn't be able to sleep if I didn't.

OF COURSE, EVERYTHING in Van Alst House feels like it's two miles away. The library is on the first floor, down not one but two endless corridors. I keyed in the security code, closed the door behind me and switched on the light. Even when I'm in a hurry, I always have to pause to admire the rosewood and the perfect shelves filled with perfect books. I always inhale the scent of old leather and paper. This library is one of my favorite places on earth, especially when Vera isn't in it. I quickly climbed the wrought iron circular staircase to the mezzanine. Sure enough, despite my desperate desire to see them, the Sayers first edition novels were not there. The short story collections stood all in a row. I ran a hand over *Lord Peter Views the Body*. Some people turn up their noses at a few of these early stories, but to me it was a thing of beauty. Vera must have thought so too, because I knew she'd paid a thousand dollars for it, without so much as a blink. There was also a copy of *Striding Folly*, a collection of the last three Wimsey stories. I liked the long introduction by Janet Hitchman, with its blend of biographical details for Dorothy Sayers and Wimsey. Not complete, but interesting. I'd even bought a copy with a slightly psychedelic cover for myself, the New English Library 1980 mass-market reprint. I loved every one of those over-the-top covers and snapped up several in that reprint series. They were still on display on the coffee table, so I could admire their funkiness. Ten dollars a pop, well spent at the book fair.

I was getting to enjoy the hunt as much as Vera did,

although at a much lower price range. I didn't care so much about pristine first editions or books that had never been read. I loved to plunge into the era the books conveyed.

I turned back to the shelves and the large gap that had been left when the Sayers books had been stolen. Of course, the books would most likely have all been in the same room at the Adams house, and now, somehow, I'd ended up with three of them missing. Why was that? And more to the point, I wondered how much hair pulling I could take before I would need to invest in another wig.

AS I REVERSED my trip down the two endless hallways and back up the steep stairs to my quarters, I thought hard. The missing books were either in the Adams house or they weren't. And if they weren't, then the absconding Adamses had taken them for some reason. As the Adamses had vanished—and in fact were not even the Adams family to begin with—if the books had gone with them, I had a really big problem, in a week of massive problems.

So, I had no choice really but to head back to 87 Lincoln Way. Officer Candy was keen to have a girls' night, but I could hardly ask her to join me in a bit of lighthearted midnight breaking, entering and book pilfering. Even though the Hemingway was worth more than the whole haul of Sayers, a court might not see it that way. Definitely no Officer Candy for this gig. The same thing went for my friend, Smiley, wherever he was. That thought stopped me cold. Where was he? All I could do was hope he was all right.

Who could help me? I would have liked someone to keep watch and give me a heads-up if the cops showed up. Lance came to mind. Of course, as he had career plans in the library world, he'd want to avoid certain types of controversy, such as being tossed into the slammer. Tiff was completely off the grid. And I really preferred not to tell Vera that I may have left some of her precious babies alone in a house that probably had lousy climate control to begin with and worse now that it was unoccupied.

The signora's talents lay elsewhere.

Karen was too fragile.

Well, the possibilities were shrinking, but I didn't have much choice. I decided not to involve my uncles. They never wanted to encounter the police unless a major payoff made the risk worthwhile. And they needed their beauty sleep. Plus Uncle Kev was still missing.

At least I had my fictional role models.

I wondered who was the better advisor for this: Harriet reflecting alone on the situation and perhaps having a word with . . . well, herself. Or Lord Peter, man of action, expert lock picker who never avoided an unauthorized entry. For sure, he'd dress nattily and head into the thick of things. If he needed a helper, Bunter was the perfect person. I didn't have a valet, a butler or any kind of person Friday.

I was on my own.

I dressed in a black cashmere turtleneck (very Audrey Hepburn), black skinny jeans (a bargain at Goodwill) and a black pashmina wrapped rather fetchingly as a scarf. I popped a black beret, one of my mother's few remaining hats, into my jeans pocket. I took my lock picks (a sweet-sixteen gift from my uncles) and slipped them into the special slot on the side of my black messenger bag. It would take a pro to find them there. The messenger bag had been a gift from Uncle Lucky for my college graduation. Up until tonight, the special slot was a bonus that I'd figured I'd never need. Over my outfit and the bag, I added a very loud, plaid cape, a vintage prize from the early seventies. I'd be hard to miss in the cape, but I'd be ditching it soon enough. Between the cashmere sweater and the pashmina I'd still be a nice combo of warm and invisible. I had my old black Converse on my feet and I'd used a black marker to get rid of the white rubber around the soles.

Fifteen minutes later, I pulled up in front of Michael Kelly's Fine Antiques and parked the Saab under a street-light where it couldn't be missed. Wearing the plaid cape, I couldn't be missed either. I chuckled to myself as I'd gotten the clever idea from *Five Red Herrings*, but sadly, I had no one to share my cleverness with.

I still had my key, but I tiptoed so as not to wake the uncles. Scavenging in Uncle Mick's shelf of useful gadgets at the back of the antique shop, I came up with what I'd remembered seeing: night vision goggles joined the tools in the messenger bag. I ditched the cape and, black as the night, headed out the back entrance and two doors down where the uncles always have a collection of "extra" cars stashed. I took a set of keys from the hook and headed out in a bur-gundy Honda Civic that was nearly as old as I was.

IN LESS THAN fifteen minutes, I had parked around the corner from 87 Lincoln Way and was creeping through a series of backyards, hugging the fences as I went. Of course, I avoided the crime-scene area. Obsessed: maybe. Nuts: no.

Soon I was at the back door of the Adams house. Like the front door earlier, the back door was not locked. I hadn't needed those lock picks after all. So it seemed likely that no one had returned to set the security alarm. It had been off when Officer Candy and I "visited," and I figured it still was. I pushed the door all the way open, and waited before easing in. I held my breath for two minutes and then slowly exhaled. Almost all security would have engaged by then if it was on. The security system being off was a good indication that the Adamses didn't plan to return and didn't care what happened. Or was it a clue that they'd been taken by surprise by someone they knew and trusted and from whom they fled or were taken? In which case, it was possible they might return if that danger was past.

I slipped on the night vision goggles and adjusted them. They were tight, making my eyes feel nearly suctioned out of my head. And they smelled like an army surplus store, rubbery and musty. But I still felt very Nikita in them. I stopped every few feet to listen for footsteps, breathing or other sounds.

Nothing.

It felt like an unoccupied house.

Nothing had changed as far as I could see. A few dozen books remained scattered on the floor and in the bookcases. This time, I searched carefully for the three missing titles. I peered under the overturned chairs and under the sofa. I checked under all the seat cushions and ventured into the dining room. But there was no luck. I felt like I'd been robbed. Vera sure had been.

Slowly, I crept up the stairs, hoping that the quality of the Craftsman house would mean that the stairs wouldn't creak. The Converse didn't let me down, soundless as long as I didn't drag my feet.

On the second floor, I felt my way around. In my humble opinion, night vision goggles are overrated, except if you want to give someone else nightmares. It didn't take long, although I double-checked upstairs and even looked under the beds and in the bathrooms. I didn't care for my role as a light-fingered housebreaker, even though the Adamses were most likely long gone and probably had different names by now. Whoever would deal with the contents of the house, it wouldn't be them. Still, I was reluctant to follow my uncles' path. I needed to be honest and aboveboard, although this might not have been immediately obvious by my visit to this house in the night sporting dark clothing and night vision goggles. Still some loose ends to be worked out, you might say.

Once this was over, if Randolph showed up, Karen and I would hand over the Hemingway with smiles on our faces.

After another close check to make sure I hadn't over-looked the books, I decided it was time to go. I headed downstairs. I needed a new plan, but my brain wasn't cooperating. As I tiptoed through the kitchen, close to making my getaway, a voice came from the dark.

"Gotcha!"

CHAPTER ELEVEN

⊰•⊱

I SHRIEKED AND careened into the kitchen table, knocking over a chair as I went. Something crashed onto the floor. Delilah's teapot, maybe. I tried to skitter away from the voice.

"Stop right there!"

Stop right there? They had to be kidding. I turned and headed for the front door and safety. Some people think everyone else is stupid. Even though they shocked me with "Gotcha!" I wasn't foolish enough to "stop right there." I grabbed a lamp as I dashed through the living room. I could always throw it to trip my assailant or bean her. *Funny, I wasn't expecting a woman*, I thought in my panic. As I lunged for the door, the lights came on.

"Fancy meeting you here."

I whirled. My brain whirled with me.

Officer Candy Mortakis was the last person I expected to see.

"Candy?"

"Uh-huh." She glowered at me, not a good look for her. Although my goggles may have made her look worse than she really did.

I decided to try for the upper hand, although it is possible I appeared to be a bit underhanded what with the night vision goggles on and the floor lamp in my hand like a javelin, although with a cord dangling on the ground. "What are you doing here?"

She sighed. "Really? Don't you think that I should ask you that? You are the person who is unlawfully in a dwelling. Were you planning to steal that lamp?"

"What? Steal the lamp? Of course not, why would I steal a lamp?"

"It is in your hand."

"I don't even like this lamp." I put it down on the floor. After all, I wasn't going to bean Candy with it.

She sighed dramatically. "You could see why I'd ask."

"Sure I can, but I wanted it as a weapon in case I had to bean you! Well, not you, but the person who was chasing me, or that I thought was chasing me because I didn't know it was you. How could I know?"

"Easy enough if the light was on."

"True, true. But there has been a murder on this street and my friend is missing. I thought I'd like to see if I could find some kind of . . ."

There was no way I could fill in the missing bits of this puzzle without implicating myself.

"Yes?" She raised an eyebrow. "Some kind of . . . ?"

I noticed that the friendly, slightly goofy Candy had disappeared, replaced by someone too cop-like for comfort.

I sighed. "Evidence. Some indication of where Delilah and Mason had taken Randolph. I know it's a job for the police, but you guys are busy trying to find out about the victim and track down whoever killed him. Except for you, no one was in the least bit interested in Randolph." Of course, I knew that unless Candy had told them, most of her colleagues had no way of knowing about the Adams drama. I added, "I'm so worried and I know that Mason and Delilah and maybe even Randolph are probably crooks, but he's just a fragile old man. What if they hurt him? I'm sure you understand."

"I understand that you've broken a few laws."

"Not actually," I said. "But . . ." My heart was still thundering. What if Candy decided to arrest me? How do police keep any friends anyway?

She said, "Couldn't you have told me you were coming back? Or that you were still so worried? I thought we were friends. I could have helped you. I could have done an additional search. You didn't have to break the law."

"Oh. That didn't occur to me. I'm sorry, I wasn't thinking clearly. And this was sort of a spur-of-the-moment decision. I couldn't sleep."

"Yet here you are, wearing night vision goggles."

"Right. They are neat, aren't they? I mean, not an attractive look for a woman, but still amazing what they can do."

"Burglars do find them handy, but they imply premeditation."

"They do? Why would that be? Oh, you're implying I'm a burglar because I was wearing them and not turning the lights on?"

"Got it in one."

"For sure that must look planned, but in fact, these goggles were in a pile of junk that I found in a closet in my attic apartment. I think my predecessor left them there. I kept them to use as a Halloween costume. They are ridiculously creepy, aren't they? He was a bit weird. So it seemed like a fun idea to wear them and not worry about alarming the neighbors. Everyone's so jumpy."

I had had a predecessor, and he might have had goggles, no way to prove or disprove that, but I was very careful not to go dragging my uncles into this situation. They were innocent for once.

"Whatever. Face it. Stop babbling. You made a plan to come here. And you didn't include me."

"Fair enough. I'm sorry. I haven't been very good company because I'm so worried about what might have happened to Randolph. I just wanted go home and go to sleep after the day we had. Then after I went to bed, I couldn't sleep after all and, then, I got this idea."

"You could have called me."

"True, but you *are* a police officer. You would have told me not to do it."

"I guess. But I might have come up with a solution. Now look at the pickle you're in."

"Yes. Although I didn't do any harm. Didn't hurt anyone. Didn't damage the property. Didn't steal anything." It was a good thing I hadn't found those books. "Check my bag if you don't believe me. I have nothing to hide." Said the woman in the night vision goggles.

She glowered at me. "I guess no harm was done."

A wave of relief washed over me. "Were you responding to a call? Do you have to make a report? Oh, you're not in uniform."

She shrugged. "I'm on my own time."

I felt a little shiver of relief. "Did you call it in?"

"No. I didn't know what you were up to. I didn't want to . . ."

"Of course, you didn't. That's what friends are for. They don't jump to conclusions about people they care about."

"Care about" might have been pushing it, as we hadn't known each other a full day at this point, but it seemed to work with her.

"I was at loose ends," she said. "I went over to Dani's Diner and had some fries then decided to rent a DVD to watch by myself." Wow. She could have run a guilting class. She was a master.

"Sorry again. I suppose we could have watched it together," I said, trying my best to look like I meant it. I pulled off the mask. It wasn't doing me any favors.

"I rented *Bridesmaids*," she said. "I heard it was funny. Anyway, then I thought I wouldn't be able to sleep after all, so I drove by here."

I stopped myself from saying sorry again. "So you couldn't sleep either."

"I couldn't, but I didn't expect to find you. I never thought you'd do anything illegal."

I opened my mouth to protest.

She kept on talking. "Now it makes me wonder if you took advantage of me when you got me to show you the house yesterday. And again when I found out about the Adamses for you. I could get in a lot of trouble for that."

She was right, of course, and it had occurred to me that Officer Candy, with her desperate need for friendship and her inability to see criminal activity—even when it almost beaned her with a lamp—was not going to shoot up the ladder to make detective here in Burton any more than she would have back at home.

She finished by saying, "I'm sure you understand that."

"I hope you won't get into trouble. I wasn't up to anything bad, but you told me that the Adamses were not who they said they were and I started to worry what if Randolph was a prisoner, something like that. A hostage? A kidnap victim?

Maybe that's why he disappeared three years ago. Perhaps it was under duress. Maybe he was forced to—anyway, I was looking for clues. I thought if I could just stand in the house for a bit, I'd gain some understanding. It was stupid, I know."

She shuddered. "You know what? The whole thing with the murder and the Adams family disappearing is creepy. This is not the kind of thing we deal with here in Burton. It's a pretty tame little town. It's why I wanted to work here."

Officer Candy wouldn't have lasted a minute in any major city, even with the best of contacts. I wasn't even sure how she'd survived the police academy. She was just a lonely girl in need of a friend.

I put on my best lost-kitten expression, the one my uncles could never resist. "So what now?"

A tiny hesitation on her part told me my strategy (such as it was) had worked.

"I know you're not a criminal. You were just trying to help your friend. And I did let you in here earlier. But you can't do anything like this again."

I was pretty sure that Candy's decision was against all the policies and procedures of the Burton police, but I was grateful. I'd definitely watch a DVD with her at some point. *Bridesmaids. Baby Mama. Identity Thief.* She could pick. "I appreciate it. And of course, I'm not a criminal."

She sniffed. "I just hope next time you'll keep me in the loop."

I said, "Really, I don't plan on doing this again, but even if, um, something happened, I wouldn't want to get you into trouble."

She smiled. "Don't worry about me. I can look after myself. It's you, my friend, that I'm worried about."

Seriously? Between the two of us, my money would always be on me.

"So," she said, "do you feel like pizza? Maybe at Domenico's All Night?"

I absolutely did not feel like pizza, especially from Domenico's All Night, but what could I do? At least it was in Harrison Falls. "Sure thing. I'll meet you there. I might need to get gas, so go ahead and order if you get there first."

She snorted. "Of course I'll get there first."

TWENTY MINUTES LATER, I pulled up in the Saab, having dropped off the Civic at my uncles' extra garage. I made darn sure that Officer Candy wasn't following me.

For some reason, my teeth were chattering and I'd put on the vintage plaid cape. Officer Candy had already ordered two large pizzas, one all dressed and the other double cheese and double bacon. She widened her eyes as she spotted the cape.

"A steal at a vintage shop," I explained. "I love the era." As we sat there, she kept smiling at me. I did my best to smile back. I am not a person who likes to take advantage of other people by feigning friendship. Give her a chance, I reminded myself. She's new here and she's desperate for companionship. Those good old boys on the force would probably be pretty hard to take. Of course, there was no evidence that the other cops were anything but pleasant and professional, good solid colleagues, but I had a feeling that all wasn't going well.

"So," I said brightly, "how do you like this new job?"

She shrugged. "It's all right, I guess."

"Are the other officers good to work with?"

She fixed me with a glare. "Do you mind? I'd just as soon not talk about it or them while we're eating."

"Oh. Sorry. Just making conversation, not trying to be pushy."

She snorted. "Don't worry. I won't let you push me."

I guessed I'd reattach my head later.

I worked my way through my pizza for a while. It seemed weird to be eating pizza at one thirty in the morning after one of the signora's dinners and a super snack. I felt breakfast looming.

After a long silence, Candy said, "So do you want to hear the latest about this dead guy?"

Uh, yeah! "Sure."

"I went by the station when you left to get gas and I got the latest."

"Awesome." I nodded encouragement.

"He's associated with . . . Maybe I shouldn't share this with you."

"Only if you feel all right about it, Candy. No pressure here." No pressure? I thought my hair would catch fire, but I had to be cool. Better if it was Candy's idea rather than mine.

"Doesn't matter. I guess it's not a secret. The guy was Pierre Gagnon. He's French from Canada."

"Oh."

"Mean anything?"

"French from Canada? No, it doesn't. Nothing."

"I mean his name."

I shook my head and tried to keep the cheese from dripping down my chin.

She said, "Serious criminal."

"Oh. I'm not in the loop about that kind of—"

"I suppose not. He's supposed to be a hit man, although he's never been charged. I hear he works for very bad people in Albany and Buffalo. Cops know who he is, but they never managed to prove anything in court."

I put my pizza back on my plate. "A hit man? Really?"

"Would I lie to you?"

How would I know if Candy would lie to me? We'd been

"friends" for about ten minutes. And it was a strange and one-sided friendship.

"Makes you think, doesn't it?" she said.

It sure did. What was a hit man doing watching Randolph's house? It had to be connected to the stolen money and those high-level mobsters.

"That must have been why they kept to themselves," I said. "Someone was after them."

"Looks that way."

"And they knew it. That's why they were so reclusive. With all that security. Delilah and Mason were jumpy as cats."

"Yup."

I said, "So possibly they weren't kidnapping Randolph. Do you think they might have been fleeing from a hit man?"

She nodded.

I blurted, "But who killed the hit man?"

"The big boys of Burton are working on that."

Yes, and I really didn't want Uncle Kev or Officer Smiley to come up on the radar while the big boys were on the job.

She added, "Do you think Delilah or Mason or Randolph was the type to stab someone?"

"No! I mean, I don't know. I don't have any way to know. Obviously, they were practically strangers. Wait a minute, what am I saying? I'm sure they would kill a hit man if he was trying to kill them. Randolph might not have been capable of it. But Delilah would defend her son and herself—I'm sure of it. Mason would defend himself. And a young guy would definitely defend his mom too." Actually Mason had seemed extremely sullen and self-centred to me, but you never know. "But to stab someone? That seems hard to imagine. If he'd been shot, now that seems more defensive to me, somehow." I stopped talking and shuddered.

"That's my line of thinking too."

I said, "But if they got close enough to stab him, he could have shot them. Why didn't he?"

She hadn't actually stopped eating her all-dressed pizza throughout our conversation. She could shrug and eat. She shrugged. "They thought they had to deal with it. And they did."

But most people don't ever have to deal with a hit man. What had they been involved in? Whatever, it went way beyond books. And it was very bad news.

"So if he was coming for them it would be a good defense. Then they couldn't hang around to tell the police, because they were on the run from someone."

"Exactly."

"But we don't know who."

"We have some ideas."

"Well, that's good."

I didn't ask and I wasn't sure I wanted to know who that someone might be. I hoped that whoever it was didn't get the idea that I was involved with the Adamses. And that I didn't have something he wanted. It would be terrible if Karen was in danger too. We might need some protection, although I was pretty sure my new best friend wasn't the most effective first line of defense.

"I really hope Randolph is all right. I can't believe he could be involved in anything dangerous or criminal. And even if he was, I really don't think he'd be able to fend off any would-be assassin."

She said, "Of course, that wouldn't be necessary now, since the would-be assassin is in the morgue."

"Right. And I guess they got away and may be able to steer clear of whoever hired the hit man. Because that person could just as easily hire another hit man. Do you have any idea who the person behind the hit would be?"

"Nope. Not a clue. There's no chatter about it anywhere.

No gossip out there. I checked around with my friends on other forces. Nada."

"So nothing about the mob and the money Randolph stole? I guess that's good news."

"We'll see," she said with a wide grin and a bit of green pepper in the gap between her teeth. "Feel like cheesecake for dessert?"

Not even I could manage cheesecake. Still, I wanted to keep the so-called friendship going. I didn't know when I'd need some more information from her.

I said, "I don't think I can. But I love to watch people eat dessert, so I'll get one and save it for later."

Domenico's All Night had pretty good cheesecake too, according to Candy. The extra time while we were waiting did leave me with the challenge of making conversation.

"So, are you back at work tomorrow?"

She shook her head. Still off duty.

"Really? But there's been an unsolved murder and Burton is such a small place, I figured . . ."

She shrugged. "You thought the new girl would be right in the thick of it?"

"I thought everyone would be pressed into service."

"I've got a bit of overtime piled up and they want me to take it. All the big boys want in on this. I talked to my sarge, but he said to save my energy for after, when they get tired and discouraged."

I supposed that made sense. "So what do you do on your days off?"

"Not much. I'm new here. The guys keep to themselves. Most of them are married or living with someone, so having a new friend like me isn't an option."

"Right." Candy was the most unglamorous, unseductive, ungirly girl I'd ever met. So I figured the wives and live-ins might not have too much to worry about, but then attraction is a funny thing. And I was beginning to see her appeal. Kind of like a Labrador retriever. She couldn't take no for an answer, and nothing could shake her optimistic good humor. I suppose you'd have to love her or hate her. "I can see where that would be a problem."

"It has been."

"But you'll settle in, become part of the community." Listen to me, like I would ever settle in and become part of the community. I had my job, my uncles, my tame librarian and my long distance friend, Tiff. Also Walter. That was it. I tried not to think about Tyler Dekker. I didn't have him. And in fact I didn't know what had happened to him. I didn't know if he was all right. I was surprised at how much that ate at me.

"I suppose. I thought small towns would be a bit friendlier, but this one isn't."

I nodded, being fresh out of advice for her. I watched the tired server set the cheesecake in front of her. I watched Candy's eyes light up.

"So," she said, "what do you do on your day off?"

"I guess I don't really have days on and off. I do what I need to do and lots of times I have to be at sales or book fairs on the weekend."

"Oh yeah. What are you doing tomorrow?"

"Tomorrow?"

"Yes."

"Oh, this and that. I have a lot of errands and whatnot for Miss Van Alst."

"Tell me about her? What's that like? Tons of money, right?"

She lifted a forkful of Bailey's cheesecake to her lips. Maybe that was to draw my attention away from the gleam in her eyes. For Candy, this would be like an episode of

Lifestyles of the Rich and Famous. In reality, more like *Lifestyles of the Crabby and Newly Impecunious*.

But I know where my loyalties lie. There was no way I'd let anything slip about the state of the Van Alst estate. The missing paintings, the lack of repairs. The fact that all Vera's money went to her collection and that, of course, included me.

I was actually surprised that I felt so much loyalty to Vera. She wasn't exactly the supportive or motherly or friendly type. She was a dragon, but she was *my* dragon. Her dignity needed to stay intact. Maybe mine did too.

"Old family, old home. Everything in it and about it means something to my employer. She doesn't spend a lot though, just on her collections." And her employees.

"So you're working all day?"

I didn't want to say that my time is my own.

I shrugged. "I get my job done and I work diligently, but it's on my own schedule, except for breakfast and dinner at eight, attendance compulsory."

"Huh."

"And I have to dress for dinner," I added sheepishly.

"You probably like that."

"I do actually."

"What do you have to do tomorrow?"

She was pretty relentless.

"You'll make a great detective some day," I said with a grin.

That surprised her. "Sorry. I didn't mean to push you. I can see you've got things to do and you don't need me pushing my way into your life."

I relented. "I'll be making the rounds of the best charity shops and secondhand bookstores in the area. It's supposed to be a nice day for a drive tomorrow, so I'm planning to do Fairlawn and Ainslie. It's easy to check Harrison Falls, Burton and Grandville frequently."

She laughed out loud. "Tough job."

It was my turn to shrug. "Someone's got to do it."

"No, they don't. Why do you choose to do that? And what do you do there?"

Easy answer. "People are always donating books. I scout through them and see if I can find something that's undervalued. If I do, I pick it up cheap and then we resell it online. I take care of that."

"Huh."

That "huh" thing was kind of annoying. I really loved this part of the job. If I had to defend it to Candy and she still didn't get it, there wasn't much hope of a friendship.

"I found a signed first edition of Dick Francis's *Driving Force* for a quarter."

"Okay."

"But it's worth four hundred bucks."

"Huh. Well you can sure go shopping on that."

"Not really. It's part of my job. I bring in these little treasures and they get sold. If it's something I can sell to a dealer, any profit from this goes straight to Miss Van Alst's credit at the dealer."

"Hardly seems fair."

"Oh, it's fair, all right. I get paid, regardless. I get my little apartment, meals and a job I love." I didn't bother to add that I uncovered a few magnificent vintage clothing and handbag finds at the bazaars and charity shops, including what I was wearing. Vera had no interest in vintage fashion or fashion of any kind for that matter. Those finds were all mine.

"Guess I can't argue."

"Different strokes for different folks. I don't want to give out parking tickets. You picked a job that you enjoy, right?"

Her expression took me by surprise.

"You don't enjoy it?"

"I don't know yet. I'm pretty new. There's more than giving out parking tickets to the job, but it's not as interesting as I thought it would be. It's kind of lonely too. Like I said, I'm not fitting in all that well. So I don't know if I'll stay on."

"That's too bad. And you don't want to try for the force in your own town? Or where you know people?"

"Nah. Too dangerous. A cop could get killed there. Plus my relatives are all in town and I'd just get picked on all the time. No one thought it was a good idea for a girl to join the police. They give me a hard time and my mom cries about it. She wants grandchildren. And she says I look like crap in the uniform. My own mother! I can't stand it. So I'll give Burton another six months and if things don't look up, I'll probably retrain."

"I'm sorry to hear that."

She poked at the cheesecake. "Although in this economy, a person wants to think twice about that. I could go out to California. Good climate."

By now, I was feeling like a total jerk. Here was a lonely person, pleasant to be around if a bit nosy. A woman with troubles of her own. Why didn't I just give her a chance?

Candy said, "So I'm off duty tomorrow. And I'll probably die of boredom."

I caved. "Any chance you want to come with me when I make the rounds of the junk stores?"

"Hell, yeah." She lit up like a high-end Christmas tree, the surplus kind my uncle Danny was selling out of the back end of his truck last year.

So that was settled. I figured I'd have to be careful about my uncles. Better they didn't meet Officer Candy. They were all still reeling from my relationship—better make that "association"—with Tyler Dekker. Which reminded me yet again, where the devil was he?

She grinned and said, "Want me to pick you up?"

Ah, the first snag. "I thought we might each go in our own vehicles."

"No way. Half the fun will be traveling together."

Relax, I told myself. You can pick her brains on the trip.

"Why not. Maybe we can go by the police station and find out the latest on the killing of . . . What was his name? Pierre Gagnon?"

"Mmmm. Bad idea."

"Oh?"

"I already don't fit in, so if I start bringing my gal pals along for tours, the guys will never let me forget it. I get called enough names. I can't just look into a computer file without sending up red flags."

"Oh."

"Listen, I'll drop in on my way, pretend I forgot something in my locker, whatever, and I'll see what's happening. Find out more about this Gagnon."

"We need to know who he's connected to. And maybe you could talk to contacts in your hometown."

"Yeah, sure. I'll do my best."

"The Adamses' lives might depend on it."

"And if they are alive, they're going to make sure no one finds them to charge them with killing this guy."

"I can't imagine Randolph killing anyone. There will be a story there that might vindicate them."

She made a face. Might have been Vera's twin for a minute. I said, "What?"

"You don't want to be too—"

"Naïve?"

"Maybe not naïve, but trusting. There's something off about them."

"I know that, Candy. But between something off and killing someone there's a lot of territory." I thought of my uncles, crooked as you can get, but gentle and kind. And never in the least bit violent. If the Adamses were crooks, I figured there was a good chance they were this type. And yes, even I knew that was probably wishful thinking.

"Then we can talk about it on our way. Where to first?"

"Fairlawn and then on to Ainslie. There's a bit of money in those communities and they are less likely to hang on to things. Although the downside of that is they may have a better sense of the value of the good stuff."

"I getcha. When shall I pick you up?"

I felt my back stiffen. I am used to being in control of a vehicle, making my own way and my own decisions. This I didn't intend to cave on.

"I like to drive. I hate being driven. Never get used to it. What time should I pick you up?"

There was a little flash of resistance in her eyes, then a grin. "Sure thing. I don't make a great passenger, but you're letting me come along. How about I come by your place and leave my car there and we go in yours. Only thing is, if I get called in, we'd have to get back PDQ."

This was turning into a pain. I could already imagine one of my favorite parts of the job being ruined by this curious, insistent and irritating person. And maybe having my day's work cut short if she got called to work on some police matter.

"What are the chances you'd get called in?" I figured they were pretty high. Even if they didn't think much of her abilities, the force must have been stretched with this murder. On the other hand, they were pretty lax in a lot of ways. Maybe the Burton cops just investigated murders from nine to five, weekdays. That wouldn't have surprised me a bit.

"Hard to say. I'm not used to their ways yet and, you know, there was a murder." She chuckled.

"That's funny?"

"Not where I come from, but they're kind of laid-back in Burton, so who knows. If there's more media coverage or something, they might get energized. I'd like to get called in. I need the experience and I want to work my way up to detective. You can't do that if you don't have a chance to watch them in action."

I wondered if the Burton force would be the best kind of experience, particularly when they had an enthusiastic new hire and they were not making use of her in what had to be the most significant crimes in the community in memory.

Fine. I could always drop her off and head out again. The worst that could happen would be that I'd lose an hour. I could live with that.

"Okay, well, we'll play it by ear. No point in starting too early. I'd like to begin at Once More with Feeling, which is the furthest point. It supports a women's shelter and a school breakfast program. It's in Fairlawn. It's closed on Monday and Tuesday and opens at noon on Wednesday. They always have a team of volunteers stocking the stuff that they received over the weekend, and they won't open until they're ready. We'll be their early birds."

"Cheep, cheep," she said. I wondered if maybe she meant "cheap, cheap."

CHAPTER TWELVE

— ❖ —

A S WE HEADED back to our vehicles (as Candy called them), I stoked the idea of visiting the police station in Candy's mind.

"So you're going to pop in to the station and check around to see if you can find some connection between Randolph and this Pierre Gagnon. Depending on what you find out, it could change what we do tomorrow."

She gave me a hurt look. "Okay, I get the message. Part of the deal, is it?"

So I hadn't been too subtle. I gave her my winningest smile, as the uncles would call it.

"Oh no, am I being pushy again? I'm just looking forward to our little road trip. I always do this alone, so it will be good to have company."

She nodded, mollified. "Okay, I won't let on that I don't know anything about antiques or whatever, but yeah, I'll pop in and see if there's any news. Like I said before, I can't bring my friends to see the 'cop show.'"

I made a small show of protest.

She rolled her eyes. "Spare me. I'm used to it with other girls I know. It's like feeding time at the zoo. Chance to see a man in uniform. Didn't I tell you these guys are taken? Even the guy who's gay and still in the closet."

"Oh, I didn't really mean to—"

"Yeah, yeah. It's all right. Human nature. Listen, I'll call you if there's anything interesting."

"Don't worry about it. I'm pretty tired anyway and I need to sleep for a few hours."

In my midtwenties and I was already starting to sound like Vera, except even Vera couldn't go to sleep with all this going on. But I found Candy quite intense and, frankly, a bit needy. I needed to recharge for the next day.

As we said good-bye in front of her dark-blue Tahoe, Candy said, "Since you're going to sleep anyway, maybe I'll wait and check with the detectives tomorrow before we head out. They're not guys to work all night if you know what I mean."

I felt dirty exploiting her desire for friendship, but what choice was there? I figured I could make it up to her when everything, whatever everything was, sorted itself out. I resolved to accept Candy for what she was: an exuberant, loud, needy person who was apparently my new BFF.

"We should leave around ten," I said. "It will be fun."

"Sure," she said. "Good times."

I SLEPT LIKE the dead. If I dreamed, I had no recollection. The way my dreams had been going, that was a good thing.

Vera was under the weather and didn't show up for breakfast at eight. After an uneventful breakfast of ham, eggs and sautéed zucchini, I popped into my uncles' place to find out if there was any word on Uncle Kev. It was now about thirty-six hours since he'd last been seen.

My uncles' place was now Walter's place too. And apparently this new nameless dog had a home there as well, although I had hopes that Tyler Dekker would return and the dog would go back to where he belonged. He nuzzled my car as I sat at my uncles' kitchen table. That dog wasn't the only elephant in the room.

Uncle Lucky had a faraway look in his eye. He wasn't paying any attention to me, Mick or the new dog, although Walter was getting his ears scratched in an absentminded manner. I knew what was behind this. Uncle Lucky's relationship with Karen had moved to a new level and Uncle Lucky was a man in love. But that wasn't something that I could ask him about. I adored Lucky and I thought Karen was great. The spoiled little girl in me wasn't sure she wanted to share. *Get over yourself*, I told myself.

But I still felt that Walter and I were caught in the middle and who knew where that left Uncle Mick.

Uncle Mick had produced a package of gummy bears and some Oreo cookies. The perfect breakfast dessert.

"Thanks, but I couldn't," I said, "much as I'd like to. I have been stuffing my face in the interest of my job and of finding out something more about that murder before Uncle Kev gets fingered by the fuzz."

It only takes a few minutes before I start to talk like the uncles and their friends.

"Kev? Why would he get fingered?"

"He was there the night it happened. You already know that and you know he clobbered a cop thinking he was saving me. Then, of course, he hid out in the area. Shortly after, somebody was killed."

I had all their attention now.

"Uncle Kev was there. I don't think he's capable of killing someone and particularly not this way. I mean, maybe in self-defense or to save someone else or even by accident, but not in cold blood."

I felt that familiar knot in my stomach. The Uncle Kev I knew was fun and funny. Not at all cold-blooded, but he was already on the run from some dangerous people before he'd stumbled into a situation with another batch of dangerous people. He might have needed to defend himself. Would he have the nerve to kill someone? Could he actually use a knife? It seemed so personal and so vicious.

I shuddered and stared at my uncles. "I mean, he would have had to look the guy in the eyes."

Lucky shook his head. Uncle Mick's ginger hair seemed to stand on end. "Kev is a pain in the entire anatomy of anyone who knows him, but he's harmless. Well, he's not harmless. He's a disaster waiting to happen, but he's not violent. Never was. Never did a thing to hurt anyone deliberately, although . . ."

I gulped. "I don't think this could have been an accident. How could it be? He would have had to have a knife in his hand. Unless the other guy had the knife and Uncle Kev wrestled it from him and—What if this hit man was after Kev?"

"Don't even imagine that, Jordan. If he had been, Kev still couldn't kill him. He's a runner, not a fighter."

I slumped in relief. I'd known that, but life was so wacky lately that I needed to hear it from someone I trusted. And the only people I really trusted were the men right in front of me. Walter too, of course. The jury was out on the new dog, but it had trustworthy eyes.

I took a deep breath and said, "As long as no one else starts thinking it."

Lucky's inch-thick eyebrows shot up as did Mick's color.

"Why would anything think that?" he huffed.

"Well, some of the neighbors might have spotted him around there. He spent a lot of time lurking. He must have left traces. A fingerprint. DNA. For sure his prints would be in the system and, for all I know, his DNA is too."

They exchanged glances and Walter snuffled in sympathy.

I continued, "The Burton police don't seem to be efficient in the least, but they will have a forensics team and it could end badly for Kev, unless they're total idiots. Of course, that's possible, based on my limited experience."

"They couldn't make it stick."

"People get wrongly charged and convicted all the time. You should know that." Of course, Uncle Mick and Uncle Lucky are from the other side of the story where the guilty don't get caught, or if caught, they don't get charged, or if charged, they don't get convicted.

I had to make my point. "And if Kev's charged or even if the cops are looking at him and they put out an all points bulletin or some public message, then the wrong people will find out he's in the area."

That hit home. Mick and Lucky might find Kev a giant boil on the family butt, but he was one of us and he needed to be protected, preferably in someone else's dwelling.

"So here's the thing. The guy who was killed was Pierre Gagnon."

They shrugged together. I swear Walter lifted his shoulders too.

I added, "A suspected hit man."

Uncle Mick said, "What?"

"You heard right. Hit man."

"Really? A hit man in Harrison Falls?"

"Burton."

"Burton? That's even more ridiculous."

As there was nothing funny or ridiculous about this, I said, "Let's say it's unlikely. So, who killed the hit man? We all agree it couldn't have been Kev. Not even in self-defense."

"Kev wouldn't stand a chance against a hit man."

"Agreed."

"So who killed this Pierre whatever his name is?"

"I think it was someone from the Adams family. They flew the coop and my new cop friend—"

"Your what?"

"Candy. Officer Candy Mortakis. She's been a good source of infor—"

"Cop?"

"I'm sorry, but she already let me into the Adams house, where I found out some interesting stuff. And she's the one who told me about Pierre Gagnon."

"Why's she doing this?" Uncle Mick crossed his arms and glowered, while Uncle Lucky shook his head the way he might if I'd suggested jumping off a high building without out a net. "Doesn't make sense to me."

"I hear you, but you have to know her to understand. She's lonely. She's not from around here and she's not fitting in with the force. She's not the greatest cop either, and I doubt if she'll last long. Anyway, she tells me stuff because she wants to be my friend."

"We are not friends with cops." Uncle Mick was still cross-armed. Uncle Lucky still had that look on his face, and even Walter was disapproving.

"I'm not really her friend. I'm just—"

"It's dangerous and you should know that, Jordan."

I tuned out the gentle admonitions and tried not to feel rotten about Candy. She genuinely wanted to be my friend, and I was diminishing her and using her information to protect those on the other side of the law. That's not like me. I'm a straight shooter when it comes to friends. Loyal and steadfast and all that good stuff. I wasn't comfortable leading her on, not that she gave me much choice. The uncles were right. Cops and Kellys are not an easy mix. But this time I was going to have to make it work. "Well, she's my pipeline into that investigation and I'm going to make the most of it. We'll just have to man up. You do realize that if Kev was there, he might have witnessed the hit man being killed. And he could be in danger from whomever killed Pierre Gagnon as well as from the police. We need an inside source."

Uncle Mick just couldn't drop the cop angle. "Bad enough that other guy, Tyler Dekker."

That reminded me. Before I took off on my day's hunting and gathering with Candy, I had to make an effort to find Tyler Dekker. Where was he? Not at home. Not at work. Not in the hospital.

"Sorry, I have to run," I said. "Just wanted to fill you in. Maybe you can make inquiries about this Pierre Gagnon. He's a Canadian, but apparently he has connections in the Albany area. Oh, and Buffalo, I think. It would help if we knew who he worked for. Or who he might have been working for this time. It might have something to do with a family currently named Adams, who went missing along with a large amount of money about three years ago. Is there any way you can nose around without . . ."

Oh boy, as the words came out of my mouth, I realized that would be a mistake. It might attract attention to our family. And put my uncles in danger. "Maybe you shouldn't."

"Let me see what I can find out without letting on it's anything more than idle chat," Uncle Mick said.

Lucky nodded.

"Well, be careful," I said.

"We're supposed to say that to you," Mick harrumphed.

I made tracks.

I HAD NO choice but to go back to Tyler Dekker's tiny ranch house. Again. This time I had a potted plant as a sort of cover. Every bachelor needs a jade plant. Hard to kill them. I had considered my lock picks, but I figured that woman across the street would dial 911 in a flash. I banged on the door again. This time I planned to leave a message. I was hammering for the third time, and may have shouted something like "don't make me break the law," when the door was whipped open and I tumbled in. The jade plant went flying.

Tyler Dekker stared at me—red-faced—as I picked myself up off the floor and stuck the jade plant back in its decorative pot.

"Most people just answer the door on the first or second hammering," I said. To my astonishment I felt tears sting my eyes. Not because it was embarrassing to have landed on the floor in front of a police officer—I'm made of sterner stuff than that. I realized it was because Tyler Dekker was obviously alive and seemingly well. Apparently, I cared more than I'd been admitting to myself.

The red flush continued to spread up his face. I hoped he'd never try to work undercover until he got that blushing issue under control.

"I'm sorry," he said. "Let me help you up."

"Never mind. I'm already up."

I repackaged my dignity as I dusted off my knees. Of course, my knees were sore but not in the least bit dusty because there was no dust anywhere in Tyler Dekker's place. He could pass any white-glove test. It was unnerving.

"What's going on?" I said.

"Don't know what you mean," he said. The tips of his ears were practically glowing.

"Yeah you do. And your ears are betraying you."

He touched the top of his left ear and frowned.

"And you are just getting into your explanation, so tell a few more lies and you might never recover physically. While we're at it, I'd like to say that you scared me. You were not home. You weren't at work. You never answered the door or the phone or any texts. There was a body behind that house on Lincoln Way and for all I knew you were that body."

"I'm sorry I didn't answer you, but you must have figured out that I wasn't dead. I know they told you I called in sick. You can hardly call in sick when you're dead."

"But someone could have called in for you, sounding sick. Maybe the same person that might have killed you. Did you think of that?"

"But it didn't happen. Exhibit A: Me standing here." He smiled, the chip in the incisor adorable as usual.

"Well, how could I know that?" I was getting grumpier by the second, despite his being alive.

"I appreciate your concern."

Concern? Was that a synonym for worry and lack of sleep?

"Maybe you killed him."

"What?" That sandbagged him. "Of course I didn't kill him. How could you even suggest something like that?"

"Well, you were obviously hiding afterward."

"I wasn't hiding."

"Were."

"I had my reasons, but not because I killed anyone."

"It might have been in self-defense. Then you panicked and went to ground."

He stared at me. "I'm a police officer. If I killed someone in self-defense, I'd file a report and go through all the internal procedures. I wouldn't go to ground. And I don't panic. We're trained, you know."

"Well, what did happen?"

"I can't tell you. I can't believe you think I killed him. He was stabbed. Do you really think I'd stab a person? Do you actually imagine that I carry a knife?"

"Maybe he lunged at you and—"

"No stabbing. No lunging. Not me."

That was a relief, to tell the truth. No other comment came to mind for once. I bent over and rubbed my sore knees.

Finally, he said, "Do you want to come all the way in? Have a seat."

"Yes." I straightened up.

"As long as you don't grill me on what I was doing."

"I don't grill you. When do I ever grill you?"

He shook his head. "Would you like something to eat?"

"Nope. So far I've had ham and eggs and zucchini, with gummy bears and Oreos for dessert, and it's not even ten o'clock."

He gestured toward the small, neat love seat. I sat. He took the recliner at a right angle to it. "I'm sorry, I can't talk about it. I hope it won't make a difference between us."

Between us? That phrase insinuated that there was an "us." Was there? It was news to me if there was, but I wouldn't have been unhappy with "us," except for the biggest problem. And I couldn't say anything about that. Naturally, as was so often the case, the biggest problem was one Kevin Francis Kelly. Was Tyler Dekker investigating Uncle Kev? That was the only reason I could imagine for him to be sneaking around after us. Kev was mixed up in some bad situation and Dekker was on the case. If it had been the Adams family, surely Smiley could have mentioned it, without naming names or giving too much detail. If he'd been on the trail of that hit man, he could have just told me so. No. He was after my uncle and that was going to be a deal breaker. Just when I was starting to understand how I felt about him. Very tricky. Let's face it: you can't throw your uncle under a bus merely because some tomato-cheeked cop makes your heart thunder. No part of that would be acceptable under any circumstances in the Kelly clan. Ever.

"I can't stay," I said. "I just wanted to know that you were all right."

"Why can't you stay?"

"I have some places to be. Book places. You know. Work."

"Oh. Maybe I should join you." There was that grin again.

"What? No. You can't."

"Why not? Is the formidable Miss Van Alst along for the ride?"

"Vera? You know she never leaves the house. No, I have a friend who's coming."

"Right. And who's he? Lance?"

"No, not Lance. It's a girlfriend. She needs a bit of company and I need help lugging things. Anyway, shouldn't you be at work?"

"Still sick," he said. "I was just kidding about joining you. No need to get quite so defensive."

"Speaking of defensive, are you going to be defensive about your dog?"

His eyes widened. "You have him?"

"Of course I have him. Well, he's in a safe place."

He ran his hand through his blond hair. "I've been to the SPCA and I've been in touch with the rescue sites. I put it out on Facebook and Twitter. I put signs up on every telephone pole in that neighborhood."

I frowned. I hadn't had time to get on Facebook or Twitter since all the stuff with Randolph and the books and the dog had been found. I certainly hadn't checked the telephone poles. Too busy trying not to get arrested.

"Oh. What were you doing with that dog anyway? I figured you just borrowed it as a cover for whatever you were snooping for on Lincoln Way."

He flushed. "He did come in handy, but that's not why I have him. I wouldn't take a dog just as a cover story."

"Wouldn't you?"

He scowled at me, not something that came easy to him. "No. I would not. What do you take me for?"

"Then where did he come from?"

"That's a story for another time and he's mine now. His name is Cobain. Anyway, what are you talking about? You were there with a fake dog."

I didn't think I'd ever seen Smiley get upset before.

"Walter is not a fake dog. He's Karen's and he needed some exercise. We're . . . I'm helping, as she hasn't fully recovered."

"Right. Exercise. In the pouring rain in the next town, miles from where you live."

"I had a reason to be there. Karen had a client and she accidentally sold him some books that had been stolen from Vera. We were trying to make a trade to get them back. The family was being difficult and I wanted to try to get to see the client without them. That's all. At least I can say why *I* was there."

"Good for you," he said.

"Well then," I said. "Now that I know you're alive, I'll be on my way."

CANDY WAS OUTSIDE her Tahoe when I pulled up in the long driveway near the back door of the Van Alst House. She was pacing in the driveway, while talking into her cell phone and snapping her gum. Her bleached hair was pulled back in a ponytail and she had a Yankees hat on. Although it was a nippy fall day, she wore a pink fleece jacket over a sequined T-shirt, cropped jeans and open-toed sandals with heels. Her toenails were bright, each one a different color. She was sporting hoop earrings too. Big ones.

I was wearing a light-green wool shift (parish jumble sale) and a lovely pair of herringbone tights that I had saved for.

At least it wasn't raining for once. The sun was starting to peek through the clouds, although the temperature seemed to be plummeting.

Candy clicked off the phone and waved merrily to me. "Ready, girlfriend?"

She offered me the package of gum.

I barely managed not to flinch. It was going to be a long morning.

We were dickering over whether to take the Tahoe or the Saab when the signora came flapping out of the house with a picnic basket, full of sandwiches, cookies, two Thermoses of coffee, carrot and celery sticks and fruit salad.

"For you friend, Jordan! Picnic! Eat! Eat!"

"Sure thing," I said.

In the end, we took the Tahoe.

I figured I'd live.

I HOPED TO make five stops. If Candy got called back, I planned to pick up my car and return.

The first stop, Once More with Feeling, was near a good area of Fairlawn. We had lots of time to chat on the trip.

"So, you got a boyfriend?" she said.

I shook my head. Whatever Lance and Smiley were, they weren't boyfriends.

I said, "You?"

"Broke up." She chewed hard on the gum.

"Oh, sorry."

"Don't be. He was a jackass. He left me for an older woman. That's part of the reason I'm here. Needed a change of scenery afterward. Didn't want to be running into him with her hanging off his arm. The urge to arrest might come over me."

I laughed out loud. "My ex was a jackass too. He maxed out my credit cards and cleaned out my bank account before I caught on and ditched him. And you know what? That's why I'm here too. I needed to make some money to get back to grad school. I hope to get a PhD in English."

"Oh, a PhD? Well la-*dee*-da."

"We have that in common," I said. "Bad boyfriends. And if you ever run into mine, feel free to arrest him."

"My mom blamed me for the breakup, said I shoulda took better care myself, been more feminine. To hell with that."

"I hear you."

"*Defer* to him."

"Be glad you're out of that."

"You said it, girl. It's good to be able to talk about these things."

"It is." I meant it too.

"You got other buds around here?"

I shook my head. "I have a best friend, Tiffany. She's somewhere in Africa. She's a nurse working on a clean water project. We've been close since we were college roommates. Now, I can't even reach her. I miss having someone to vent to. What about you?"

"Well, I used to have a bestie back home, but she screwed me over."

"Oh!" Have I mentioned that Candy was a person who could surprise you and often.

"You know how it is."

I didn't but I laughed anyway. "Maybe you should have slapped the cuffs on her."

I was getting comfortable with Candy. We didn't have much in common, but she was growing on me. She was big and bold and she scared me a bit. It's not like I was drowning in friends. Candy took my mind off things I couldn't do anything about: Uncle Kev and the Sayers books and whatever Tyler Dekker was up to.

We arrived at Once More with Feeling before I even knew it. The store manager's name was Annie and she greeted me by name. I introduced Candy.

"Lots of good stuff, Jordan. People are cleaning out closets. We got a good haul from some downsizers too. Have fun."

I didn't head straight for the books. There was no reason for them to know that the books were the main reason for this visit. Instead I made my way down the rows of coats, suits and jackets and finally to my favorite spot: sweaters. As it got nippier, I was on the lookout for top-of-the-line cashmere at rock-bottom prices.

Candy followed, managing to get in my way a good deal of the time. It was easier when she was in the car. At least she stayed in the driver's seat.

"What are you doing now?"

"Checking for vintage clothing. People get rid of things and they don't know they're vintage."

"What about the people who run the shop?"

"They're not in the vintage business. They get donations and they want a lot of turnover. That's how they fund their charities."

"Huh. Well, I don't know how you could wear somebody else's old stuff."

"They're clothes. They can be washed or dry-cleaned, and you'd be surprised at how many pieces still have the tags on."

It didn't look like I'd make a believer out of Candy, but I managed to score a royal-blue cashmere twin set that had quite obviously never been worn. I worked at not looking too excited.

"Still gives me the creeps," she said.

I hung on to the blue cashmere twin set as we wandered the aisles.

Candy's face lit up. "Look at that Barbie! I never was into Barbie dolls, but Police Officer Barbie came out when I was eight years old." She was pointing to a Barbie wearing a police uniform. The doll was still in its dusty box. If the box hadn't been crumpled a bit, the doll would have been pricey. Now it was three dollars.

"You should get it," I said.

She shrugged and said, "What about the books?"

"We'll make them look like an afterthought. I have to wander around for a while." Of course, I was holding the doll. Candy was busy scowling.

I said, "Maybe try not to look so intense. You're making people nervous."

The resulting smile probably made them a bit more nervous. I decided to quit while I was ahead.

I cut my losses and went over to the books. The usual bestsellers. A few tattered Reader's Digest Condensed Books. Some vintage cookbooks. A dozen pristine Hardy Boys books for a dollar each. I knew I could get eight to ten for them online. I'm always on the hunt for the 1931 first edition of *What Happened at Midnight*, which I happened to know was worth about a thousand dollars. I did locate a copy of *Strong Poison*, a Sayers book from the New English Library reprint series with the psychedelic covers, but the paper was badly foxed and it smelled too musty to buy. Too bad, because it was the one where Lord Peter decides to save the mystery writer, Harriet Vane, from the gallows, when she was on trial for poisoning her lover. One of my favorites. But musty books are a no-no for me. Even though burying them in clean kitty litter for a couple of weeks can help take out some of the mustiness, I preferred to wait for a better copy.

Candy answered her cell, which was a relief. It was hard having her in my space. All that intensity.

"I got called back in," she said. "Gotta go. Sorry. I know you're having fun, but duty calls."

"No problem. That was our arrangement," I said, wishing we'd each had our cars. But then we wouldn't have had those conversations on the way.

She headed out. I took my finds to the cashier. I realized I still had Candy's Police Officer Barbie. I paid for the doll and grabbed the bag with the sweaters, the Barbie and the Hardy Boys.

Candy was surprisingly quiet on the way home. Whatever she'd been called back to, she didn't want to talk about it.

I considered asking her thoughts about the Smiley situation. But she was not in a warm and receptive mood. And I reminded myself that she was a police officer and if Smiley's activities violated policies, Candy had no ties to him.

As we approached the Van Alst property, she practically had a black cloud over her baseball cap. I didn't think I'd done anything to bring that on. So what, then?

If it was related to the murder investigation, she would have been suppressing excitement. She was itching to get in there. No, it must have been something else.

Maybe she was just sleep deprived. I knew I was.

I felt a sinking feeling in my gut. What if she'd found out something about Tyler? Or Uncle Kevin?

CHAPTER THIRTEEN

＊◆＊

T HE VAN ALST House was a perfect fall vision of brilliant foliage. I said good-bye and Candy responded with the barest of grunts. And no eye contact. I wasn't sure what had happened. I hopped out of the Tahoe and Candy vanished with a spray of gravel. Still, the day was so gorgeous, nothing much could dim its effect. The Van Alst House was showing signs of age, and the property was in need of a decent gardener, but the vivid swirling leaves on the property looked amazing. What was even more amazing was the signora jumping in front of me.

She motioned wildly back at the kitchen door. "*Il gatto!* Oh, *Madonna!*" Her eyes were wild. At the door there were two bowls and a plate of cold cuts and what looked like bratwurst, from my best guess.

My Italian being limited to food items, I thought perhaps we were talking about cake. "*Gateau?*" I asked hopefully. "You want me to eat it?"

I tell you, it really does something to your self esteem

when a person behaving this erratically looks at *you* like you're the one who's lost your marbles.

"Meeeoooo! Meeeoooo!" She seemed to be petting her arm, and grimacing in desperation. Her round little body shook. Then she motioned behind her to the dishes at the door again.

As I approached her, she began wailing like a kicked sheep. I held her by the shoulders, hoping that if I waited long enough, I'd be granted understanding.

She was petting her arm again. One last time she let out a "Meeeoooo" then her shoulders fell in defeat.

"I believe Fiammetta is trying to tell you that someone kidnapped my cats."

The voice from behind and below us sent a cold jolt through me.

"What?" I said stupidly, whirling to gaze down at Vera in her wheelchair.

"*Dio mio!*" Signora crossed herself.

Vera had somehow managed to make her way out of the house and across the gravel without either of us hearing her approach. I figure the crunch of the gravel had been drowned out by the racket.

"The cats, Miss Bingham. The cats are gone. They are no longer in this house. While you were out gallivanting, Fiammetta and I have searched the entire house. Every. Single. Inch." Her voice was calm and icy cold.

It finally dawned on me that the bowls at the back door and plates of salted meats were intended to lure the felines home. Unless someone had kidnapped them, not that the idea made any sense.

"And you've checked the—"

Vera did not let me finish. "Yes! Did you not hear me just now? We have checked every square inch. They are not here. Not. Here."

"It's just that they are often under the beds or tables. I know that the hard way. Check my ankles."

"They are not. Fiammetta has checked everywhere, crawled under everything. They are gone. They are such creatures of habit and now, they are gone. Vanished."

I knew those cats. They liked nothing more than a firestorm of emotion. They could be reveling in all this attention and drama. I said, "There's the dumbwaiter. They like hiding in that."

"Vanished, Miss Bingham. What will it take to convince you?"

FOR ONCE, THERE was no sumptuous lunch in the conservatory. It was every girl for herself as the signora roamed the Van Alst estate calling for the cats. Vera rolled after her in the wheelchair. In the distance, I could hear her saying, "Pull yourself together, Fiammetta. The cats are Siamese, not Italian. They won't understand a word you're bleating."

Of course, I joined in the great cat hunt, but inside the house. I started in my own attic garret and searched the third floor and then worked my way down.

Obviously, the signora had been in my room already, as there were small things out of place. She knew that one cat liked to hang out with me and the other one was interested in slashing at my legs from under the bed.

I was sure she'd done her best to search, but I was younger and more flexible. I could crawl right under beds and into attic eaves. I could even fit into the dumbwaiter. I did these things and many more, but after a couple of hours, I conceded defeat.

By then, the signora was glumly busying herself in the kitchen. I gathered that she was making some enticing treat for the cats. Vera was glowering at the *NYT* crossword in the conservatory. She hadn't gotten far. Not like her at all.

I didn't want to depress her more by saying that my long search had been for nothing.

She glanced up at me. "Have you had any success in finding your missing people, Miss Bingham?"

This took me by surprise. I felt a lump in my throat. It was so unlike Vera to be concerned about anyone.

I shook my head and then managed to say, "Thank you. One has shown up and I am sure the other one will too. And so will the cats."

But in reality, I wasn't sure. Where could those cats be? They were spoiled and indulged and weren't likely to find a better situation anywhere else. We had no near neighbors and anyway, the felines were skittish around strangers.

I didn't say anything, but I was worried about predators. There had been coyote sightings in our area. But coyotes don't roam inside houses. What could have caused the cats to exit the house in the first place? That was the question.

I stepped into the kitchen to see if I could offer the signora a hand. She was in a flap and very distressed. However, I found myself shooed out of the kitchen in short order. I figured she found her cooking domain therapeutic.

I had lots of other things to do and to think about:

Was Uncle Kev alive and all right?
What was Officer Smiley up to?
Where were the three missing books?
What had happened to Randolph, Delilah and Mason?
How was the dead hit man connected to them? Or was he?
Was there a connection between him and the other death in Burton? It was too coincidental otherwise.

What about Harry Yerxa? Had the nosy old neighbor wit-
nessed something? Had someone threatened him to shut
him up? Was he hiding out?

What was Karen forgetting to tell me?

Why did Officer Cundy's mood change so abruptly on our
trip?

Not in the least, where were the damn cats?

And why were all these terrible and inexplicable things
happening to us, all at once?

VERA WAS BACK in her regular vinegary mood. To tell the truth, I was a bit relieved. At least I know how to deal with the familiar Vera. The glimpse of her compassionate side had been a bit unsettling. Just before our regular dinner at eight, I ran into her as we headed down the endless corridor toward the dining room. I wasn't sure if the signora had been able to produce a meal given her state of mind.

She looked up and raised an eyebrow at me. "Don't think I have forgotten about my missing Sayers and your role in that."

"I have not forgotten my role in repatriating the books that were stolen from you before I ever set foot in this house, if that's what you mean. I am making progress too."

I used my calmest voice—just to keep her from going on about it—when the long chime of the front door sounded.

We whipped our heads toward the noise. Vera spun around in her wheelchair. The signora came barreling out of the dining room. I was barely ahead of them both. And reached the door only mildly out of breath.

"Well, what are you waiting for? Open it!" Vera barked. "I'm sure it's not the Girl Scouts selling cookies!"

No, I was equally sure the Girl Scouts had been warned on their first try not to ever attempt to sell cookies here again on pain of something dire. I swung the heavy door open to reveal Uncle Kevin.

My jaw dropped.

The signora burbled some unfamiliar syllables, but Vera was silent.

Uncle Kevin was holding a small pet carrier containing a blue point Siamese. An elegant paw with sharp claws was poking out of the front grate. Uncle Kev carried a friendlier Siamese cat on his shoulder, like a parrot.

My job and accommodations flashed in front of my eyes.

"Buh!?" was all I could manage before the signora pushed past me and Vera nearly ran over my foot getting out.

Good Cat leapt gracefully from Uncle Kevin to Vera's lap. Kevin grinned. I wasn't sure what was happening.

I leaned forward and whispered, "Where have you been?"

He whispered back, "Long story. For another time."

Kev turned from me to face Vera and the signora. He twinkled. Shazam! He pulled out all that ginger-haired Irish leprechaun magic that is in the Kelly genes. They didn't stand a chance.

Kev was saying, "Oh, hi, Jordan. Glad you're back. Heard you were worried about me. I came by today to talk to you, and Miss Vera and Miss Fiammetta here were in a state about the kitties going missing."

Really?

Why did that not strike me as the whole truth?

"And the cats?"

"I had nothing better to do, so I went looking. I found them down the road a bit. They jumped right in the car."

I felt like I'd swallowed a stone. "You found them heading down the road and they jumped right in the car."

"Yes. That's what I said. How weird is that?"

"Oh, very weird." The thing was, I knew my uncles, and for this uncle, in particular, the word "found" had a different meaning in his dictionary, as in, you might "find" a Rolex or another man's wife in your bed.

By now, the signora had pulled Kevin and Vera inside and pressed the handle of the pet carrier into my hand. The feline in the carrier managed to lash out and slash my herringbone tights.

Stunned, I watched my worlds collide.

No questions asked. There were no accusations of wrongdoing. Vera stroked Good Cat, while the signora fussed over Uncle Kevin. He was radiating Kelly charm in her direction. You could practically see it: golden beams headed toward her. As many people have learned, that charm was enough to turn a person's brain to mush.

"I noticed you have some beautiful landscaping. I saw a spectacular specimen of burning bush," I heard Kevin say as they entered the dining room, toward his reward of homemade Italian food.

It was about three minutes before I could unhook Bad Cat's claw and then gingerly set down the carrier. I was careful to stand safely behind it when I released the latch and a very unhappy Siamese raced, rowling, into the corridor. My tights were ruined, but I was happy to have escaped with only minor blood loss.

"Cats." I muttered. At least you could trust dogs. Walter would never have done such a thing.

Kevin's laugh boomed from the dining room and along the corridor.

I wasn't sure if it was wise to race back to my quarters to remove the tights. But I did. I also applied antibiotic cream and bandages and put on fresh tights and the high dress boots I usually wore to dinner. Too bad I hadn't thought of that before.

By the time I arrived back, Kevin was seated at the Sheraton table like a king, surrounded by delicacies and delights and two smiling women.

The signora had outdone herself this afternoon, probably in an effort to calm herself.

Kev's hand gripped a crystal tumbler filled with expensive-looking amber liquid. Cognac? Who drinks cognac by the tumbler? Never mind with dinner. But we weren't dealing with just anyone here.

"Here's our girl!" Kevin trumpeted. "Beautiful thing, ain't she!" He beamed with pride, but my spirits were sinking fast. I began mentally packing my bags.

"Quite." Vera's tone, terse as ever, made it impossible to know if she truly thought I was a beautiful thing. Maybe she was thinking about replacing me with Kevin.

"So, we're going to be workin' together, my girl!" Kevin said with a mouth full of pasta.

"What?" I practically choked. I hadn't left them alone with him for more than ten minutes.

Vera said, "Yes, after speaking with your Uncle Kevin, we've decided that there could be a mutually beneficial arrangement made. And I've been sorely disappointed in Eddie's so-called gardening skills."

"Huh?"

"Please, Miss Bingham, if you are not prepared to speak in complete sentences, at least you could try and use *actual* words."

Kevin continued grinning and chewing, pausing every now and then for a slug of cognac.

Lucky for Eddie. He was off the hook, even though he'd volunteered.

"Your uncle has impressed me with his extensive knowledge of horticulture, and as you know, that has never been a strength of mine."

Had Kevin picked up a knowledge of horticulture in some minimum-security prison or diversion program? No other Kelly had the foggiest notion of plant life or gardening, if you didn't count cannabis. Of course, I wasn't going to mention that.

Vera pivoted the wheelchair to face out the multipaned window. "Kevin will stay here in exchange for maintaining the grounds. Eddie can't keep up with it, and not a single person has responded to our advertisements."

I could barely squeak. "Here? With me?"

Vera shot me a querulous glance. "Doesn't that suit you, Miss Bingham?"

"Oh, absolutely, it does."

"He will have his own accommodations of course. There are rooms over the garage. They used to be the chauffeur's and gardener's quarters. Mr. Kelly has said he'll be able to fix them up quickly. He'll be very comfortable there."

"Terrific," I said with a sinking heart.

I had no idea what kind of conversation had passed between Vera and Kevin that could have gotten him moved in and employed here in the ten minutes it had taken me for first aid and a change of tights. Kelly charm strikes again.

The signora was so taken with him that she forgot to serve me dessert, and Vera didn't even notice that the green in the sauce was clearly zucchini.

I knew I was the only person in that room who had made the connection about the cats going missing and the cats being found with Kevin's need to have a new place to live. And Vera and the signora were never going to hear that from me.

I was very glad that Uncle Kev was alive, even though I felt like killing him.

Life would never be the same.

BACK IN MY room, I tried not to dwell on exactly what life with Kev would be like. Vera and the signora might be besotted, but they'd learn soon enough. I had plenty to do and at least I didn't have to worry that he was dead or that he'd killed someone. Not even Uncle Kev could be so vacuously cheerful if he had.

I unpacked my bag from Once More with Feeling. There was Police Officer Barbie, staring at me. I hoped the doll would cheer up Candy since our outing had been cut short. And then I realized I had no number for her, because it was kind of a one-way friendship. She had my address and my phone number and I had only her work information. I glanced at my watch. Good thing I'm a night owl.

I wanted to check on Karen anyway. And Burton wasn't far from Grandville. As Candy had been called back to work, she might still be there. I wrapped up the Barbie box in pretty paper and then covered that with plain brown wrapping. I didn't want to embarrass her in front of her colleagues.

FIFTEEN MINUTES LATER, I parked the Saab in front of the Burton Police Station and walked in.

I smiled at the officer sitting at the desk.

"I'd like to speak to Officer Candy Mortakis. Do you know when she'll be back?"

"Sure thing," he said. "She's here now. Name?"

"Jordan Bingham."

He picked up an old-school interior phone. "Candy, there's a young lady to see you.

"A Jordan Bingham."

"No idea."

"All righty."

He looked back at me. "Go right through. Second desk on the left."

Wow. Candy had a desk?

He buzzed me through an interior door.

An attractive blonde in a crisp white blouse and trim charcoal wool pants looked up from the file she'd been working on. She wore small gold hoops and a good leather belt. I approved.

"Yes," she said as I approached.

"I'm looking for Candy Mortakis."

"You found her."

"What?"

She frowned. "Who were you expecting?"

"My friend, Candy."

"I am Detective Sergeant Candace Mortakis."

I blinked. "But there can't be two people in this police department with that name."

She chuckled. "Probably not in the whole world. Tell me, why do you think someone else had my name?"

"Because she told me."

No chuckle now.

"She told you she was Candace Mortakis?"

"Officer Candy Mortakis."

"Where did this happen?"

"Could I sit down? I think there's something very bad going on."

She gestured to the empty chair by the side of her desk. "Where?"

"Over at 87 Lincoln Way."

"You mean 89."

I shook my head. "No, I was looking for Mr. Randolph Adams at Number 87 and she came around and helped me."

"She told you she was a detective?"

"Officer. She was wearing a uniform."

"And she gave you my name?"

I nodded. "I don't understand what was going on. Why would she—?"

"Why would she what?"

I paused and thought. There was so much wrong here. I couldn't trust the "other" Candy, whoever she was. "Randolph Adams and the entire family have disappeared. All the other cops were busy with the crime scene in the backyard of Number 89. She took me into the house and helped me search to see if Randolph was injured in the house."

"Without a warrant? No homeowner there?"

"The door was unlocked. The place looked like it had been ransacked. She said it was all right if an old man might be in danger."

She ran her hand through her nicely highlighted blond hair.

"You find anything?"

This bit I modified. "No. But she gave me some information about the Adamses."

"Hang on," she said. "Hank, get over here. You got to hear this."

Hank, a more rumpled and stereotypical detective, ambled over. He was pleasant looking and pudgy. Perhaps the pudginess was new, as his gray suit was stretched tight over his arms and middle and his white shirt gapped between buttons.

Candy filled him in as far as I'd gotten.

"Do you think she's a reporter?" I asked. "I wouldn't have thought a reporter would impersonate a police officer. That's against the law, isn't it?"

Hank leaned back against Candy's desk and crossed his arms over his chest. He gave me a hard look. "You bet it is. So she gave you some information about the Adams family?"

"She said that there was no record of the family until about three years ago."

Candy might have wanted Hank to hear what was going on, but she wasn't letting him take over. "And what is your involvement with these people?"

Oh well. I suppose it had to come out. "I work for Vera Van Alst, the wealthy book collector. Her Dorothy L. Sayers collection was stolen some months back and sold to a bookseller who then sold the books to Randolph Adams. The bookseller was not aware that the books had been stolen. I have been tasked with getting them back and once we tracked down Randolph Adams—"

"Who's 'we'?" Candy said.

"The bookseller, Karen Smith. She had a brain injury in an attack a few months ago, so her memory is faulty, but we did track him down and were ready to trade the collection for another valuable work."

"And?"

"And Randolph's family was very suspicious of us and seemed to want to block the sale. To tell the truth, we thought they were drugging him or something. We noticed he got disoriented and drowsy after drinking some tea from his daughter."

Hank rolled his eyes. "What is this? Some kind of soap opera?"

"I know it sounds crazy. It even seemed bizarre, being in the middle of it."

"What else?" Candy said.

Maybe it was a mistake, but I had to leave out the part where I went back to the house with night vision goggles and let myself in and was caught by the imposter Candy.

Hank fiddled with a pen as I spoke. "She said she was lonely. She had no friends here on the force. She wanted to get together for a girls' night. She talked a lot."

"What did she talk about?"

"She told me what she'd found out about the Adams family not existing. She told me about the murder victim."

Hank dropped the pen. Candy's eyes widened. "What did she tell you?"

"That he'd been stabbed. That he was a contract killer."

"Contract killer?" Hank used his outside voice. "What do you mean, he was a contract killer?"

"Down boy," Candy said. "Let her talk."

"She showed me a picture."

"We haven't released a name or photo."

"I realize that, but she had a photo of a man. He was obviously dead. She said his name was Pierre Gagnon and he was a hit man."

"Why did she show you the photo?"

"I don't know." I didn't plan to drop either Uncle Kev or Smiley into the soup. "This other Candy was very intense and there had been a murder. She asked if I recognized him."

"And?"

"I'd seen him in front of the Adams house on my last unsuccessful attempt to see Randolph. He was parked next door, I guess in front of Number 89, just waiting and watching."

"You saw his face?"

"My pooch ran off and I asked this guy in the Impala if he'd seen my dog. I had no idea who I was talking to, before

Candy told me he was a hit man. I guess that was dangerous."

They exchanged glances. Meaningful glances.

I said, "What? Was he a hit man?"

They were probably decent detectives, but they never
would have made a career in theater.

"He wasn't, was he?"

They weren't talking.

Actually, they didn't have to talk. Their expressions were
deadpan, but they couldn't hide the emotion in their eyes.

"Tell me he wasn't a police officer. There was nothing in
the news or—I'm sorry. What's going on here? I hope he
wasn't a colleague."

"We need to talk to you about what you saw there."

"Of course." Talk about a sinking feeling. There was so
much I didn't want them to know. Uncle Kev's presence.
Tyler Dekker's. My own extra visits, unauthorized entry and
book pilfering.

"We'll take you to an interview room," the real Candy
said, not unkindly.

My feet dragged. How long would it take for my web of
omissions to be revealed? And people I cared about hauled
into interview rooms? That would be very hard on Tyler. Of
course, I doubted they'd actually catch up to Uncle Kev.

Halfway across the room, the intercom squawked. "All
units. Shots fired and multiple suspected shooters at farm-
house just south of the junction of Appledoorn Road and
Crawford Road. Hostages likely. All available units."

I didn't like feeling grateful for someone else's tragedy,
and I hoped nothing happened to the hostages, but I was
thrilled to get out of the station. I gave the real Candy my
address at Van Alst House, my cell number and Vera's number too. I promised not to leave the county.

As I collapsed in my Saab, Candy and Hank pulled out in a Tahoe. Now what? I wanted to get away from the police station.

I passed a silver Audi as I left Burton and did a double take. But of course, the Adams gang would have ditched that car long ago. The driver was a young, dark-haired woman, not Delilah, for sure. Not Mason either, and definitely not Randolph.

I pulled over and took out my cell. Kev and Tyler needed to know. So did Karen and Uncle Lucky. We could make sure our stories made sense later. I figured the cops would be tied up for quite a while at the shoot-out.

For once, Kev was where he was supposed to be. "Thanks for the heads-up," he said. "I'll be gone if they show up here."

"Yeah, well, leave the cats this time."

Tyler did not pick up. His recent track record with phone messages and texts was terrible. It wasn't the sort of thing I wanted to leave a message about.

I tried Karen's number. No luck. Then I tried her cell number. "Oh, Jordan! I am so glad you are calling. I remembered what I needed to tell you."

I made sure not to interrupt. I knew how easy it was for her to lose her train of thought.

"It was Randolph!"

"Yes?" I said encouragingly.

"He slipped me some books in a plastic bag."

I wanted to shout, "What books? What bag?" But I merely repeated, "Yes."

"You were on the other side of the room with Delilah. And that creepy Mason was keeping an eye on you. Randolph slipped me three books and signaled me to keep quiet. He asked me to keep them safe for him. So I did. I slipped them into my tapestry bag and . . . I am sorry to say, after I checked them at home and put them in a safe place, I forgot all about them, until today. Mason was so hostile to us and then all the upsetting news about the murder and everything. I knew there was something I was supposed to mention but I couldn't bring it to mind. I've been tired out by all this."

"That's great, Karen. You remembered. I wonder why he wanted you to keep them. What books were they?"

"You'll never guess!" she said. "They were three of the Sayers books."

"Let me guess. *The Unpleasantness at the Bellona Club*, *Clouds of Witness* and *Have His Carcase*.

She gasped. "How did you know?"

"Long story, but I'll fill you in later." I didn't want Karen knowing any of the illegal things I had done to find the rest of the collection. It would have put her in a tough spot with the police. It would put me at a disadvantage too. "Where are the books?"

"Safe with me."

"Great."

"Well, not so great, really. I remember the titles but I don't exactly remember where I put them, but it will be a safe place. Don't worry. I'm sure it will come to me. Do you want to have a hunt for them?"

"Thanks, Karen, I'll do that. Are you home now?"

"No, I'm visiting Walter at your uncles' place. I miss Walter so much. Mick is making dinner. He's cooking."

"Really? Cooking?" Did that mean opening a can?

"Yes, tuna casserole with mushroom soup and crumbled potato chips baked on the top. I love that."

So did I, but it was much more cuisine than I expected from Uncle Mick. Something was going on over there. As soon as I got out of the mess I was in, I'd have to find out what was up.

"Karen, the police are going to question me about my involvement with the Adams family and 87 Lincoln Way. They'll want to talk to you too."

"Oh dear! What will I say?"

"Just tell the truth. You did nothing wrong."

"All right, I'll tell the truth if I can remember it. If not, I hope I don't cause you problems."

"You won't. They won't suspect you of anything. And your head injury is a matter of record. Don't worry. I'll go hunt for those books now."

I tried Tyler again. This time I used a different tactic when he didn't answer. I didn't know what he was up to, but I knew that I could trust him not to do anything that would harm me.

"It's me," I said, sweetly. "I need a bit of advice from you. Some very strange things are emerging about the murder. You may not know that I was in the vicinity and also that a fake police officer befriended me. She was pretending to be Candy Mortakis from the Burton police force. The real Candy is a detective over there. The story is so wacky the Burton police are looking at me strangely. They want to interview me about everything. If they hadn't had a shoot-out in the town, I'd be locked in an interview room right now. Can you offer me any reassurance? Or at least a shoulder to cry on? I'll be over at my friend's place late tomorrow afternoon if you have time to talk. Upstairs over the shop."

There. In case he was also undercover, and the wrong person picked up his phone and got my message, they wouldn't figure out he was a police officer. And he would know exactly which friend it was.

I decided to interrupt Uncle Mick even if he was making tuna casserole, a challenge to any Kelly.

"I may need a lawyer soon," I said. "And it's possible Kev

might too. Just giving you a heads-up. We may have been in the wrong place at the wrong time. Do you want to set something in motion?"

I don't usually get silence from Mick, but this day was special.

I added, "It's because I was in the neighborhood of the murder. I was in the house next door. I don't think I saw anything that can help, but they want to question me because of this bizarre situation." I filled him in on the Candy ordeal. Neither Mick nor I gave much away on the phone. You never know who can get a warrant for what.

"I'll get on it right away," he said. "It's not like you've ever done anything that wasn't on the straight and narrow, my girl."

I exchanged a few quick texts with Lance to arrange to meet at eight the next evening for dinner and dishing. I stifled a few yawns. It was too late for any more driving or sleuthing or surprises. Time to catch up on my sleep.

CHAPTER FOURTEEN

＊✦＊

V ERA KEPT ME busy with a plethora of errands the
next day. She must have used a lot of energy dreaming
them up. But by late afternoon, I had nothing left to do but
head over to Karen's and hunt for the three books she'd
hidden. I loved Karen's cluttered apartment with its books
and china and chintz. Despite the clutter, her home was
small enough that the books couldn't stay hidden long.

During the drive to the Cozy Corpse, I kept worrying
about inconsistencies that had been bothering me. It was not
only the Adams family. But I would have to try to figure it
all out later. I hoped I'd have some insights before the Burton police got out the rubber hoses (to use a term from Uncle
Mick's lexicon) and "interviewed" me.

Now added to the mix was the imposter Candy, whoever
she was. It finally occurred to me that if Candy had deceived
me about the dead police officer, it was because *she* was the
real danger. If anyone was a contract killer, it must have
been Candy. She had to be pretty cocky to hang around the

crime scene dressed as a cop. This woman had an insane kind of courage. She had wanted something. But what? The Adams family was gone. A cop was dead. What had she been searching for?

I kept a sharp eye out for the navy-blue Tahoe and the treacherous woman who had pretended to be my friend. I did spot a silver Audi going the opposite way. It seemed like they were everywhere. So much for a faltering economy.

Karen was off with Lucky. I parked the Saab on the street to leave room for the Cozy Corpse van when Karen returned. I glanced around but didn't see any suspicious-looking vehicles. The miserable guy next door was in his backyard, piling leaves into bags near the driveway. He gave me the stink-eye, as usual. His wife stuck her nose out the back door and added her version of the dirty look. I didn't give them the satisfaction of appearing to notice. I was feeling pretty good in my cashmere coat with my favorite wide-legged trouser jeans. I continued through Karen's backyard to the back door. At least Karen had left the door locked. I unlocked it and dropped my keys into the pocket of my jeans.

Upstairs, I surveyed the tiny apartment. I planned to search for the books in the living room, then the bedroom and finally, and only if necessary, the basement. I was inspecting the stacks of elderly volumes by the easy chair when I heard a noise from the staircase.

I turned and stared at the entrance to the room. The woman pointing the gun at me looked vaguely familiar. She was a curvy brunette with a mane of shoulder-length chestnut hair. It looked very good with a fresh blowout. She was wearing skintight Levi's and a black tee with a plunging neckline. Her complexion glowed and her green eyes seemed to glitter. It was the odd little gappy smile that gave her away.

"I don't know who you are, but you'd better put that gun down," I said with fake bravado.

"You can stop with the act," she said. "I can read you like one of these moldy old books."

"Candy! You've had a fabulous makeover. I never would have recognized you. What a surprise."

"I bet it's a surprise."

"How did you know I was here?"

"I've been looking for nosy girls who now have to be dealt with."

"What? Dealt with?"

"That's right. Now, go sit in the chair."

I had nothing to lose. "Candy, I thought we were friends. What are you talking about? Are you really pointing a gun at me?"

"Yes, I am, because you are too smart for your own good. Don't bother lying. It's too little, too late, and it won't work."

I wanted to kick myself. She must have followed me. I'd been watching for her vehicle, but of course, she had probably ditched that without a blink. The world was full of cars that I hadn't been watching for.

No one knew I was here except Smiley, assuming he picked up my oblique message from the night before. Karen and Lucky were in their own little world, and Mick would assume that I was at Van Alst House. Vera and the signora probably still thought I was in my attic. Tiff had fallen off the face of the earth. Lance wasn't expecting to meet up until eight in the evening.

I was on my own. Well, not exactly on my own. I was facing a gun-wielding Candy and that was definitely not a good thing.

The Kellys do not do guns, so that part of my education was sadly lacking. This one looked heavy and dangerous though. And it was pointed right at me. The fake Candy was definitely very comfortable with handguns. That much was obvious. She wasn't a police officer and it was clear that Candy's connections were not law-abiding ones. I figured her training included learning how to shoot. Mind you, in the small confines of Karen's apartment, Candy could hardly miss. Even though I knew she wasn't the real Candy Mortakis, I still couldn't stop thinking of her as "Candy."

I thought hard. Was there anything I could use against her? She was going to have to silence me. There was nowhere to run, so my only hope was to find a weapon. Aside from the teapot, the china cups and the books, everything was soft and cozy. Useless in this scenario.

"It's been fun, but fun's over now," she said.

"Can't we discuss this?" I decided to play it as if she really was a small-town cop and not, as I had belatedly figured out, a hired killer.

"I don't know what you think you're arresting me for, but I can get a great lawyer with one phone call. So this won't advance your career in Burton."

"Cut the crap. I'm not arresting you and you know that. I think our little game has played itself out. Now, what I need to know is, where is the information that Randolph gave you?"

I stared at her. "I don't know what you're talking about."

"Don't waste my time. Where is it?"

I did my best to steel my nerves as I told the truth. "Randolph didn't give me *anything*."

"I'm not fooled by that for a minute. If you can't produce it, you're of no use to me alive. So, where is it?"

My steely nerves were somewhat hampered by the fact I knew she had already killed at least one person. In fact, she'd probably killed a lot of people. I didn't want her to know that I'd figured that out. The problem was I didn't know what "it" was.

"Honestly. Randolph was drugged or something. He didn't give me anything. He could barely stay awake."

"This is getting old. Tell me where it is."

"Believe me, I would if I could."

She sighed theatrically. She was one hell of an actress and I supposed she really liked the dramatics. The sigh sounded very professional. Maybe she'd had a bit of stage training, unlike the real police. More likely she had the easy gift for manipulation and deceit of a natural-born psychopath. Whatever, it wasn't good.

"He had to have given it to you. It wasn't in the house. Where else could it have gone?"

What did this mean? Had Candy been the person to ransack the Adams house after the family had fled? Was that why she was hanging around in her fake police uniform? But why? Was she looking for a clue to track them down?

"It would help if I had some idea about what you're looking for," I said.

"No more of your cute tricks. I'm running out of patience and you're running out of time."

"Look," I said, anxious to change the topic. "Randolph could have dementia. He might have intended to give me something, but he didn't. If he had, would I keep looking for missing books?"

"Who said it was a book?"

I blinked.

She narrowed her eyes at me.

"Well, the only thing *I'm* interested in is books. I'm just doing my job. I need to retrieve a collection of Dorothy L.

Sayers first editions that were sold to Randolph by mistake. That's my only connection to him."

"It may have been your only connection, but not anymore. Did he give you a book?"

I shook my head. "No, he didn't."

Bad enough I was facing down the barrel of some kind of gun, I didn't want to dump Karen into it. I was grateful that Karen wasn't at home, but it was just a matter of time before she returned. I prayed that when she did, Candy would be gone.

I thought hard. What could she be talking about? If I could figure that out, I'd have some leverage.

"Still stalling," she said,

"Again, if I knew what you're looking for, I could work with you."

"Work with me?" Her green eyes were not warm or pleading or filled with the need for friendship. I figured they never had been, but I had fallen for her pretense.

"Because I don't want to get shot. There's no love lost between me and the cops."

I kept my voice light as if I actually believed my own words.

"In that case, tell me where it is."

Well that just went around in circles. "I don't know. For me it was all about the books. That's all."

Of course, it finally dawned on me. "It" must have been the books that Randolph slipped to Karen. Perhaps he'd placed something in them. Something he was trying to keep from Delilah and Mason. Or maybe just Mason. That relationship continued to unsettle me.

Why would those books be important to either of them? I thought back to our visit to see Randolph. Mason's arrival during our talk explained why Randolph had quieted down suddenly. I hadn't thought much of that at the time. Just a confused elderly gentleman. But instead of an overprotective grandson, Mason was something else entirely. And Randolph was well aware of it.

What would Wimsey do? He certainly would have reminded me that people are not who or what they seem to be. Perhaps he'd have mentioned that money and family strife are a recipe for trouble. Of course, I doubted Wimsey would find himself in such a dangerous situation in the first place. And if he had, surely Bunter would have shown up. Or Inspector Parker. Most likely with the books in hand. Obviously, I needed more and better sidekicks, maybe some that walked upright.

A movement in the doorway behind Candy gave me hope and then, panic. What if it was Karen coming home? There was no way that Karen would be a match for Candy. It would take Candy a minute to get the information out of her about Randolph and the three books. Then Karen would be dead. If she remembered about the books. And if she didn't remember, she'd probably be just as dead.

I shuddered and Candy raised an eyebrow. "Got something to tell me?"

I needed to stall. "If it's a book you're looking for, I can probably help."

"I don't know what it is. You do."

"I wish I did."

"Not as much as you're about to."

Behind her a shadow blurred. The reassuring bulk of Officer Tyler Dekker moved on surprising cat feet behind Candy, his weapon raised.

As he reached her, I ducked behind the armchair, hoping it would absorb any random gunshots.

"Put the gun down." Smiley meant business.

I could see her weighing the options.

He said, "Officer shoots hired killer in murder attempt."

She stood still.

"Or you could try your luck with the judicial system. With the right lawyer, you might get a reduced sentence. Hope for the best in prison. But you'll be breathing. Not that you deserve to be."

Candy leaned forward and put her gun on the floor.

I inched farther behind the chair and out of the line of fire. I didn't trust her not to turn and start blasting. "Be careful," I said. "She's a real weasel."

"I know that."

"And she's not a police officer."

"I realized that as soon as I pulled her over last week."

"What?"

"Routine stop for a traffic offense in Harrison Falls."

"And?"

"Her ID was in order. Candy Mortakis from the Burton force."

I said, "That's a real officer's name, that's why."

Candy grinned. "You'd be amazed what you can find on Google."

He ignored her. "She was driving a navy-blue Tahoe and she was in uniform, but something bothered me. I couldn't put my finger on it, so I had to let her go. Kept an eye on her though."

"Of course, the Tahoe. That's what all you law enforcement types like to drive."

"My gut told me that she wasn't what she looked like."

"Was that why you were creeping around Lincoln Way?"

"I've been keeping an eye on her. I tailed her to where she was staying. And then I followed her to Lincoln Way. I knew she was up to something. I managed to get a photo of her from a distance. No one in Harrison Falls would listen. I passed the photo on to a friend at Quantico to see if he could run it through their database. My friend said she's a suspected gun for hire. I gave him everything I knew. Next thing, I'm politely asked to take a hike. I'm infringing on an active organized crime investigation."

I said, "But you didn't take a hike."

"How could I when every time I turned around, you showed up. I'm not good at minding my own business and neither are you. I needed to save you from whatever you were mixed up in."

I could hardly say I didn't need saving, given the circumstances. My feminist pride had to take a hit. I said, "The dead undercover cop must have been FBI."

"What?"

"The guy who was killed was undercover. The real Candy Mortakis let that slip."

His face turned ashen and his jaw tensed. A fallen officer hit all cops hard. Even I knew that.

Candy sneered. "You could smell bacon a mile away. Just like the first guy."

I said, "Bacon? Oh, of course, you killed the first guy as well and he was undercover too. You're more of a knife for hire than a gun. And you threw in the bit about the second victim having no fingerprints just for the hell of it. All fun for you, as was the dressing up and fooling me."

"Get yourself over here, Jordan, away from her. I'm calling for backup. We've got her now."

He grinned a bit at that.

Before I could move, I spotted a shadow in the doorway from the stairs.

"Look out!" I shouted. "Behind you!"

I reached for something to lob at Candy as Smiley whirled.

Candy dove for her weapon. Mason Adams raised his gun and pointed at Smiley's head. He nudged Smiley's legs with one of his Blundstones. He said, "Don't try anything."

I aimed the antique china teapot at Candy's head and hurled it hard. Missed. Candy dodged it, bumping into the wall as she did. The teapot crashed to the floor. Candy was back in charge. Now it was two guns to one. And she was royally ticked off.

"Drop your gun or I'll shoot your little girlfriend," Candy said.

Without a word, Tyler lowered his weapon to the floor.

Mason said, "Good news, babe."

My head swam. Babe?

Mason and Candy. I thought I'd had her figured out, but this came out of nowhere. I was missing a lot if I hadn't figured this out. What else didn't I know?

"It better be good news because now we have another cop to get rid of on top of this nosy girl here," Candy said.

"He's a cop? I thought he was just her stupid boyfriend." He gave me a dismissive look.

"And?" she said.

"And what, babe?"

"Tell me the good news, because right now it's all bad news."

"Oh yeah. Randolph thinks he remembers giving it to the woman. But he's losing it. Sometimes he remembers things, other times he doesn't. Sometimes he hardly knows who he is."

"Well, she's here and she claims she doesn't know anything about it. You sure he's not just putting one over on you?"

"Huh? Oh, her? No, not her, the other one."

"What other one?"

"The older one, with the red hair. The woman that sold him the books in the first place. I forget her name. Karen something. She owns the store downstairs: the Cozy Corpse."

"Oh, right. Jordan, you told me about her, didn't you? She has it?"

"He said he gave three books to her. She put them in some kind of a flowered bag."

"What books are they?"

Mason blinked. "He called them the Sayers books. He didn't tell me their names."

"Titles, not names. Books have titles," she snapped. "Are you sure he's telling the truth?"

"Yeah. I had to play rough with him. He knows that once we have it, we don't need him, so he held out."

"Keep in mind that without the money, there's no new life for us. Just you going back to being Jason Pecelli with the mob gunning for you."

"I know that, babe."

"I'm all that stands between you and an unmarked grave somewhere. You realize that?"

Mason licked his lips. "I do, babe. And you've been amazing. The cop routine was priceless. No one would ever recognize you in a getup like that."

She giggled. "Right under their noses. I actually enjoyed it. Those Burton cops were too stupid to breathe. But fun's got to end now. We need to find the books and then it's just a matter of putting Randall and Dawna out of their misery so we can make a new life for us. That reminds me, did you track them down? I can't believe you were stupid enough to let that old man get away."

Changing their names to Randall and Delilah and hiding out in Burton wasn't nearly enough to save the former Randall and Dawna from the relentless Candy. Especially with that snake Mason in their midst. I actually felt sorry for them.

"You don't have to kill Dawna, babe. She's not responsible for any of this. She's just—"

I'd never seen a smile as cold as the one on Candy's face. "She's just the woman you left me for. Do you think I'm going to forget that she played me for a sucker?"

Mason might have been planning a life with Candy, but I figured he was fully aware that she was a psychopath. "I was just crazy, babe. Scared about the mob. Out of my depth. I didn't realize how much I'd miss you. Dawna wasn't responsible. She's not the sharpest knife in the drawer. She was stuck there with that old husband. You can let her live. She can't hurt us."

Candy smiled. I figured poor Delilah had just been consigned to a more painful death.

She said, "Enough about them. Does this woman, Karen, know what she has?"

"He said he didn't tell her anything. She thinks it's just ordinary books."

"Well, either way, we need to get it. And get rid of her."

Mason didn't show any desperate need to save Karen's life. I figured he still had some feelings for Delilah. He'd do whatever he could to save her.

"I tracked Karen down. I know where she is. There's an antique shop in Harrison Falls. She's there with some big bald guy. She's still carrying that flowered bag. We'd better get there fast."

I thought my throat would close.

"Look around here first and take any books you see that are by this Dorothy L. Sayers. Then we have some business to tidy up here," Candy said. "Two busybodies."

I said, "If you kill a police officer, they will hunt you down. They already know who you are and what you look like."

She snorted. "Nice try. It won't be the first time."

I knew she was telling the truth about that. She'd killed the undercover cop who was watching the Adams house.

Had he been waiting for Candy and not the Adams family as I had assumed?

Mason turned to me. "You wouldn't ever recognize her. You see how much she can change her appearance."

"The books," she said. "Check carefully and fast. We need to finish up here."

As Mason checked each stack of books and bookcase, Candy headed for the kitchen. She glanced around and scratched her wig.

Still keeping his eyes and guns on us, Mason turned to the bedroom and began rummaging around.

Candy hummed as she lifted a pot from a hanger, placed it on the stove, poured some olive oil into in and turned on the burner. She draped a tea towel near it. What was that about? As she walked back in and gave me an evil, self-satisfied grin, I had a horrible feeling that I knew.

Mason emerged from the bedroom. "Nothing here, babe."

"All right. We're on our way. This job will only take a few minutes," Candy said. "Poor old absentminded red-haired lady went out and left the stove on. Happens all the time. No sign of arson. Just good-bye house."

That's what that grin was about. She had done this before, just as Smiley had suggested. And she'd been successful.

I said, "No one's going to believe that story."

"You'd be surprised what people will believe. Anyway, we'll be long gone and no one outside this room has any reason to connect us." She turned to Mason. "Let's get these two where they can't make any more trouble."

"Should we tie them up?" Mason gave a nervous glance at us. His normally smooth voice sounded a bit raspy.

"Nope. Nothing that will tell the investigators that their deaths weren't accidental. Too bad they got locked in by the brain-damaged old lady. She sends her little friends to the basement to get a jar of preserves and forgets they're down there, locks them in and leaves the house.

I said, "No one is going to believe that."

Candy sneered. "You can't imagine how easy it is to lead the police astray when old ladies are involved. It's almost comical. Of course, for you, it's tragic, really." She turned to Mason. "Hand me his gun, then get their cell phones. And take her bag too." It was obvious who was top dog in this relationship. I wondered if Mason—like me—had been deceived by Candy and if she was just using him as she used everyone.

With my phone in Mason's possession and a gun in my back, I followed Candy's orders and walked out of the apartment and down the stairs to the basement. Tyler was right behind me. I imagined he was feeling the barrel of Mason's gun in his back. There was no chance of escape. Mason shoved me forward. I barely managed to grab the railing. Tyler was pushed in behind me. As he stumbled on the stairs, the basement door closed behind us.

Mason said, "Do we really have to . . ."

Candy shouted out merrily, "Yes, we do. Remember rule one: don't leave witnesses. And you'd better decide whether you are with me or against me. As for you two, I'm locking you in now. Hope you don't mind the heat."

I heard the dead bolt engage and something else. Was that the key being tossed across the entrance floor? No chance of getting out now.

"And the dark," Candy called from the other side of the door. Her laugh faded as she left the building.

I gasped. "She turned off the light. The switch is in the entrance. I don't remember seeing another switch in the basement."

"That's bad."

"Right. And I thought Candy was just needy, but all along she was a murderous psychopath." I put my ear to the door. Silence. I assumed that Candy and Mason were gone.

"Let me see if I can get it open," Smiley said.

He heaved himself against the heavy wooden door. He tried again and again. "It won't budge," he said.

"No hope," I said, fighting my instincts and trying to keep calm. "It will be solid. And Karen hides her valuable books down here. She doesn't want anyone to find her treasures. Who'd suspect her of hiding them in a damp, buggy basement?"

He said, "We'd better get going if we can't get out this way. Maybe there's a light source somewhere down here."

We felt our way down the stairs. My heart was break-dancing now. There was no easy way out of the basement. "Be careful. This place is full of booby traps." It wasn't easy to stay calm. The pan of oil was probably reaching the boiling point on the top of the stove. How long before that pan caught fire?

"What's down here?" he said. "Another exit?"

"I don't think so. I never saw one. But there are windows on the side. Maybe we can get out through one of them," I whispered. Just in case.

I could feel the warmth of Smiley's arm as we leaned together and slowly descended. At the bottom of the stairs, he put his arms around me. "I'm sorry. I should have been able to stop them. I should have been able to protect you from this."

Jeez, he smelled good. You'd think my life would be flashing before my eyes, but no, I was too busy huffing the cop.

"Don't be sorry. It's my fault. I'm the one who first made the contact with that crazy killer. I did stupid things to recover a collection for Vera."

"I think we both did dumb things."

"Great. Tied for worst place."

He held me tighter. I didn't need that. I needed to think about the likelihood that I didn't have long to live. I needed to work on Houdini maneuvers to get out of there. I needed to kick at the doors and scramble to break windows. I did not need to be so aware that I was so close to Smiley and that he smelled like a fresh mountain stream. More important than the fact that we were completely unsuitable for each other, we had only a few minutes to live.

I employed some moves that I'd learned at an interpretative dance class—for credit, of course—and disentangled myself. "We have to get out of here."

"I'm so sorry," he said.

"Me too. Not as sorry as we'll both be if we burn to a crisp. Feel around. We need a hammer."

"Okay, but I'm not sorry. I wanted to put my arms around you and if not now, when? This could be our last chance."

"Look, we need to get out of here before we asphyxiate or burn. Whichever comes first."

"I know that. I am a police officer and I will get us out of here."

"You could see me roll my eyes if it wasn't so dark here."

"Trust me."

"Better if you trust me. You said it's your fault that we're here in the first place."

"Well, you're the one who can't mind her own—"

"Stop it."

"What?"

"Running your fingers on my neck. I told you—"

"I'm nowhere near your neck. What kind of a person do you think—?"

"Well, if you're not—" Then I knew it really was the

worst-case scenario. I was fighting for my life and simultaneously living through emotional turmoil *and* an arachnid
invasion. My arms flailed wildly in the darkness.

Smiley shouted, "Stop screaming and jumping around.
We need to work on getting out of here."

"But I hate spiders. I hate them. Help." I managed to get
a grip. Smiley was right. Work on how to get out. Don't
think about spiders. Or him. "Are you all right?" Smiley
said from a safe distance.

"Yes. We just need to get to one of the windows."

"Hurry. How long do you think it will take for that pan
of oil to ignite?"

"She set it up to accelerate a fire without looking like it
was deliberate. The pan was quite full. Maybe it won't catch
right away."

He said, "Yeah, well, once the fire starts, this old place
will go up in no time. After that we'll have a couple of
minutes. Tops."

"We need to get to the windows."

He said, "Where are the windows?"

"Stop pressing against me."

"Sorry, sorry. I can't see anything and I don't know how
to avoid you."

"Work it out. I'm thinking if we can knock a hole in a
window—"

"What window? Where?" Smiley sounded grouchy, not
like him at all, but the threat of death can do that to a person.
Forgivable.

I said, "There are at least two windows along the driveway
side of the house. If we find them and break the glass, one
of us can crawl out and get help." From my memory of the
size of the windows, I figured I would be the one crawling.

"Fine. Let's find them."

Not so easy in the dark. I said, "We have to get oriented."

Smiley said, "I just banged my knee on something. A dresser maybe?"

"There's a worktable in the middle of the room. With a ton of craft stuff on it. Right. So the wall with the windows visible from the driveway would be on our left. We were facing the front of the house as we came down the stairs and didn't turn."

"We don't have all the time in the world, so let's give that a try."

We felt our way, slowly, painstakingly, toward the far wall. It was a relief to feel the dank cement walls. "We're feeling for a window frame," he said.

"I know that. Please stop breathing on me."

"Believe me, I'm not trying to."

"I think the windows must be fairly high."

"I'm aware of—wait. I feel a frame!"

I moved my hand around the area where he seemed to be. Sure enough. A frame.

"So there are curtains covering the window. Karen was paranoid about people seeing what she had down here."

"Not so happy about that right now," he said.

"I hear you, but—yes! There's the curtain. Feel it?"

"And I'm yanking it off." That clatter that followed must have been the curtain rod hitting some empty paint cans, before landing on the packed earth floor. I couldn't see the cloud of dust from the decades-old curtain, but it stung my eyes and clogged my throat. Soon we were both coughing. Bad news indeed.

I gasped for air and tried to say, "We still can't see out. What's going on?"

"Bars," he said, before giving in to a hacking cough.

I felt. Sure enough. "Oh no."

"Oh yes. This window is barred."

"I didn't notice bars before. Of course, I wasn't looking for them. But anyway, we should be able to see outside. Oh, wait! There's something else blocking out the light on the other side of the bars, not just this incredibly dusty curtain."

"That has to be it," he said.

The Kelly family does not give up. "Let me see if I can find the lock on the bars." Too bad I wasn't quite tall enough to do that. No choice but to ask Smiley. "Can you feel a lock?"

There are not too many simple household locks that I couldn't open with the right tools. I chose not to mention that to him.

"Well?" I said after too much time had passed.

"Nothing. I can't feel a lock. I think it's been screwed into the frame."

"That's bad."

"Real bad."

"But what goes in must come out. If we can find the place where it's screwed in, we can unscrew it."

"With what?"

"Do you have a screwdriver on you?"

Who has a screwdriver on them? I didn't have my lock picks either. There was probably something to use on the worktable, but who could see it?

I said, "Why are you making that noise?"

"I'm trying to squeeze my hands through the bars, so I can get rid of the paper or cardboard or whatever it is. But they're too big, or the bars are too close together."

"Let me try. My hands are smaller."

"Don't get stuck," he said. "We need to be able to move around."

I may have snorted. "And trip over things?"

I heard an "oof!" And an "ouch." "Right," he said.

The good news was that I was able to squeeze my hands between two of the bars. The bad news was it wasn't paper on the windows. I could have ripped paper and pulled it through. No, this window had to be covered with a piece of cardboard and it wasn't going to come without a fight. I struggled and pulled. Just made things worse. "Okay. I don't know what I'm thinking. It won't come in. Easier to push it out," I said. "What can we use that's narrow enough to fit through the bars, but strong enough to break the glass? Is there a hammer there?"

"You mean is there a hammer here in the pitch-dark?"

"Yes, that's what I mean. Is there?"

"Not that I can feel. We need something long and narrow and tough enough to push through the cardboard and break the glass."

I moved backward and started an avalanche of stuff. I went flying forward with a wail. I banged my knee on something hard and jagged and scraped my palms as I landed on the earth floor. An image of the cold packed earth in a grave flooded my mind.

Smiley was right there. Speed of light sort of thing, not that we had any light. He did his best to help me up, inhibited by my own attempts. We grunted and pushed. I may have snarled.

"What happened?"

"I must have tripped over the stupid curtain rod. Wait— the curtain rod!"

He said, "We have to do this together. I don't know how sturdy this rod is, but if we both grab tight and lunge together, we might be able to do it."

Lunging together sounded like it might have its downside, but I agreed. We managed to grip it and to practice a bit.

"On the count of three," he said and we lunged.

"Let's try it again."

After five lunges, we felt the pop. If you've ever broken a piece of glass you know how easy it is to break it when you don't want to, but if you ever do really need to shatter glass, that's a different story.

There was the satisfying crash as the glass hit the asphalt driveway. The cardboard flopped out on top of the glass.

It was dark out already, but there was enough light from the streetlight in front of the Cozy Corpse to dimly illuminate the section of the basement closest to the window.

Our eyes met. "We're still stuck because of those bars," he said.

"But now we can see enough to find something to pry them off." We glanced at the curtain rod, but it was now beyond use for anything, let alone a crowbar.

"Let's check those screws," he said, peering at the frame. "I'll try to find something to use for that." A second later he said, "It's still too dark to see over here."

"There are matches on the shelf. And there are candles. I'll light one."

"We don't need more fire. Why don't we just yell for help?"

"Because . . . You're right. We can try to attract attention. Especially with the crabby neighbor. He was outside when I got here."

"Help! Fire! Please help!" We both yelled at the top of our lungs. "Help! Call the fire department! Call the police! Please!"

A man's voice came back. "Help yourself." Then we heard the door slam.

What now? What would Wimsey do? He certainly wouldn't engage in an argument. Way too smooth for that. On the other hand, Wimsey wasn't here and I wasn't sure how happy I'd be if I was in this situation with someone who was wearing a top hat and a monocle. Just seemed wrong, that's all. Wimsey also had his "man" Bunter with him as an assistant. Smiley wasn't much of an assistant. He wanted to run the show.

"How can we get their attention?"

"I told you he was nasty."

"There must be some way."

"It would probably take a Molotov cocktail tossed in their yard."

"What?"

"That's it! We can do that."

"That's an incendiary device, Jordan."

Suddenly he was very cop-like.

"I know it goes against what you stand for, but dying down here in this spider hole goes against everything I stand for too."

"Point taken. What do we need?"

"Something flammable, a rag and the matches. That should get their attention."

"Sounds like you've done this before."

"Absolutely, I'm just that kind of girl," I snapped defensively.

"No need to yell. It's just that you know how to make one." He raised his hands in surrender.

"Are you serious? Everyone who's ever seen an action movie could figure it out. Stop arguing and let's find the right kind of bottle."

"What's the right kind of bottle?"

"I don't know. Big enough with a narrow neck? I think that's the key. Let the pressure build up. There were wine bottles on the craft table. And grab the Mason jar with matches from the shelf."

"I got the matches. And how about this one?" he said, brandishing what looked like an empty wine bottle with a candle in it.

"Too wide for the bars, I think,"

"There are others. This one's better. More slender. But we better double-check it." A quick test showed that we could fit the bottle through the bars.

"Perfect," I said. "Let's pick up the pace. Gasoline?"

Of course Karen had not been foolish enough to keep gasoline in her firetrap cellar. Just paint stuff and . . . Yes!

"Turpentine!"

We yelled it simultaneously, which was a weird form of togetherness.

"Now what?" I said.

"You're the one who knows how to make these things."

"Obviously I just know what I've seen in the movies."

"Okay. Grab a rag."

"I don't see any rags—"

"The curtains!"

The ripping noise was almost drowned out by the coughing racket as we ripped the curtains into strips, stirring up a storm of dust.

"Let's just hope for the best," I said, probably the first time anyone has said that before tossing an IED.

He said, "We have to light it outside and make sure there's no chance it can bounce back on us."

"Well, I know that. My hands will fit through the bars. I just need to be calm enough to throw it at the target."

"This looks like a chair. It's sturdy enough for you to stand on."

"Now to figure out where to throw it, not that we have a lot of choice. That garbage can looks good to me, and it will attract the neighbors' attention."

"And it's not close enough to the house to set it on fire."

"They'll call the cops in a New York minute, maybe before they call the fire department. Let's do this thing."

Pulse racing, I held the bottle and he lit the trailing fabric.

"Here goes nothing," I said, sounding like my uncles just before one of their "outings."

The arc of the bottle with its flaming tail was glorious to watch and, indeed, my uncles would have been proud. It soared through the air and landed with a splat in the closest bag of leaves by the near edge of the neighbors' yard. Wimsey couldn't have done better with all that cricket playing.

"Good going," Smiley said. "I'll probably lose my job over arson."

"But maybe not your life. Anyway, blame it on me. I led you astray."

His round, pleasant face hardened. "That will never happen. It's on me."

"Oh, for Pete's sake—"

The *whoomph* of the leaves put an end to the conversation. Seconds later, the nasty neighbors banged open their back door. He started yelling and swearing. She screamed long and loud.

"Call 911, you stupid woman," he shouted.

The scream stopped abruptly.

Smiley said, "If we're lucky, it will only take a couple of minutes for the first responders to get here. We might make it."

"The waiting might kill me. I'm going to check and see if I can find where Karen hides her books. Maybe I can save the Hemingway and with any luck the Sayers."

"Don't be crazy! There's no time for that. We need to stay by the window."

"One minute," I said, stumbling toward the far wall. I was

pretty sure that's where Karen hid her valuables. Her house was about to be engulfed, but if there was an opportunity to save her Hemingway and Vera's Sayers books, I was going to take that minute to do it. There was no chance that reinforcements would arrive that fast. The light was still too dim to see well, but I felt around. Sure enough, there was a metal case tucked inside the huge old stockpot near the shelf where the matches had been.

Of course, the box was locked and I had no picks.

"Hurry up," Tyler shouted, "or I'm going to drag you back."

I was starting to push my luck. I grabbed the metal box and managed a stumbling return. Luckily, it wasn't very heavy. Enough for about four books, I thought.

"I can't believe you did that," he said, running his hands through his hair. "If the house goes up, the floors are going to collapse and you need to be near a solid outside wall if you have any chance at all. You need to stay right here."

A minute later the shriek of sirens cut through the air. We peered through the window as the first firefighters trooped down the driveway, clomping along with their heavy bunking pants and carrying the hose for the leaf fire.

Of course, with the neighbors bellowing and the thunk of boots, there was so much noise that no one heard us shouting for help. Through the racket we thought we could hear the angry neighbor giving the cops an earful and shrieking about where Karen could be found, as if poor Karen would ever do anything like this. I thought I heard a "calm down, ma'am."

We kept shouting. My throat was beginning to hurt by the time two Grandville police officers started down the driveway.

Of course, we needed to snag the cops before they got to

the back door. I teetered on the chair while Smiley on tiptoes was tall enough. We both hollered. I tried to grab at pant legs, but no success. "Help! Down here! Hurry!"

The pair turned and the closest got down on one knee and peered in. "Officer Tyler Dekker. Harrison Falls Police Force," Smiley said. "My friend and I are trapped, locked in. The perpetrators set a fire on the second floor. Go through the back entrance and open the basement door on your left. It's bolted on the outside. If you can't find the key, the firefighters are going to need axes or the battering ram."

The cop frowned. "I think I know you. Both of you. Wasn't there some breaking-and-entering issue here in the spring?"

"A misunderstanding," I said. "Maybe we can discuss it when we're not locked in a burning building."

Smiley added, "What she said."

I wasn't sure what they'd remembered about that encounter, but let's just say this wasn't the first time Smiley and I pulled a fast one on his colleagues. Job one was to get out of the basement. Job two would be avoiding charges about the Molotov business.

I said, "This house is ancient and it's full of old paper. If it catches fire it will burn in seconds and the whole street will probably go up."

Smiley said, "Tell fire. We could have a flashover situation here. Accelerants on a stove. Call gas and power and clear the area."

The first officer headed for the back door. We heard him calling it in. At least he'd believed us. The second officer headed to talk to the firefighters. Next the sound of the glass in the back door splintering. The first officer came out again, moving quickly and gesturing to his partner. "I can smell smoke from the upstairs. We need to get them out." The rest was lost in the confusion. Whatever it was, it worked. Two firefighters redeployed to our side of the driveway and lumbered for the back door.

"Hey! What the hell!" the nasty neighbor bellowed.

I clutched the metal box to my chest as we rushed over to the stairs. From behind the door at the top, we heard, "Stand well back!"

We stood at the foot of the stairs until the basement door was shattered with the axe.

"You first," Smiley said, pushing me ahead.

CHAPTER FIFTEEN

❖

I DIDN'T ARGUE. I scrambled up and out to the backyard. The smoke was acrid now, choking us even outside.
Was it just the bag of leaves, now smoking and smoldering,
or had the worst happened upstairs?

As smoke began billowing down the stairs, a firefighter,
burly in his bunking gear, started to guide us away from the
house.

"You'll pay for this!" the neighbor shouted as we crossed
the street.

Smiley walked back toward him. "Not as much as you'll
pay for refusing to call for help when people were trapped
in a burning building. See you in court."

All along the street, people were spilling out of their
homes. Some stared. Some wept. Smiley returned and held
me tight. I won't lie. I liked the embrace. I don't cry often,
but as we stood and watched the Cozy Corpse go up in
flames, my face was wet with tears. "Karen's lost everything.
Her home and her business."

"You're alive," he whispered and tightened his hold on me. The box dug into my chest. "That's what matters now."

All I could concentrate on was *Don't kiss the cop. You cannot kiss the cop. Whatever you do, do not kiss the cop.*

Kellys do not kiss cops. Nor do Binghams.

Ever. Under any circumstances. Even if they think this is their last day on earth.

I kissed the cop.

All those "don't" thoughts flew away. Vanished. All I was thinking was . . . Well, I wasn't thinking, really. Just folding into reassuring arms, soft lips, breathing in the dust from each other's hair. Every rule was broken.

Was it the lure of the taboo that caused me to forget I'm allergic to the police?

I wasn't sure when I became conscious of the TV truck and camera crew. But it wasn't soon enough.

"It's over," he said.

I shook myself and pushed away. "But it's not over. What am I doing? I have to go save Karen."

"But Karen wasn't home. She's all right," Smiley said.

"She's not safe yet."

"But you're safe and you're alive. Plus you're not so bad for a woman who keeps almost getting me killed," he added, holding me tighter.

"And you're not so bad either. For a cop." I sniffed and held him back.

We watched as the police officers slowly approached. Now we were out of the fire and back into the frying pan.

What was the matter with me? "There's no time for making out. We have to stop Candy and Mason." I pulled away just before the cops reached us.

"You've been traumatized," Smiley answered, reasonably.

"They think she has the book and—"

"What?"

"They know she's at Lucky's place. We need to warn her before they find her."

"These officers are going to want statements from us."

"We can't afford the time to be interviewed."

"No choice. If we leave now, we'll be suspects immediately."

Even though I've done my best to stay on right side of the law, I found myself saying, "Maybe you can suggest that Candy must have thrown the Molotov cocktail."

He shook his head. "You want me to *lie*?"

"I know there will probably be a price to be paid for doing that—although it saved our bacon—and maybe they'll even lay charges, and I'm willing to pay the price, but right now, we need to find Karen."

"There will be forensic evidence and we are going to tell the truth eventually."

"Fine. You stay, explain everything to them and I'll go find Karen."

"You can't. You *need* to give a statement."

"I'm going."

"We have to tell them what happened. Those perps took my weapon. I have to account for that. That's more than just a little paperwork. The Burton police are going to insist on a debriefing."

"You talk to the police. Tell them what happened. Make sure they get people over to Michael Kelly's Fine Antiques right away. Get a phone and let the Harrison Falls police know. Candy and Mason are going after Karen and Uncle Lucky. I have to stop them." I sprinted away from him and toward the Saab. Luckily it hadn't been blocked in by the fire equipment. And just as lucky, I had put my keys in my pocket instead of my purse. Smiley caught up to me. "We'll send the Harrison Falls police. We just escaped with our lives. These people are just too dangerous. Wait for the cops. Wait a second, don't go anywhere." He turned to one of the uniformed officers who had helped us out and who seemed to be keeping a close eye on us. "Look, this officer is going to let you use his phone. You don't need to leave. Call them. Tell them to be careful." He must have been feeling his promising career vaporize.

My hands shook as I keyed in Uncle Lucky's number. Straight to message. In Uncle Lucky's case, that's merely a beep. Uncle Mick didn't answer either, and Karen's cell phone was not available. I found myself hyperventilating. I tried the special number. No answer there either. By now, I was shaking all over. Smiley wrapped his arms around me once again. It helped but not enough.

From across the street we heard a series of long cracks and then there was a glowing wave of sparks and embers. The house began to collapse. The crowd gave a collective gasp and seemed to surge. That was such a bad idea. The police pushed them back. I thrust the officer's phone back to Smiley and jumped in my car before Smiley could try to stop me. I tucked the metal box under the seat.

"And after you call your colleagues, please call Vera for me. Right away."

"Call your boss?"

"I know you have her number. Tell her what's happened. Tell her I am going to Uncle Mick's and Uncle Lucky's because they are in danger. Tell her to send her gardener over."

"Her gardener? What—?"

"Trust me. She has to send the gardener. Has to. He's very resourceful. And he will know where to go." I didn't mention that he was Uncle Kev. Even after our close encounter, I didn't want Smiley knowing too much about Vera's gardener, and I sure didn't want Smiley making any connection with the crazy man who beaned him with the shovel. Kelly habits die hard.

"Call police. Call Vera. Get the gardener," I said as I pulled away in the Saab.

"You can't take on these killers on your own," he yelled. "I don't care about the rules. Aw hell. I'm coming." Or at least he said something like that, carried away on the wind.

I BROKE EVERY speed law getting back to Harrison Falls. Near the shop, I saw the navy Tahoe and the silver Audi. My chest tightened at the sight. The cars were empty. Candy and Mason were already there. Was I too late to save Karen? And what about my uncles? They were very resourceful, but they wouldn't have been expecting visitors with guns.

I parked in an out-of-the-way spot, raced toward the shop and slipped around the side to the back. The small shed near the rear door had always been my point of entry as a child. At last the secret parts of the Kelly quarters were going to pay off. I wasn't quite as limber as I'd been in my teens, but I managed to climb on the portable storage bin and heave myself onto the shed and approach the window that opened into what had been my bedroom closet, now Uncle Kev's bedroom closet. The window still opened easily. That was the whole idea. I slid into the closet, leaving it dark. I managed not to yelp with pain when I banged my shin on something on the floor. Uncle Kev's beer cooler? Next I slid on a T-shirt and hit the wall. Thanks, Uncle Kev. Still hanging up your clothes on the floor at your age? I held my breath. Had anyone heard?

I took a few seconds to feel around in the drawer of the bedside table, in case Uncle Kev kept a spare burner phone there. That is another Kelly tradition. Sure enough, my hand closed around a small and most likely untraceable phone.

No one would call this phone, so that was good. Clutching it tightly, I tiptoed out into the hallway.

Everything was quiet, except for a sad snuffling sound that I took to be Walter. I would have expected a hum of printers as Uncle Mick worked on his latest scheme and whatever sounds Uncle Lucky would make on whatever his project was. But I heard nothing. Silence except for Walter. Sad little Walter sniffing and snuffling.

That didn't make sense. There was no way Mick or Lucky would just leave their new object of adoration alone and neglected. Couldn't happen. Not with that level of infatuation. Walter would have to have a dog sitter. Therefore, something was wrong. Uncle Mick and Uncle Lucky were indisposed, as they used to say, mostly about colleagues who were doing hard time.

I stopped to listen again. Nothing except the sad snuffle and a sorrowful whine. I figured that was Cobain. I clicked a small lever and slid a section of wall outward. Pulling it closed behind me, I tiptoed down the hidden staircase. I hadn't explored these special Kelly spots since my childhood. I used to enjoy the Nancy Drew feeling, but now I felt only fear for my uncles.

I keyed in Uncle Mick's number and waited. The phone rang on and on and on. There was no way Uncle Mick would not answer the phone. Unless he couldn't. Unless he was . . . I couldn't let myself think about that. Next, I tried Uncle Lucky's number. It too rang on and on.

Nothing could happen to my uncles. I couldn't imagine life without them. I felt a wave of hatred for Candy. For her greed, her duplicity and her murderous tendencies. I had to put that bad emotion to work.

At the bottom of the staircase is a small peephole—charmingly disguised in a vintage clock on the kitchen side—where I used to peer at my uncles as a small child. Uncle Mick would always be trying variations on favorite foods, like fried Mars bars, which added to the fun. I felt tears sting my eyes as I tried to crouch low enough to see through the peephole.

Uncle Mick was sitting on the floor, feet straight out, silver duct tape on his mouth and securing his hands and feet. His ginger hair stood on end and his face was redder than the hair. I almost gasped out loud at the sight. That would have been a mistake because Candy was sprawled on one of the dinette chairs, a smirk on her face. The gun in her hand was pointed straight at Mick.

If she took her eye off him for a nanosecond, Mick would have sprung across the room at her. But she didn't appear to be letting down her guard.

Where was Uncle Lucky? And Karen? Were they in Uncle Lucky's rooms? Were they also prisoners? I had to find out. Carefully, I crept back upstairs, fighting the urge to cough from the dust in the staircase.

Candy would be listening, waiting for someone to come and rescue Mick.

Nancy Drew might have been jealous of the house with two hidden staircases. Even Agatha Christie might have been impressed. Dorothy L. Sayers was a bit more cerebral, but it was her books that had landed us in this predicament. If Karen hadn't sold the Sayers firsts to Randolph, we'd be having a normal life at this point rather than facing death at the hands of a sociopath for hire. I tiptoed into the hallway, again closing the wall section, and into the linen closet.

From there, another panel, and I began my descent down the second, even more rickety stairs to Lucky's living room. His room also had a matching peephole, hidden in Uncle Lucky's vintage seventies' stereo system. I bent and peered out. I was startled to see that the sitting room had been moved around. The rug was rolled up and the furniture pulled to one side. A roll of duct-tape and the scissors sat on the coffee table. Karen was crouched on the floor. Even from where I was hiding, with my limited view through the peephole, I could tell she was shaking. Lucky strained his mighty arms against the duct tape. Normally, Lucky was the largest and mildest of my uncles. Tonight, I could feel his anger rolling off him in waves.

Karen whimpered, "I don't remember. I keep telling you, I don't remember things. I don't remember being given books. We tried to find them but—"

A gruff voice said, "Shut up. I told you to shut up. When you're ready to tell us, then you talk. You have ten minutes left or I shoot the hulk here."

Who was she talking to? I couldn't see anyone. Then Mason's Blundstones came into view. Pacing. Nervous, unstable Mason.

By this time I had concluded that Candy—obviously the boss—was keeping Mick and Lucky separate, so they couldn't communicate with each other or collaborate in an escape. A smart move on her part, but something that could work for me. I figured the nervously pacing Mason was the weak link, but on the downside, he had two prisoners instead of one.

While Mason was yelling at Karen, I knocked twice, softly, on the wall. Karen was sobbing, so Mason didn't hear.

Uncle Lucky turned his head slowly to the stereo, and I

saw the almost imperceptible nod. If I had a chance to tackle Mason, Lucky would be right there hurtling through the air.

I was now at the point where it didn't matter if the cops burst in and found whatever project Mick and Lucky had going. It only mattered that they would live.

I knew if Karen did remember what she had done with the books, that would be the end of all three of them. After all that time, hoping and urging Karen to remember things, now I prayed she wouldn't.

I crept back up the stairs and into the closet again. Smiley was without his cell phone, so I dialed Lance and asked him deal with the police. I kept it short. The less I spoke, the less likely that the two downstairs would hear me. I explained what was going on. "Let the police know that there are hostages and two armed criminals inside. One hostage is in the kitchen directly in back of the shop and two are in the room on the side. Karen is one of them. Tell them to be careful with her. No sirens. If Candy hears police, she could shoot them and run. I have to go."

Lance shouted into the phone, "Jordan, no! Wait for the police."

"Sorry, she's given them ten minutes. I can't wait."

"You'll get yourself killed!"

"Just make sure the cops get here in time."

"Be careful. You know how I feel about you."

No time to think about that. I crept from the closet back to the hallway and along to the linen closet with the subtly hidden door that led down to Uncle Lucky's broom closet. Uncle Lucky kept the space clear for ease of getting in or out. This small, neat closet led to the hidden stairs and also to a door outside. Always thinking, the Kellys.

I feared for happy-go-lucky Mick and for Lucky, who

had finally found happiness with Karen, and for Walter. If anything happened to any one of the three, I would never be able to forgive myself.

Of course, there's a peephole in the broom closet door. Mason's back was to me. I channeled my anger toward the man with the gun. And that was easy. I couldn't hesitate even though I am not the kind of person who attacks another human.

Slowly, I let the door open an inch. Naturally Lucky kept it well oiled. We were getting close to the ten-minute mark. I frantically searched for something I could use as a weapon against the vile Mason. Nothing but a broom, a mop and a bucket. I was out of time and still short a weapon. The only thing I had going for me was the element of surprise. I lunged from behind and dropped the bucket over Mason's head. Uncle Lucky leapt like a giant ballet dancer and used his bulk to bring Mason down onto the rolled-up carpet without a sound beyond the *ooof* of Mason's breath being knocked out of him. I used the scissors to free Lucky's hands and feet. I grabbed the gun as Lucky let Mason experience being restrained and gagged by duct tape. For added security, he unfurled the rug and rolled Mason in it. I figured it wouldn't kill him, but he'd never get out of it on his own. I would have been happy to hand the weapon to Uncle Lucky, but he was bending over Karen and picking her up. "Shhh," he whispered.

We were thinking as one Kelly when we hustled though the broom cupboard in less than a minute, Karen in Uncle Lucky's arms. As we exited, we could hear Candy shout.

I said, "Get Karen to a safe place. We have to go in for Mick. Candy is vicious. He doesn't know anything and she has nothing to gain by keeping him alive. I'll go in through the shop. You take the back stairs."

Lucky nodded and hurried away. I didn't wait for a

response. I hoped the police had arrived. I would have been very glad of reinforcements at this stage, but Mick's life was too close to the line to delay.

I crept around the edges of the shop, careful not to trip over the piles of objects strewn here and there. Too bad there were no peepholes from the shop to the apartment. The door was opened a half inch. I peered through. I could see Uncle Mick, but not Candy. She was probably distracted, looking for Mason and, if she found him, unrolling him out of the carpet. Maybe she was pistol-whipping him as she went. Time was short for Uncle Mick. I dashed through the door, keeping low and leaving the shop door open behind me. I hoped for enough time to get the panel to the hidden staircase open. I couldn't lift Uncle Mick. He is, as we say, a man of substance. I grabbed a serrated kitchen knife and sawed through his duct tape bonds.

"Push," I whispered as we made it through the opening, pulling the false wall closed behind us. The space that was tight for one was now painfully crowded with a man of substance, a hyperventilating adult woman, a snuffling Walter and a gangly Cobain who kept trying to climb into my arms. If Candy heard us, we wouldn't be breathing for long.

I was absolutely sure that she'd hear us trying to escape through one of the upstairs exits. I peered through the hole. She was back, glancing around the room, checking under the table. She actually scratched her head. Could she hear Walter snuffling?

I was surprised she couldn't hear my heartbeat. I had a weapon in my hand but of course I had no idea how to use it. She stared at the slightly open door to the antique shop and then turned her head to the visible stairs. Which way would she go? Whichever, we would be taking the other.

After a couple of seconds, she pivoted and headed for

the shop. That was our chance to get out. But of course, it was not to be. Boys will be boys.

Walter couldn't resist talking back to the mean lady. Cobain added his two cents.

With a reverse pivot, Candy was now facing our hiding place. While our staircase was hidden, the thin fake wall wouldn't protect us from a spray of bullets. Being a dog, Walter didn't need a peephole to know that she was coming for us. He barked all the way up the stairs.

We Kellys are lovers, not fighters, and we will always pick the path of least bullets.

I collided with Uncle Mick as we crashed up the stairs in the dark. I heard the wall splinter as the first bullets came through.

It would have been good if Walter had stopped the racket. The sound of the gunfire just revved him further. Still, the gun made enough noise to drown out our departure and probably Walter's protest. Mick picked him up.

How long before Candy figured we were upstairs? We made it to the top and scuttled down the hallway to the linen closet. We thundered down those stairs to Uncle Lucky's sitting room again, then we heard her in the hallway.

"Might as well come out, if you want to live."

Not likely we'd fall for that. Walter helpfully yipped back at her. It wouldn't take long before she found the opening in the linen closet. All we needed was a minute head start.

Mick was breathing like a locomotive when we made it to the downstairs utility closet and fumbled to open the door into the side yard. We staggered along the side of the house into the crisp October evening and into the view of a bouquet of police cars. Tyler Dekker was in the first one. He must have charmed his way through his statement.

I raced toward him. He sprang—and that is not too strong a word—from the car and grabbed me in a bear hug. "Candy's still inside. And armed."

If the scramble to escape from Candy didn't kill Uncle Mick, the sight of me in Smiley's arms might do him in. Sure enough, he was bent over, hands on his knees, his face as red as the Heinz ketchup he loved so much.

Police in riot gear were assembling outside the house. Candy was in for a real reception if she emerged and a worse one if she didn't.

She had found the secret staircases. Did we need to reveal the Kelly family secret hideouts to the police? It was a high price to pay to get her out of there, but I saw no choice.

Again, Smiley wrapped his arms around me. I looked to the side and I did a little double take. A crowd had gathered. Some of them looked familiar. Vera sat stone-faced and silent in her wheelchair, arms crossed. The signora seemed to be dancing a hysterical little jig. Uncle Kev moved like a blur toward Mick and grabbed him in a bear hug, lifting him right off his feet. As I moved into view, the signora shouted something and I swear that Vera grinned. Past them at the edge of the crowd I caught a glimpse of Lance hovering.

The police were holding back the crowd as teams prepared to storm the building. I moved to meet Lance.

He wasn't smiling. He approached me slowly and without his usual twinkle. He thrust a bag of books into my arms. The Sayers books.

He said, "Judging by what I saw on TV, I guess our date's off tonight. Here are the books. Your secret's still safe with me."

Oh no. I had really hoped our kiss wouldn't have made the news coverage. I opened my mouth too late. Lance slipped through the crowd and vanished.

A phalanx of cops moved forward. The door to the shop disintegrated as the SWAT team entered.

As I joined the crowd of police, onlookers and relatives, Vera wheeled forward, grimly. I straightened my back as she approached.

"Miss Bingham," she said.

"I'm sorry. I did my best to get your collection back and—"

She raised a hand to silence me. "I was remiss."

What?

She continued. "Your Uncle Kevin has been speaking to us. I realize now that your life and Karen Smith's life and your uncles' lives as well were in jeopardy. Although he didn't say as much, I must acknowledge that I pushed you into a dangerous situation to satisfy my desire to possess my collection again."

"Officer Dekker was almost killed too."

She glowered. This apology probably wasn't coming easy to her. Apparently, I'd gotten all that was coming. Lesson learned: don't push your luck with Vera.

I said, "I appreciate what you're saying, but of course there was no way for you to know where the search would lead."

She had pressured me into a dangerous situation, but I was my own woman and had to admit, I could have stood my ground a bit better. If she could manage that apology, then I could be gracious.

I hoped like hell that the metal box actually did contain the missing three books from her Sayers collection.

"IT WAS VERY kind of Vera to offer her guest room," Karen said, the next day. She was bundled up on the love seat in my cozy garret and starting to get her color back after her ordeal. It had been worth the two story climb to get her there. The signora had already arrived with hot chocolate and delicious pastries. Karen could have some recovery time at Van Alst House, leaving Lucky and Mick to start dealing with the damage to the Kelly "homestead."

"Open the box," Karen said. "I can't wait any longer. I hope the smoke didn't damage them."

"Me too."

"I'm glad we can do this together," she said.

"Yeah me too, although we're running out of places to hang out together. Let's hope Van Alst House doesn't burn down or get riddled with bullets."

"I sure hope the police release the crime scene soon. Lucky is very distressed."

"Shame. I guess it's not a surprise anymore that he was renovating his place to make a love nest for the two of you."

Karen nodded. "After losing my home and my business and almost being killed yesterday, I could go my whole life without another surprise."

"Hard to believe that all that happened. Seems surreal now that we're safe." I eyed Karen for signs of fragility. "I am so sorry about everything that happened. You seem to be taking it in stride." I was worried that it hadn't all sunk in.

"It's only stuff, Jordan. I'm happy to be alive and now I have a future with Lucky." She leaned over and squeezed my hand. "And you escaped too. I couldn't help noticing you and Officer Dekker are, um, getting along very well."

I changed the subject to one we both agreed on. "Did you ever think you'd be so happy to see two people led away in handcuffs? I was almost sorry they didn't try to resist arrest."

"But we got the Sayers books back."

I paused to think about Randolph for a minute. "I wonder if Randolph also made it. Or if . . ."

"We may never know. Try not to think about it. Let's make sure the collection is all here and unharmed."

I was overwhelmed with relief when I opened that box and found the missing volumes. "They're all here. The three Sayers books. The Hemingway. And your two Edith Wharton firsts."

"If you hadn't been on the ball, they would have been lost in the fire."

"But they weren't. Let's make sure they're in good enough shape to make Vera happy, and while we're at it, we should try to figure out why Candy and Mason thought they were worth killing over."

Karen and I pored over the Sayers books, flipping through the pages gently. They didn't smell like smoke. But there was another odor I couldn't quite place. They had made it through pretty much unscathed, except for a bit of damage to the spine of *The Nine Tailors* from being thrown across the room. There were no obvious answers when we finished.

Karen shook her head. "It's very strange. The three Sayers books are collectible and in great shape, reasonably expensive but not . . ."

"I know what you're saying. I don't understand why Candy and Mason were so desperate to get them. There are Beanie Babies that would get a better price. But at least Vera will be satisfied."

CHAPTER SIXTEEN

***

A PPARENTLY VERA DIDN'T do satisfied.
"Miss Bingham," she said in her best voice of doom
as I slowly deflated in the conservatory later that morning.
She was closely examining the Sayers collection as Karen
and I perched on the edge of our chairs, holding our breath.

"Yes?"

"I believe you said the collection was in the same condition as when it vanished from the safety of my library." She
shot Karen a dirty look, possibly thinking about billing her
for her stay.

"That's right except for the slight damage to the spine of
The Nine Tailors, which I already mentioned to you."

"No, not that. This." She held open *The Unpleasantness
at the Bellona Club.*

"I don't see what's wrong."

"Water damage. Can you not see the buckling here on
page sixty-four?"

I leaned forward. She was right. Not that anyone else

would have noticed the minute damage on the inside margin of the page. What a strange place for water damage. How could water get in there and miss the rest of the page? Smoke damage, I could see, but where would the water come from? When Karen left with the three books, they were safely in her bag.

"How could that have happened?"

"A better question, Miss Bingham, is why is there water damage on all three?" She pointed to *Clouds of Witness* and *Have His Carcase.*

I picked up *Clouds of Witness.*

Vera said, "It's on page sixty-four."

Sure enough. The same kind of mark. The same page. A long, skinny rectangle of rippled paper.

"And observe *Have His Carcase.*"

I sighed. Of course, it also had a long, thin, rectangular wrinkly bit. "What about the others? Is there any water damage there?"

"Lucky for you there wasn't."

So how did the same type of damage get on the same page in three different books? I stared at the three books. The marks were similar, but not identical. One short. One medium. One longer.

"But the books didn't go near any water. They were perfectly safe once Randolph gave them to me," Karen said.

Vera said, "And it certainly didn't happen when they were in my possession."

I said, "It can't be a coincidence that these were the books Randolph gave to the Karen. And it looks so uniform. Almost as if it was done deliberately."

"Ridiculous. Who would damage a book deliberately? Only a fool or a child."

Candy and Mason didn't have the books, and Kev, our

resident fool, never got near them. There were no children involved. If there had been, I could have seen it. How many times had I doodled in the margins of a dusty book from Uncle Mick's shop? But this wasn't doodling. It was something else. I picked up *The Unpleasantness at the Bellona Club* again and sniffed page sixty-four. I was rewarded by a sharp and pungent scent. I passed the book to Karen.

"Do you smell that? We noticed it in the box. Do you think it could be vinegar?"

Her eyes widened. "I do. But why?"

Vera roared. "Food substance? On my books?"

At the roar, the signora swept in from the kitchen, clutching some freshly cut herbs. "You hungry?"

"Travesty," Vera muttered.

"Why indeed? Why would someone put vinegar in a book?"

"And only on page sixty-four."

Something tickled my brain. "When I was a kid, Uncle Lucky showed me how to make invisible ink out of vinegar and lemon. You could use either one. It was a lot of fun. All you had to do was hold it up to the heat of a lightbulb to reveal the hidden writing. We would leave secret messages for each other."

Vera barked, "Who would dare write a message in my books?"

"Randolph!" Karen and I said it together.

I added. "He was desperate, a prisoner. He knew you'd look closely at those books. That must have been why he gave them to you."

Karen said, "But how do we see what the message says?"

"We need an incandescent bulb for the light and the heat. We've changed most of our bulbs here to CFLs, but I think Vera has some in her study."

I picked up the three books and took off down the endless hallway to the study, with Karen at my heels and Vera gaining in her wheelchair. "Miss Bingham! Do not damage my books further!"

I ran faster. I needed to do this. In the study, I flipped on the desk lamp and held page sixty-four of *The Unpleasantness at the Bellona Club* up to it. Slowly, the paper browned and a string of numbers was revealed.

Vera squawked. I lifted *Have His Carcase*. Page sixty-four. Paper browned. A shorter string of numbers.

Vera said, "This is unacceptable!"

Karen said, "She has to. A man might have died because of those numbers. And Jordan, Tyler Dekker, her uncles and I almost did too."

A grunt. I took it to be permission and held up the last book, *Clouds of Witness*. Four numbers this time.

We had our answer. Of course, we didn't know what the question was. What did these numbers mean?

We copied them down so Vera could get her precious books back. Karen and I stared at them.

I said, "Is it some kind of code?"

Karen said, "Not my strength."

"Mine either."

Vera rolled closer and glared at the three groups of numbers. "Obviously, twelve digits is a bank account number."

I said, "But what about the others?"

"Really, Miss Bingham. The nine digits must be a routing number for the financial institution. The four could be anything. A check number. A PIN."

I said, "But why would Randolph, assuming it's Randolph, write banking information in a book?"

Vera said, "My books."

Karen said, "He was having memory trouble. I know what that's like. You have to write down everything or you'll lose it. And you might lose it anyway."

It was starting to become clear. "How about this? He was afraid he'd forget these numbers. He couldn't write them down and leave them where Delilah and Mason would find them. So he gave them to Karen. It was obvious he'd taken a shine to her and felt he could trust her to take care of the books."

Karen laughed. "But not enough to tell me what was in them. I wonder how much money there was. Maybe I'm not so trustworthy after all. I did just lose my house and business."

I said, "But you did find true love. That's good because I think there's a ton of money. Candy told me that Randolph was a mob accountant who skimmed a lot of cash from some dangerous people who wanted their money back and Randolph dead. So of course, he'd have known how to move that money around. Mason and Delilah must have assumed he couldn't remember the account information. There'd be no way to get the money without it. That's why Mason said he'd roughed up Randolph."

"Even if Mason roughed him up, the stress would just make it harder for him to remember."

"So we have these numbers, but no way to find out what bank they belong to."

Vera said, "Of course you can find out. You have everything you need. The transit number is a matter of public record. That will identify the bank. With the account number and the PIN, what else would you need?"

I said, "Right. You could do it online."

Vera said, "It shouldn't be difficult. The important thing is that I have my Sayers books back."

My mouth dropped open. I said, "Yeah that's the most important thing, all right."

She had the grace to look abashed. "And of course, I am appreciative, Miss Bingham. And Miss Smith."

"And you're glad we're still alive, along with Officer Dekker and my uncles."

"Indeed."

It was as good as it was going to get.

And what would we do with this mob money even if we did get access to it?

Karen's home and shop had been insured to a degree and she'd now be having a wonderful life with Lucky. I could have used the money for grad school, but it was dirty and dangerous. I didn't want to go through the rest of my life looking over my shoulder. That potential pile of cash was a death sentence. The only shopping you'd do was for a pair of cement shoes.

KAREN'S VOICE WAS breathless. "He called me! On my cell phone."

"Who? Lucky?"

"Randolph!"

"What?"

"He still had my number and he called—"

"Why?"

"He wants to meet to get his books."

"When? That could be a problem."

"Tonight. At seven."

"Oh boy. What did you say?"

"I said yes. But we can't give him the books."

"We'd never pry them out of Vera's grasp. But he doesn't

really want the books. He wants the numbers. And we can sweeten the deal with the Hemingway so that I haven't actually stolen the books from him. I don't want that on my conscience anymore."

"Even though he's a crook himself."

"A charming crook though and not a murderer like the people who are after him. Where?"

"The library in Ainslie, if you can believe that."

LUCKY DROVE. WE weren't completely at ease with the idea of meeting Randolph, even though we knew that Candy and Mason were behind bars and had been denied bail. Randolph did still have a price on his head.

In the library, we glanced around, but saw no sign of Randolph. We were lurking in the reference stacks and just about to give up when an attractive, sporty-looking middle-aged man edged in beside us.

"Ladies, I am eternally in your debt," he said.

Randolph's voice, but where was the silver hair and fragile old man? Transformed, it seemed.

"Thanks to the miracle of a haircut, a box of Just for Men and a chance to detox from the wrong medication, I am a new man. If you'll hand me the books, I'll be away for the rest of my life."

"We don't have the books," I said. "But we have what you need. You'll find it written on the bookmark tucked in page sixty-four of *The Old Man and the Sea*. We couldn't bring ourselves to deface the book. We're keeping the Sayers books, but you don't need to worry about us. We won't go after the money."

He stared at me and at Karen. Then a smile broke over

his face. "I should have realized that two such brilliant women would figure it out. And I am prepared to offer you something for your continued discretion."

I said, "No, thanks. We're all right. We've seen what it can bring."

Karen nodded vigorously.

He said, "Thank you. They'll be after me with or without the money, so . . ."

"You may as well have it. But there's something I need to know. What about Delilah?"

"Ah, my dear Delilah. She has a history of such bad decisions."

Karen and I exchanged alarmed glances. We hadn't liked Delilah much, but that didn't mean we wished her dead.

Randolph seemed oblivious. "I think all that's all out of her system now. Mason really manipulated her. But we've worked through it." He turned to gaze at a woman seated fidgeting with a magazine at one of the reference tables. She had giant Jackie O glasses. She ran her fingers through her hair, smoothing her short, blond bob. Her slender, elegant figure was impossible to mistake. I hoped she'd find a better disguise in the future. Now that Randolph didn't have to hide his stash from Mason.

They might have been slightly left of the law, but Karen and I hoped they'd make a life somewhere safe. Karen, Lucky and I would keep this meeting our little secret.

"YES, IT SEEMS that Mr. Kelly was able to sniff out some rare flowering shrubs that were native to this area. And would have been part of the original garden plan when my father built our home. I daresay he is having more success in one day than you have had had in the past month, Jordan."

I guess risking my life repatriating her collection didn't count for much. But that's Vera for you.

On this beautiful late October afternoon, Vera, Kevin, the signora and I stood facing the gardens, as we waited for Uncle Mick to arrive. I twisted my peep-toed heels in the pea gravel.

Vera pressed on about Kevin's virtues, while he primped the bushes. I had a knot in my stomach. Vera said, "He managed to find, procure *and* deliver the specimens from a reputable nursery in Somer's Point."

"Somer's Point, New Jersey?" *Oh no.* Somer's Point was where Gus the Screw lived. Gus the Screw and Uncle Kevin have been known to hit Atlantic City from time to time and test their "system."

The knot got tighter as I thought about it. I wished my mother's emerald-green shantung suit didn't require such a wasp waist.

"Yes, your uncle was kind enough to pick them up himself. He's ensured that they were planted before frost. He insisted on making the journey immediately despite all the unpleasantness last week." Vera sniffed. "I wish you could be as efficient, Jordan." She smiled a little when she said it, though. I'd helped her pick out a deep-coral blouse, simple pearls and gray trousers. When I wasn't looking she pinned a subtle diamond circle brooch to her coat. If I didn't know better, I'd think Vera was starting to enjoy herself and maybe even take a shine to me.

Uncle Mick arrived and loaded Vera into the Navigator and the wheelchair into the back. Little crepe paper bells dangled from every possible attachment point. The signora fussed over Vera, demanding that Mick "Go slowly, slowly!" Then she checked and double-checked the seat belt around her employer.

"Get off me and into the car, Fiammetta. We're not preparing for a space launch."

Vera's departure left me alone with Kevin. "Somer's Point? Really, Kev?"

"Yeah." Kevin was oblivious.

"Flowering native shrubs?"

"*Myrica pensylvanica*, the common Northern Bayberry." Kevin winked and sparkled at me. "Don't worry though, we dug them up from the side of the turnpike, totally free." He was preening the shrubs like Vidal Sassoon might fluff a fresh bob.

"Wait, we? You got Gus the Screw to help you dig up flowering shrubs?"

"Gus? Ah, no, he doesn't dig holes for trees usually. I went with Harry . . . You know, the neighbor guy? Harry Yerxa?"

Well, I wasn't expecting that. I couldn't believe that I'd forgotten all about Harry. "You know where Harry is?"

"Indeed, I do, Sugar Plum. He's hittin' the slots in Atlantic City. Like I just told ya." He shook his head as if I was a little slow on the uptake, but he'd forgive me because I was cute.

Kevin loaded a gym bag into the Saab. "I'm going to get ready there, so I don't get anything sweaty." I nodded and shuddered. And I thought I caught a glimpse of a braided hemp sandal poking from Kev's bag.

THE KELLYS WERE born to party. And this was going to be the party to end all Kelly parties.

The repairs to the walls and doors had been made in record time, thanks to an army of uncles. Michael Kelly's

Fine Antiques was looking its best. Everything in the shop had been moved out to the many storage places in the neighborhood or hidden under groaning tables covered with tablecloths—Kelly green, it goes without saying. This was good, as a certain police officer was in attendance and we didn't need him to spot anything that might be on a list of things that had fallen off the back of a truck.

Flickering candles lent a magical green glow. I did my best not to worry about the provenance of the polished silver gleaming on every table. This was the first family wedding I had ever been part of. My head was whirling with happiness for Karen and Uncle Lucky. We had so much to celebrate. Being alive, for example.

Karen was glowing too. Her wild red curls were caught up into a Victorian updo and accessorized with small jeweled combs. Her skin was clear again and her hand steady. The antique cream crepe organza dress with its satin trim had a high-waisted column skirt. It flattered her pale skin and vibrant hair as did the simple touches of gold jewelry. I took a certain pride in the fact I had found the dress at a vintage shop, just at the point where Karen had given up in despair. It was my gift to her.

Uncle Lucky was beaming. His head gleamed. His vintage tux was at full capacity. The Kelly green cummerbund strained against his midsection. The tux hadn't seen the light of day since the early eighties. But I hoped it would survive the night without seam failure.

Mick was holding forth to whoever would listen. As best man, he too wore a tux and a green cummerbund. The ladies were not disappointed, as his bow tie was undone and the pleated shirt open to offer a peak at the gold chain nestled in his ginger chest hair.

Walter wore a custom-made vest to match Lucky's tuxedo and a Kelly green bow tie. A variety of Kelly uncles worked the crowd: Billy and Danny certainly gave Mick competition with the lady guests. Others kept a low profile. Everyone but me steered clear of Smiley in his Dockers, white shirt and gray blazer. I was delighted to see that he'd brought Cobain in a tuxedo T-shirt. There wouldn't be any awkwardness with Lance, as he'd RSVP'd no to his invitation, not that I was happy about that. I guessed we had some stuff to work out.

Smiley gave me that grin with the chipped incisor and said, "I checked out the Church of the Eternal Musings and they are a very pet-inclusive organization. I won't go so far as to say religion. No problem with Walter and Cobain attending this wedding."

Another grin. "You look nice," he said.

I blushed. "It's my first time in a wedding party. We're not big on them in our family, except for Mick's Russian brides, but those are stories for another day. All to say, being maid of honor is great. Karen doesn't have any family so I am also subbing for the father of the bride and I'll walk her down the aisle.

The food table was groaning. The best of traditional Kelly cuisine. Vast platters of white bread sandwiches with the crusts cut off. Egg, tuna and something unidentifiable. It took me a minute to recall devilled ham. I had hoped for peanut butter and jam. I admit to a certain weakness for all these fillings. There were towers of cocktail franks and spicy red sauce. Ritz Crackers and Cheez Whiz. Bowls of sour cream and ketchup potato chips to continue the theme. And in a concession to modern times, an acre or so of wings, barbecue and honey garlic, although those were probably too trendy for Mick.

In the corner, a fiddler was beginning to tune up. Would

the roof stay on tonight? Vera was parked at an angle, staring at the mountain of food, a look of surprise on her face.

I said, "No chance of zucchini here. Or any other vegetable. You are safe for the duration of the wedding and the reception."

She nodded. And smiled. "Party sandwiches."

"Don't forget to save room for the cake."

On the other side of the table, the signora was trying to figure out exactly what the Cheez Whiz actually was. No one had mentioned that this was a food occasion to her, or she would have whipped up enough for the entire gathering. But it wouldn't have been Kelly food and I had made sure it didn't happen. I had taken the several bags she'd brought and stashed it all in Uncle Mick's fridge. Karen would be happy with it on her honeymoon.

Speaking of honeymoons, it was time for the wedding.

Turned out Uncle Kev was an ordained minister from an online church and was able to perform the ceremony. I had actually triple-checked this in order to prevent any legal awkwardness for the bride in years to come. It was hard for me to believe that the Church of the Eternal Musings could possibly be legit, but I had lost that bet with Kev.

Kevin swanned to the front of the room, arms outstretched to his flock. I rushed to the front. What the hell was he wearing?

"What?" he said. "It's religious."

"Those aren't religious vestments. That's your Moses costume from two Halloweens ago."

"Like you can tell without the staff and tablets." He shooed me to the side and boomed to the gathering, "Dearly beloved. We are gathered here together . . ."

The rest of the ceremony was short, sweet and unique, to say the least.

The crowd of uncles, friends, colleagues, crooks and cops clapped, cheered and teared up as Lucky swept his new bride into his arms.

My iPhone vibrated. I checked it and found a text from Lance with a photo attached. The text said, *Sorry I missed the wedding, but I'm sure you'll forgive me when you see this*. I opened the attachment to find a grinning Tiffany in front of the sign for the Buffalo Niagara International Airport.

It was now the perfect wedding.

So many happy endings.

Best of all, I now had a brand new aunt whom I already loved.

Vera had her collection back.

I got to keep the job I loved.

Lucky and Karen had a shot at real happiness.

Lance had forgiven me.

My best friend was coming home.

And there were all those party sandwiches.

Life after Wimsey was good.

RECIPES

People love the sound of Signora Panetone's meals. Here are three recipes from her kitchen.

POLLO AI PEPERONI
(CHICKEN WITH PEPPERS)

Although the signora would make this simple chicken dish using ripe, luscious tomatoes and juicy peppers from her own garden, it's even good in the winter with whatever passes for tomatoes and peppers. Not as good as the late-summer version, but good. And for you busy people out there, it's easy to make, reasonably quick cooking and even better the next day.

This is a typical and traditional Italian dish. Signora usually makes it this way, but sometimes she changes it to

*keep you on your toes, or because she has a little more or
less of something.*

2 chickens, cut into serving pieces
4 tablespoons extra virgin olive oil
3 garlic cloves, slivered
¼ cup flour for chicken
½ cup dry white wine (whatever you have, although in
    Rome it would probably be Frascati)
1 pound fresh ripe tomatoes, peeled, seeded and chopped
3 juicy peppers, seeded and cut in strips (we used orange
    and green to contrast with the tomatoes)
1 tablespoon fresh thyme leave or 1 tsp (or to taste)
    dried thyme
Salt and pepper

If the signora was writing this, she might say, first you catch
your chicken. Please take the easier route and buy the
chicken already cut.

In a large pan, heat the oil with the garlic for about 5
minutes. Dry the chicken and shake in a bag with the flour.
You can skip this stage if you want, but it won't brown as
nicely. Add chicken to the oil and garlic and brown the
pieces all over. If there is too much chicken fat in the pan,
you may want to remove some with a bulb baster. Then
sprinkle with wine. Cook for two minutes, then add the
tomatoes and the peppers. Season with thyme, salt and pepper, cover tightly and simmer for about 40 minutes. Don't
cook too high or too long if you want the chicken to be
tender and you do.

The signora would serve this with a crisp green salad, a
loaf of crusty bread and a glass of Frascati.

Zuppa Rustica (Rustic Italian Soup)

*The signora makes this very simple peasant soup when Vera
or Jordan need comfort food. Or if the cupboard is nearly
bare. The whole is much greater than the sum of its parts.*

2 quarts good quality chicken stock (Homemade is best, but
    there are very good boxed or frozen versions out there.)
½ cup of hot water plus 1 bouillon cube or ½ cup stock
2 cups fine dried bread crumbs
2 whole eggs
½ cup cheese, Parmesan or old cheddar (dried and stale is
    better!)
2 tablespoons olive oil
4 tablespoons of finely chopped parsley or 2 tablespoons
    dried parsley flakes
Salt and ground pepper to taste

Bring the stock to a boil in a pot on top of the stove.

While it's heating, in a medium bowl, make a broth with
the water and bouillon cube, if using (or use ½ cup stock).
Add 1½ cups breadcrumbs, mix, then allow to cool thor-
oughly, before adding eggs, cheese, olive oil and parsley.
Mix with your hands, until fully combined. If mixture is still
very wet, add more breadcrumbs until you are able to form
cherry-sized balls that retain their shape. You may not need
all the breadcrumbs. So don't worry too much about that.

Sometimes, the signora adds ½ cup finely shredded cooked
chicken to this, but if so, she uses ½ cup less breadcrumbs.

Drop the balls into boiling stock, do not stir. They are
cooked when they float to the surface,

Serve with fresh grated good quality Parmesan cheese to top and lots of crusty bread.

MAIONESA (HOMEMADE MAYONAISE)

Although this is often thought of as a French or Spanish sauce, Italians love their homemade mayo too! With good reason.

1 large egg
A pinch of salt
½–¾ cup of light and fruity olive oil
Fresh lemon juice

Place the egg and pinch of salt in a small bowl. Whisk together until frothy. The signora says you get the best results by using a wooden spoon and working very slowly. Then add the olive oil bit by bit as you continue whisking, starting very slowly, adding a few drops at a time and adding more as the oil is absorbed into the egg yolk mixture. Keep adding until you have a thick, creamy sauce. Add a few drops of fresh lemon juice at a time. Not too much or your sauce will be runny.

This is lovely with salads or poached fish or cold chicken. Take your time and get the technique right. It's worth the effort. Or as the signora says, maybe she should just do it for you.

FROM *NEW YORK TIMES* BESTSELLING AUTHOR

JENN MCKINLAY

-The Library Lover's Mysteries-

BOOKS CAN BE DECEIVING
DUE OR DIE
BOOK, LINE, AND SINKER
READ IT AND WEEP

Praise for the Library Lover's Mysteries

"[An] appealing new mystery series."
—Kate Carlisle, *New York Times* bestselling author

"A sparkling setting, lovely characters,
books, knitting, and chowder! What more
could any reader ask?"
—Lorna Barrett, *New York Times* bestselling author

"Sure to charm cozy readers everywhere."
—Ellery Adams, author of the Books by the Bay Mysteries

jennmckinlay.com
facebook.com/TheCrimeSceneBooks
penguin.com